MY IMMORTAL HIGHLANDER

Books by Hannah Howell

Only for You
My Valiant Knight
Unconquered
Wild Roses
A Taste of Fire
Highland Destiny
Highland Honor
Highland Promise
A Stockingful of Joy
Highland Vow
Highland Knight
Highland Hearts
Highland Bride
Highland Angel
Highland Groom
Highland Warrior
Reckless
Highland Conqueror
Highland Champion
Highland Lover
Highland Vampire
Conqueror's Kiss
Highland Barbarian

MY IMMORTAL HIGHLANDER

HANNAH HOWELL

LYNSAY SANDS

KENSINGTON BOOKS
http://www.kensingtonbooks.com

KENSINGTON BOOKS are published by

Kensington Publishing Corp.
850 Third Avenue
New York, NY 10022

All Kensington titles, imprints, and distributed lines are available at special quantity discounts for bulk purchases for sales promotion, premiums, fund-raising, educational or institutional use.

Special book excerpts or customized printings can also be created to fit specific needs. For details, write or phone the office of the Kensington Special Sales Manager: Kensington Publishing Corp., 850 Third Avenue, New York, NY 10022. Attn. Special Sales Department. Phone: 1-800-221-2647.

ISBN 0-7582-1292-5

First Kensington Trade Paperback Printing: September 2006
10 9 8 7 6 5 4 3 2 1

Printed in the United States of America

CONTENTS

The Hunt

Hannah Howell

One

Scotland, late Spring 1509

Rain. He loathed rain. It rained too much in Scotland. Bothan MacNachton suddenly grinned even though the chilling rain had found a way down the back of his neck and was slowly soaking his back. He could lay the blame for his hatred of rain at his beloved mother's tiny feet. Everyone knew cats hated to get wet. Then again, it was his mother's blood that allowed him to step outside of the shadowy world his father was forced to stay in, if only for short periods of time. That was not only a true blessing, it was vital to him and his clan. It was a fair trade, he decided.

He dismounted, took his horse Moonracer's reins firmly in his hands, and began to lead the huge gray gelding up a hillside. The rain had made the mossy rocks slick and treacherous. Not only did he want to ensure the safety of his prized mount, but under such conditions he was more surefooted than the horse. Halfway up the hill was one of the many safe havens his clan had found scattered along the routes they traveled on the rare times they left Cambrun. The location of such places was relentlessly taught to every child until he or she could find them in blinding snow, and Bothan could almost scent the trails left by his kinsmen, living and long dead.

Another scent caught his attention and he stopped, breathing deeply and slowly in the hope of determining if he was walking into danger. Female, he decided, and relaxed a little, despite having grown up around women far more deadly than most men. This one was not of their ilk. He could not smell even a small trace of MacNachton or Callan blood. Starting on his way again, Bothan decided he would take the risk of sheltering with a stranger. The light smell of smoke promised a fire to warm himself by, and that temptation drew him onward.

His hand on his sword as both warning and ready defense, Bothan entered the cave. It did not surprise him to find a woman seated by the fire, her mare settled in the rear of the cave. The way the sight of her affected him did, however, and he was hard-pressed to hide that surprise. He felt as if someone had punched him hard in the chest, causing his heart to miss a beat and his breathing to falter. She also did not look even faintly startled or alarmed by his appearance. She smiled in welcome as if she had been expecting him, yet he knew he had made no sound as he had approached the cave.

Bothan stood just inside the cave for a moment, allowing the rain to finish dripping off him and Moonracer, and studied the woman, trying to understand why she affected him so. He had seen, and bedded, far more beautiful women, yet this woman's face held him nearly spellbound. Ethereal in many ways, her allure was difficult to describe. She had a heart-shaped face with wide, heavily lashed eyes and a full mouth. Her nose was small and straight, her chin faintly pointed, her skin flawless and pale, and her neck long and slender. Those wide eyes were a brilliant green, the rich color only enhanced by the light of the fire. She appeared to be small and very slender, although the blanket she had wrapped herself in hid most of her womanly curves.

When one of her delicately arched brows, tinted red by

the fire, slowly rose in mute question, Bothan realized he had been silent for too long and he bowed. "Your servant, mistress. I am Sir Bothan, a weary traveler who only seeks a small respite from the rain."

Kenna Brodie merely smiled at first as she struggled to catch her breath. She had heard a great deal about the MacNachtons in the last year or so, but no one had told her that they were beautiful. Sir Bothan was very tall, almost too lean, and dark. There was a smooth, golden glow to his skin that was enhanced by the firelight. Unfortunately, that same light also enhanced the predatory lines of his face. Even though his lids were slightly lowered and his eyes somewhat shielded by his thick, black lashes, she caught the glint of gold there as well. The only feature softening that cold look of a hunter was his mouth. It was well shaped and his lips were slightly full. A mouth meant for kisses and dark, sweet pleasures, Kenna thought, and startled herself out of her bemusement over his fine looks. This man could kill her in a heartbeat, she reminded herself, and he was trying to hide who and what he was by not giving her his full name.

"Then, come, sit down and warm yourself," she said. "I am Lady Kenna Brodie of Bantulach."

"Weel met, m'lady," Bothan said as he led his horse to the rear of the cave and tended to its needs first. "Ye are far afield. Bantulach is north of here."

"Three days to the north and one day to the west, to be precise. A hard journey with poor trails to follow. I think e'en the drovers have given up on some of them."

"And yet ye traveled it all alone? Or, has some trouble befallen your companions?"

"Alone, Sir Bothan. What few companions I might have chosen to travel with me are held at Bantulach." She filled a wooden bowl with some of the stew she had been cooking over the fire and offered it to him. "Eat, sir," she urged gently when he hesitated. "'Tis made from that last of my supplies, for I felt I risked my health if I tried to carry that bit of venison any further."

Quietly accepting the offer of food, Bothan cautiously sniffed it before taking a small bite. A poison might not kill him, but it could make him dearly wish it would. It could also weaken him enough to make him very easy to kill. As half Callan, half MacNachton, he could not be exactly sure just how vulnerable he was to such things, and there had been no way to safely test them. He had learned the scent and the taste of many poisons and could detect none here.

Someone could have found a new, stronger poison, he mused, but kept on eating, not wishing to reveal any fear. These were increasingly dangerous times for his clan. The whispered rumors that had always swirled around them had grown more widespread and there was growing number of people who believed them. There were men who hunted them now, and that group showed signs of banding together. That unity would make them even more dangerous than they already were. He had heard no mention of women being part of that group, but it was not an impossibility.

"Why are ye traveling alone?" he asked.

"'Twas nay my choice," she replied as she offered him an apple. "I was sent away from Bantulach."

As he accepted the apple, Bothan stared at her. It was difficult to think of any crime such a pretty, delicate woman could commit that was so vile it would result in her banishment. A look of innocence could be feigned, but Bothan felt surprisingly certain that hers was not. Now that he was closer to her, however, he did notice that there was something a little strange about her eyes, although he could not quite put his finger on what it was. It was possible that superstition alone had caused her banishment.

"Why are ye traveling about alone?" she asked him.

"I had no need of an escort for what I was doing. A mon doesnae want an army at his heels when he sets out to find himself a bride."

Kenna thought it very strange that she should feel so upset, even a little hurt, by the fact that this man had been on the hunt for a bride. In her dreams he had been all shadow and mystery, a man with the heart of a wolf and an ancient, dark soul within him, and a man with a dark, chilling hunger. He was not a man a woman should care for. If she felt anything at all when he spoke of hunting for a bride, it should be pity for whichever poor woman he finally ensnared.

For a brief moment, she actually considered attempting to do what she had been sent out to do. Her heart twisted with horror at the mere thought of killing this man, or any man, and then mutilating his body, and she felt ashamed. Her uncle had to be mad to ask her to bring him the hand, head, and heart of a MacNachton. Even if she believed, as her uncle did, that these men were demons who fed upon the souls of Christians, she knew she could never kill someone simply to try to wrest Bantulach out of her uncle's greedy hands. It was hers by right, but she would not spill blood to regain it.

That left her with precisely nothing, she thought, and sighed. Her dreams had held the warning of her loss, her solitary future, but she had tried to ignore them. There were ways to interpret her dreams that showed the way to a happier fate, but Kenna was certain they were not the ways her dreams had truly indicated she should go. Somehow her fate was tied to this man. That was why her dreams had told her of this place and of this meeting. She just wished they had told her how and why. There was a power within this man that could help her, but it could also destroy her. Her dreams had led her here but had left all the decisions about what to do next in her hands. It was beyond annoying.

"Did ye find a bride?" she felt compelled to ask. "If she lives betwixt here and Bantulach, I may ken something about her or her clan."

"Nay, I found naught," he admitted reluctantly.

"Ah, weel, mayhap next time."

"Mayhap." He took a drink from his wineskin and then

offered it to her, oddly pleased by the way she did not hesitate to accept it and have a drink. "I have some verra specific requirements," he murmured.

Naturally, she thought. All men had *specific requirements* when they sought a wife. No one asked if the woman had any, however. She had to accept whatever was chosen for her. It was just another great unfairness that women had to suffer, she decided.

"Was there no mon to defend ye ere ye were cast out from Bantulach?" he asked, and almost smiled at the cross look she gave him over the implication that she was unable to defend herself. He suspected some of that irritation came from the sad knowledge that a man's word would carry far more weight than her own.

"Nay, there was no one. Weel, that may be unfair. There were some who wished to speak for me, but I wouldnae allow them to, for it would have endangered them and their families. Either the mon who now calls himself the laird or those whose fears he had roused and aimed at me could have turned on them."

"And who is the mon who now calls himself laird?"

"My uncle."

"I see. What fears did he rouse?"

Kenna hesitated to answer that question. Her gift had only ever caused her trouble, even amongst her own kinsmen and clansmen. She had learned at a very young age that it was wise to speak of her gift only rarely. Such a thing had been impossible to keep secret amongst those whom she had grown up with, however, and she had suffered for that, hating the wariness others revealed and the fears bred of old superstitions. It was not until her uncle had prodded at all those fears, fed them with lies, that she had actually begun to fear her own people, however.

But this man had his own secrets, she suddenly remembered. Her dreams had made that much very clear. This man held fast to secrets that made hers look as innocent as a child's. Kenna discovered that she was also intensely curious about how he would react to her *gift* and all of the accusations flung at her far too often, all those superstitions her sly uncle had made excellent use of.

"The fear that I am a witch, a handmaiden to the devil, and a sorceress," she said quietly and was a little surprised when his only reaction to that confession was to cock one dark eyebrow.

"And are ye?" he asked.

"Nay, but I do have dreams."

"Most of us do." He had to bite back a smile when she glared at him. "Ah, a seer's dreams, are they?"

"In some ways, although I think a true seer would have ones that were more precise than mine. My dreams tend to leave me with more questions than answers."

Bothan smiled faintly. "As do a seer's, but many who call themselves such are arrogant enough to think they ken all the answers. From what little I ken of such things, few such *seeings* are precise. I have a cousin who is troubled by such dreams and often curses them for telling him only part of the truth."

"Aye, 'tis exactly what such dreams do. And too often that little piece of the truth is hidden within a swirl of images, dire warnings, and curious hints of what is to come if one doesnae choose the right path." She sighed and shook her head. "'Tis difficult to choose, especially when I am left with only frightening warnings of what will happen to me or others if I choose wrongly. Too often that leaves me with such doubts I cannae choose at all, nay verra quickly leastwise. My mother always called it a gift but I have found it a torment and a curse most of the time. The only thing that pleases me about it all is that the dreams dinnae come to me too often."

Bothan could easily understand that feeling. He would not like to be haunted by dreams that carried warnings but no hint as to how to avoid the trouble being foretold—or even if it could be avoided. It certainly sounded like a curse to him. He could sense that it made Kenna feel alone, as if she was not truly a part of the life that teemed all around her. That, too, he could understand, for it was a feeling he was well acquainted with.

The wariness he always felt around Outsiders began to ease. This young woman was even more alone than he was, for she was feared and cast aside by her own people. Bothan hastily reminded himself that her situation did not mean she would accept all that made him different, but that did little to end the sympathy he felt for her. He at least had his father's and his mother's people to stand beside him, people he did not need to guard every word and action around. Kenna suddenly started to look irritated again, and he suspected he had just revealed his sympathy for her a little too clearly.

"There is no need for ye to pity me," she said a little sharply, fighting the temptation to accept such comfort.

"'Twas nay pity, m'lady, but sympathy," he said.

"I am nay sure I see the difference." And she knew he would lose that touch of compassion very quickly when she told him the whole ugly truth.

He ignored that. "So your uncle used your gift against ye, stirring up the fears of your clansmen, and then grabbed hold of all that should be yours. Is that the way of it?"

"Aye, ye have guessed it aright. My clan wasnae too certain they wanted a wee lass as their laird and my uncle gave them a verra good reason to put me aside and allow him to rule. There were witnesses to my father's dying words, the ones that made me his heir, but they were soon cowed by my uncle. I could see that it would be dangerous for the few brave ones who chose to stand with me and begged them to save themselves. One mon died and, although it could have been an accident, his death came so quickly after he spoke out on my behalf that I feared my uncle had silenced him. I couldnae let any others suffer that fate."

"But why has your uncle allowed ye to live?" Bothan shrugged. "I think 'twould be easiest for him to just be rid of ye, aye?"

"That is what he has done, isnae it?"

Bothan thought about that for a moment and had to agree. Kenna was a small woman, slim of build and delicate of feature. No matter how clever, strong, or brave she was, she was no match for any man determined to do her harm. Luck with a knife might save her a time or two, but the odds of her continuing on her travels in blissful safety were very small indeed. It was sad and unfair, but a woman on her own too often faced a hard, brutal life and a very short one. Her uncle had indeed rid himself of her and without even bloodying his hands.

"So he has banished ye from your home and your birthright."

"Aye, but he told my clansmen that he was sending me on a journey that would prove me worthy of being their laird."

"And just how were ye to do that?"

"By returning to Bantulach with the hand, head, and heart of a MacNachton."

Two

She never saw him move. Too stunned to speak, she remained absolutely still beneath his long body, staring into those golden eyes and wondering if and when the knife he held against her throat would end her life. Even more frightening was that, for the briefest of moments, that beautiful face above hers had seemed to change, to become distinctly feral, almost catlike. She had the oddest, most chilling feeling that it was not the knife that was the true threat to her well-being, but those sharp white teeth now clenched in a snarl.

It must have been the firelight that had made her believe she had seen fangs, she told herself as she fought to calm her fear. Kenna also told herself that the vision that had raced through her mind, the one that showed that very tempting mouth of his stained red with her blood, had been born of that fear. She should have anticipated that he would react quickly to such a perceived threat and not spoken so bluntly. It would have been wiser to have begun with assurances that she had no intention of carrying out her uncle's orders. The fact that Bothan had not killed her yet made Kenna hope that he would be willing to listen to those assurances now.

"I am nay armed," she said quietly.

Bothan had already realized that, but asked, "Did ye plan to kill me whilst I slept?"

"So ye *are* a MacNachton then, arenae ye?"

"I think ye kenned that from the beginning."

"From the moment ye stepped into the cave."

"Ah, of course. Your dreams."

"Aye, my dreams. I dinnae intend to do it, ye ken, e'en if I could, which I doubt."

"Oh? If ye dinnae intend to do what ye must to return to Bantulach and claim all that is rightfully yours, what do ye intend to do?"

She sighed. "Wander about and pray that I can find some place safe to live. Then, mayhap, spend the rest of my pathetic life plotting ways to oust my uncle from Bantulach without spilling too much blood."

Bothan stared at her, looking deep into her wide, green eyes. He could read her fear there, the fear born of having a knife held to her throat, but he could see no guile. She met his gaze without flinching as she spoke, her voice heavy with resignation and sadness. He believed her, yet he still hesitated. Judging wrongly now could cost him dearly.

She knew about the MacNachtons, he reminded himself in order to stop himself from easing his guard too much and too quickly. He doubted she knew everything, for she had been startled by the speed of his attack and the look he knew had been upon his face. A little knowledge surrounded by superstition and rumor could be dangerous, however. Dangerous for him and dangerous for his clan, especially considering what she had to gain from his death. Yet, he simply could not sense a lie or the blood of a killer in her and so he eased his grip on her, pulling his knife away from her pale, slender throat. He did not sheathe his knife or release her, however.

"Ye lose a lot by nay doing as your uncle has asked," he said, keeping his gaze fixed upon her face and still watching closely for any sign that she was lying to him.

"I would lose a great deal more by doing as he asked. I willnae win back Bantulach by spilling the blood of an innocent mon. If naught else, such an act would make me no better than my uncle. 'Struth, I begin to believe he killed my father."

The grief that briefly pinched her expression was real. Bothan was certain of it. He was also certain that her suspicion concerning the death of her father was well warranted.

"Why did your uncle choose a MacNachton for ye to kill?"

"He believes ye are all demons who feed upon the souls of Christians, that ye are naught but beasts disguised as men."

She knew more than that pernicious rumor. Bothan could see that in her eyes. "What else did he tell ye?"

"He told me little else save wild tales of demons who ravaged the countryside at night, always at night, for they feared the sun. Ah, and who feasted upon the blood of innocents like virgins and bairns. 'Tis the sort of thing often said about anyone who looks different and who makes people uneasy. I dinnae think ye are surprised by such ugly rumors."

"Nay, and *I* dinnae think ye are telling me everything."

"Everything my uncle said about the MacNachtons."

"I see. So, tell me, what do *ye* ken about the MacNachtons, aside from such tales or rumors as have been spouted by your uncle?"

"Just what I have seen in my dreams," she whispered, uncertain about his mood, for he still held her down and his deep voice had a cold, sharp edge to it.

"And what did ye see in those dreams, lass?"

"Ye. I saw ye." She wondered why they were both whispering now. "I saw that I would meet with ye here."

"What else?"

"It wasnae clear. Ye werenae clear. Ye were all shadows and mystery. Ye were shown to me as a mon with the heart of a wolf and an ancient, dark soul, a mon with a dark, chilling hunger and secrets. Many secrets."

Bothan slowly sat up, straddling her body. Her dreams

had shown her a disturbingly clear image of him. He was going to deny it all, of course, although he knew she would not believe that denial. She would not press him on the matter, however, of that he was certain, although he was not sure where that confidence came from. What interested him more was how her uncle had heard those tales about the MacNachtons, how much the man truly did know, and if he was one of the growing number of hunters he had heard so many whispers about.

He got to his feet and, grasping her by the hand, pulled her up to stand before him. She barely reached his breastbone and he relaxed a little. There was little chance that such a small woman could harm him if he remained wary. That was not going to be all that easy, since he truly did believe her when she said she would not and could not even try to kill him. This was not a time to put his full trust in his own judgment, however.

"Why would your uncle choose my clan as his prey? Such rumors have haunted us for many, many years. They cannae be the only reason."

"Because he felt sure that ye or someone else in your clan would kill me if I tried to fulfill the quest he sent me on." Although Kenna had thought that the most logical conclusion, she frowned for she was no longer so certain of that. "What else could it possibly be?"

"To have us rid him of you would make his life a lot easier, there is no doubt of that, but that still doesnae answer the question of *why* he chose *my* clan. Has he often spoken of us?"

Kenna stared at the man who quite possibly considered her his enemy now and wondered why that made her so very sad. She quickly shook aside such idle thoughts and tried hard to remember how often her uncle had spoken of the MacNachtons. He had, she suddenly realized, seemed grimly fascinated with all the strange tales about the clan. She could even recall her father expressing disgust over his brother's obsession with a clan that lived too far away from

Bantulach to be either a threat or an ally. She had obviously paid more attention to her uncle's words than she had realized. Before her father had died, she had accepted that she and her uncle would never be close and had thought she had fully ignored the man.

"Now that I think upon it, aye, my uncle had a very strong interest in your clan," she replied. "That makes no sense, for I am certain he has never met ye or any of your people."

Ignoring her blushes, Bothan swiftly checked her for any hidden weapons as he thought over what she had just told him. He left her standing alone near the fire as he searched her belongings as well. All she carried with her was a small hunting bow, arrows, and a dagger. Collecting her weapons, he set them down by his pack, signaled her to sit down again, and retook his place across from her in front of the fire.

"Why didnae your father name your uncle as his heir?" Bothan asked when they were both seated again.

"My father wasnae fond of the mon and I think he didnae trust him verra much. He ne'er explained why." She sighed. "And, although I am but a lass, my father felt Bantulach was mine by right of birth. In truth, my father wished me to marry as soon as possible and place a strong mon at my side. My uncle quickly made that impossible. I think he began to spread his tales about me as soon as my father fell ill."

"And it worked, didnae it."

"Aye, it most certainly did," she whispered and struggled to banish a wave of self-pity as she stared into the fire.

Only a short while ago Kenna would not have believed that anything could trouble her as much as what her uncle had done, what he had asked her to do, or the way her clan had turned her away. Having a knife held to her throat by a man with eyes like a wolf had made all those other problems seem small, at least for the moment. The fact that he did not trust her, could actually think she would try to kill him and mutilate his body, also troubled her far more than she felt it ought to. She could not blame him, however.

People had been known to commit murder for far less than she had at stake.

Even worse, the one plan she had come up with to solve her troubles was now ruined. As she had waited for the man her dreams had told her about, she had thought he would make a good ally. It had occurred to her that her dreams might have led her to him for precisely that reason. Unfortunately, giving the blunt truth about her quest without any softening words surrounding it to take the threat away had lost her his trust. He would linger in their shelter until the rain stopped and then he would walk away and leave her to her fate. Of that she had no doubt. It was what any sane man would do. This was certainly one of the wrong paths her dreams had hinted at. Kenna just wished her *gift* had given her some warning before she had boldly marched down it.

Bothan studied Kenna as hard as she appeared to be studying the fire. Either she was a very skilled deceiver or she had no idea how expressive her face was. He could almost read her thoughts simply by watching each expression that crossed her pretty face. She looked to be a very unhappy lass at the moment, and he did not think it was because she had lost all chance to fulfill her quest. Anyone who intended to murder someone did not usually announce it so bluntly, especially not when she was unarmed and thus unprepared to immediately carry out that threat.

That only eased his tense wariness a little. At the moment she was no real threat to him, but she had probably not yet fully faced all her losses. When she did realize all she had lost and exactly what she faced in the future as a woman alone and penniless, she could just change her mind about killing a MacNachton. It would then become a matter of survival. She would still require close watching.

Kenna was not the greatest threat he faced, however. Her uncle concerned Bothan far more than she did. Although the little she had claimed the man had told her or others about the MacNachtons sounded very much like the sort of rumors that had always been whispered about his clan, Bothan felt sure there was more to it all. The self-proclaimed laird of Bantulach wanted his niece dead. The fact that he had sent her on a bloody quest against MacNachtons seemed to show that he felt sure that would do the trick. Foolish rumors and superstitious whispers could not be all that gave the man such confidence in that. The interest Kenna claimed her uncle had long held concerning the MacNachtons was also dangerous. Bothan could not shake the feeling that Kenna's uncle was one of the hunters he had been looking for.

The only way he could make certain of that was to meet with the man. It was an idea that was both eminently sensible and completely insane. To go to Bantulach was to ride into the lair of a man who might know far too much about him, might have killed his own brother, and had obviously tried to kill his niece, using the MacNachtons as his weapon. The man deserved killing for that alone, Bothan decided. The possibility that Kenna's uncle knew all about the MacNachtons and was one of those dedicated to hunting them down would only make his death more personal.

The problem was, how could he get Kenna to return to a place where her own kinsmen shunned her and one of them so clearly wished her dead? And, if he could convince her to return to Bantulach, could he also convince her to allow him to travel with her? He would be in as much, if not more, danger than she would, and it would be difficult to explain why he would put himself at risk for a woman who had been sent to kill him.

Bothan was struggling to think of some way to convince Kenna that they should both travel to Bantulach when he suddenly recalled what she had said her father's deathbed instructions to her had been. She was told to marry a strong man to place at her side and help secure her rightful place as the heir. It was a common way to ensure that a daughter could hold fast to what her father had bequeathed her, although it was often the husband who ended up ruling or holding the purse. The children born of such a marriage would have the right bloodline, however, and that was usually of great importance to a man about to meet his maker.

At the moment, what most concerned Bothan was what use he could make of the final commands of the late laird of Bantulach. He was a strong man and he had been hunting for a wife with a good dowry. Although he was not sure he ought to trust Kenna Brodie even as far as he could spit, it appeared that this meeting had been fated. The fact that Kenna would be returning to Bantulach to take her place as heir with a very-much-alive MacNachton at her side to oust her uncle had a sweetness to it that was very hard to resist. So, too, did the thought that marriage would put Kenna Brodie in his bed. Despite everything, he still felt a very strong attraction for her. Bothan suspected that touch of danger that now clung to her only heightened it.

"So there was no mon at Bantulach with backbone enough to marry ye?" he asked.

"A few, but only one who I would have considered accepting," Kenna replied. "Howbeit, he was promised to one of the few women I could call friend. The others? Weel, their greed o'ercame their fear of me, at least it appeared to. I think that fear was still there and that would surely have caused me trouble in the end."

"'Tis weel kenned amongst your clan that your father told ye to wed a strong mon? E'en your uncle kenned it?"

"Aye. Interest in my father's dying words was verra keen and his instructions to me were quickly repeated to everyone at Bantulach. If I wasnae cursed with these dreams and my uncle hadnae convinced so many that I was a witch, I would have had a wider choice of husband. Yet, that may be for the best. If a mon cannae stand firm afore a wee lass such as I just because someone whispers the word *witch*, ye cannae really call him a *strong* mon, can ye? If he cannae face me, how can he face any other threat?"

"E'en a mon who can face an army without flinching can feel a tremor or two of fear when facing something that may harm his immortal soul," Bothan said quietly. "Something thought to be of the devil can send even the bravest mon running for the hills. After all, if 'tis magic, or 'tis a trick of the devil, it cannae be defeated with a sword or a brave heart, can it?"

Kenna grimaced. "Nay, it cannae, and, if I am a witch, I must be both."

"Weel, although I certainly believe there is evil in the world, I dinnae much believe in witches."

"Nay?" There was an odd look in his eyes that made Kenna feel far more uneasy than cheered by his words.

"Nay. And, I am a strong mon, trained as a warrior."

"Aye, ye do appear strong."

Bothan almost smiled. She looked so adorably confused. "So, I shall marry ye and we will return to Bantulach together."

Three

"What?"

A wide-eyed, blank stare was not the most flattering response to the only marriage proposal he had ever uttered, Bothan thought, and yet he was hard-pressed not to laugh. "I said I will marry ye and we will ride to Bantulach together."

"Was holding a knife to my throat and snarling your idea of wooing a bride?"

"Be fair, lass. Ye had just said that ye had been sent to kill a MacNachton and take a few pieces back to your uncle. And I didnae snarl," he added, although he suspected he had.

Kenna struggled to calm herself. He was right. She had invited that attack with her ill-chosen words. He could have killed her right then, and few would have questioned his right to do so. No one would question his right to see her as his enemy now, either. That the man was speaking of marrying the woman who said she was sent to bring his hand, heart, and head back to Bantulach as trophies could make many people question his sanity, however. Even though she was really no threat to him, Kenna suspected her uncle was. She also suspected that Sir Bothan was very much aware of that. That made a marriage between them and a return to Bantulach pure idiocy, as far as she was concerned.

The sad, and somewhat alarming, thing was that, once she had fully understood what he was saying, she had felt a very strong urge to say aye. Swiftly and loudly. He *was* an extraordinarily handsome man any woman with eyes in her head would immediately covet, but he had also just held a knife to her throat, and the attack had come so quickly she had not even seen him move. Surely a normal man could not move so fast? It was not just her dreams that made her think there was something very different about Sir Bothan MacNachton, either. Kenna knew, without a flicker of doubt, that there was something about Sir Bothan that set him apart from all others and it was something that could prove both frightening and very dangerous. Even knowing that, however, she was still strongly attracted to the man. Kenna decided it was not just Sir Bothan's sanity that should be questioned.

"The fact that my uncle wants me to bring him a few choice pieces of a MacNachton ought to be enough to make ye wish to go anywhere *but* Bantulach," she said.

"I think he is a threat to me and to my clan. That is more than enough to compel me to go there and search out the truth."

"What ye will find is that if my uncle Kelvyn says he wants a MacNachton in pieces, he means it. And, what the mon has had to say about your clan makes what he says about me seem naught but a wee tale for the bairns."

"Weel, I hadnae thought I would be welcomed with open arms."

"More like a weel honed dagger to the gullet."

Bothan ignored that. "As I said, the mon is a threat to me and mine. I cannae just walk away from that. He also sent ye out on a bloody quest against my clan. Luck may have been with ye and ye may have succeeded, but we both ken that your uncle's true intention was that we kill you for him. That, too, cannae be ignored. What if he succeeds in getting rid of ye in some other way? Will he then try to blame us?

"Nay, I must meet this mon and judge him myself. I need to see if 'tis all naught but bluster and lies and a hope that someone will rid him of a problem or if this was but the first, tentative strike against my clan."

"If it was, he chose a verra poor weapon."

"Och, nay. A bonnie lass is oftimes the deadliest weapon to use against a mon."

That was flattering in a rather strange way, Kenna mused. Quite naturally she liked to think that such a handsome man thought she was bonnie. Oddly enough, she found herself rather pleased to be thought a deadly weapon as well. A woman as small and slender as she was never seen as a threat.

She quickly shook aside that nonsensical thought and put her mind back on Sir Bothan's crazed plan. Kenna suddenly realized that her biggest concern was for his safety. The more she thought about her uncle's choice of a MacNachton for her victim, the more she realized Kelvyn Brodie feared and loathed that clan, that he truly believed the rumors he had heard about the MacNachtons. As she had dug deep into her memories, she had begun to see that Kelvyn had long been rather obsessed by the clan and what he saw as their evil nature. Her uncle may well have seen this quest he set for her as a good way to be rid of her, but Kenna began to think the man had also thought to test the strength of his chosen adversary. So, too, was there a chance that her uncle had thought to use her death at the hands of a MacNachton as a way to move against them or inspire others to do so. It was a chilling thought, but Kenna was unable to shake it from her mind.

"Now what has put that particular look upon your face, lass?" Bothan asked.

"What look?" Kenna was rather proud of how innocently confused she sounded by his question, but his expression told her he did not believe it for a minute.

"That look of fear, dismay, and a wee touch of utter horror."

A little startled by how accurately he had guessed her feelings, Kenna decided to be completely honest. "I was just realizing the harm that could have been done your clan if I had been killed. E'en worse, I begin to think that my uncle had every intention of using my death against your clan."

Bothan nodded. "Aye, I wondered on that."

"But why should he? Ye have done naught to him, have ye? Do ye e'en ken who Kelvyn Brodie is?"

"Nay, I have ne'er e'en met the mon. Dinnae think any of my clan has, either."

"Then I must be wrong. Mayhap, because of what he has done to me, I now see all he has e'er done or said as suspicious, sly, or e'en threatening."

"And mayhap ye see it that way because it is, and always was."

Kenna shook her head. "It makes no sense unless he truly does believe all the rumors about your clan."

"I intend to get answers to such puzzles when we return to Bantulach as mon and wife."

She scowled and eyed him as if he was a dangerous lunatic. Bothan suspected many of his kinsmen would question his sanity as well. Each time he spoke of marrying her, however, it felt more right. All his instincts told him this was what he should do despite the fact that she had been sent out to hunt and kill a MacNachton, and his instincts had never led him wrong before.

Of course, the very strong attraction he felt for her could easily be leading him astray, he mused, and then inwardly discarded that brief flicker of doubt. It was certainly what had kept him from immediately killing her, the feel of her slim body beneath his and her wide, lovely eyes stilling his knife hand. Searching his mind and heart very carefully, he remained confident that lust for Kenna Brodie was not blinding him. It was certainly there and it was strong, but it did not lead him.

In truth, he thought, the attraction he felt for her was the one truly good thing about his plan. As soon as they were wed he could satisfy that strong need she so effortlessly stirred within him. Marrying her would also satisfy his need for a well-dowered bride, a need that would aid his clan once it was satisfied. The MacNachtons would have yet another place to shelter in when they traveled, just as his laird had hoped for when he had made his plans to breed out all the blood that forced the MacNachtons to cling to the dark, remote lands of Cambrun. Bantulach would probably never be completely safe for a MacNachton to freely be all his breeding demanded of him, for the Brodies of Bantulach were Outsiders, but it would be better than huddling in caves as they too often had to do now.

All he had to do was convince Kenna to accept him as her husband. At the moment she did not appear too persuadable, but he did not let that deter him from his plan. Bothan knew she was attracted to him, although he was not sure of how strongly. Seducing her was a possibility, and a very attractive one, but so was simply convincing her that his plan benefited her as much as it did him. It would also help her to fulfill her father's last wishes. She had already attempted to do that, but due to her uncle's malicious whispers, she had failed. It did mean, however, that she was willing to marry to hold fast to her inheritance, and that could be useful to him. Lust and greed had placed many a couple before the altar. Later, once her uncle had been dealt with, he would find a way to make the marriage more than a union based upon gain and passion.

As he had searched for a well-dowered bride, Bothan had slowly come to the realization that he was actually looking for far more than a marriage for gain. Unless there was a true bond between him and his wife, he would never be able to trust her with the full truth about himself or his clan. Unless his wife loved him, Bothan knew there would always be the chance that she would turn against him when she finally discovered his secrets. He knew he might not be able to get Kenna to love him, but there was still one very strong advantage to taking her as his wife, one he had not found in any other woman. Kenna Brodie was also troubled, perhaps even threatened, by the fear and superstition of others. It was a bond of sorts and it would suffice for now. He would find and strengthen other bonds between them later.

"Why do ye act as if a marriage between us is unthinkable?" he asked.

"I dinnae ken ye," she replied. "I cannae wed a mon I dinnae ken, a mon I met only a few hours ago."

"Ye were prepared to wed a mon just to hold fast to your inheritance. What does it matter if that mon be a stranger? Few women get to ken their husbands weel ere they are wed."

A telling point, Kenna mused, but she absolutely refused to admit that aloud. "Mayhap, but verra few of those husbands are said to be demons who steal the souls of—"

"Aye, aye—virgins and bairns. Weel, I suspect just as few of those wives are said to be witches, eh?"

This man was dangerously skilled in the art of debate, she thought crossly. "Ye have some verra dark secrets," she said, "and dinnae try to deny it. I may nay fully understand all that my dreams tell me to do, but the ones I had about ye were all verra clear on that fact."

"Ye think me a demon, do ye?"

"Nay, of course I dinnae, but I do think there is something verra different about ye."

"There is something verra different about ye as weel, is there not?"

Kenna took a deep breath to quell the sudden urge to throw something at his handsome head. She noticed that he had not conceded that there *was* something odd or different about him. He had simply turned her words around and thrown them back at her. Even reminding herself that he had every reason not to trust her did not ease her annoyance with him by very much. She was sorely tempted to tell him exactly what her visions had told her about him, but a strong sense of caution held her back. He might think her an even greater threat if her dreams had told her the truth about him, or, if not, he might well think she was mad, something far too many also saw as a threat. Considering how this man reacted to any perceived threat, it was definitely safer to keep her mouth shut.

"I have dreams, something ye said a cousin of yours is also troubled by," she said.

"So ye must ken that I willnae condemn ye for them or think that ye are a witch. We have both been plagued by dark whispers and the fear of those who heed them. We have that in common."

"I dinnae think uniting against them will benefit us. Nay, t'will probably just incense people and cause them to build an even bigger pyre to roast us on."

Bothan could not fully repress a smile, but he quickly sobered. "Do ye mean to let your uncle win this deadly game? To spend the rest of your days cowering somewhere hoping that no one will guess ye are a seer?"

Kenna rather liked being thought of as a seer, but she struggled to ignore how flattered she felt and concentrate on the insulting part of what he had said. "I mean to stay alive."

"I cannae allow ye to do so by killing and butchering a MacNachton."

"If ye hadnae leapt at me so quickly I would have told ye that I had no intention of fulfilling that quest. E'en if I could find the stomach to do as my uncle commanded, I truly dinnae think it would keep me alive." Kenna sighed. "We both ken that this quest was intended to put an end to me. If I had actually succeeded and returned victorious to Bantulach with my bloody prizes, he would have just found another way to see the deed done. He wants Bantulach and I am in his way, just as ye would be if ye returned with me as my husband."

"Ah, I see. Ye refuse to marry me because ye fear for my safety."

"There is no need to be so sneering about it. Aye, I *do* fret o'er the danger ye would be strutting into."

"I never strut."

Kenna ignored that. "Howbeit, my refusal to marry ye is born of the simple fact that I have only just met you."

"But ye kenned I was coming."

"Aye, I did. My dreams were verra precise about that. There was naught in my dreams, however, that told me to marry ye after but a few hours acquaintance and a knife held to my throat." She just scowled when he cocked one eyebrow, silently reminding her yet again that she had threatened him first.

"I will let ye think on the matter," he said.

"What is there to think on? I will go my way when the rain ends and ye will go yours."

"Nay. *We* will go to Bantulach together, wed or no."

"Why, for sweet Mary's sake? Uncle Kelvyn wants me dead. Ye, too. Weel, nay ye precisely, but a MacNachton. 'Tis madness to walk right into his grasp."

"He is a threat to me and mine. Ye have said naught to make me change my mind about that. Mayhap it was but a whim born of some rumor he heard that caused him to choose a MacNachton as your victim, but mayhap it is more. I intend to find out. Ye need to lay claim to what is rightfully yours. If he did kill your father, his own brother, and he tried to kill you, do ye really wish him to be the laird? T'would seem to me that such a mon will treat your people with the same callousness he has treated his verra own blood kin. Did ye not say that he quite probably already killed one mon who spoke out, who said something he disagreed with or wanted kept quiet? One must wonder if he has any loyalty in him save to himself."

When Kenna fixed her gaze onto the fire and frowned, offering no reply to his words, Bothan inwardly sighed. She knew what he said was the cold, hard truth, but he could not really blame her for trying to ignore or deny it. The time that two of the Purebloods had turned against their laird, nearly killing him and his new wife, still troubled some of the clan even though it had happened over thirty years ago. Betrayal by one's own kinsmen was a wound that left a verra deep scar.

Despite the sympathy he felt for her, Bothan used Kenna's distraction to fetch a length of rope from his saddle. He did not really believe she would attempt to hurt him as he slept, but did not feel it would be wise to leave her free to prove his judgment of her wrong. He also did not want to wake in the morning to find her gone. He would be able to track her down with ease, but he did not want to have to waste time doing so. Instinct told him that they needed to get to Bantulach soon, and he never ignored what his instincts told him.

Kenna was slow to realize what Bothan was doing. The rope was already secured around her wrists before she gathered enough of her wits to protest. She stared at Bothan in silent outrage as he tied the other end of the rope to his belt and then made up his bed on her side of the fire.

"Is this another example of your wooing?" she snapped as he made up a bed for her that was far too close to his for her peace of mind.

"I just need to be certain that ye dinnae flee as I sleep," Bothan said as he lay down. "Ye are right. Ye havenae kenned me weel enough or long enough to wed with me. I will give ye tonight to think on it."

Kenna suspected she would spend the night dreaming of the many painful ways she would make Sir Bothan MacNachton pay for this humiliation and pay very dearly indeed.

Four

Kenna reluctantly opened her eyes, annoyed by her inability to go back to sleep. She could hear the rain still falling outside the cave. Since they would not be leaving the shelter yet, she saw no good reason to be awake. Then she realized that she was no longer tied, and the last vestiges of sleep rapidly fled her body.

A tense fear she did not understand the cause of crept through her body. Kenna sat up and peered toward the rear of the cave. The sight of Sir Bothan's horse made her feel almost weak with relief and that puzzled her even more. The man had tied her by the wrists and lashed her to his belt as if she were some puppy prone to meandering. She ought to want him gone. Instead, when she had thought he had left, she had felt almost painfully alone.

"How verra odd," she muttered as she stood up and stretched. "Ye have only kenned the mon for a few hours and dreams dinnae count. How could ye possibly miss him?"

The answer quite naturally should be that she could not miss such a stranger. Yet even in that brief moment that she had thought he had left her, she *had* missed him. Sharply and painfully. Shaking her head over what could only be termed absolute foolishness, she donned her cloak and walked toward the mouth of the cave. When she lifted her gaze from the floor, she stumbled to an abrupt halt, all thought of dashing outside to relieve herself fleeing her mind. Sir Bothan MacNachton stood there with his back to her. If she had not looked up at that precise moment, she would have walked right into him. There was a lightness to the sky that hinted at an approaching end to the rain and that light framed his body beautifully as he stood with his arms outstretched and his head tilted back ever so slightly. He was obviously bathing himself in the rain. He was also very obviously naked.

Breathe, Kenna, she silently commanded herself. She closed her eyes and slowly opened them again. He was still naked. The man had a beautiful back, she decided, unable to avert her gaze as she knew she ought to. Broad shoulders, a trim waist, taut, well-shaped buttocks, and long, muscular legs made for a sight that was a pure gift for the eyes. His hair hung down in thick, black ropes to the middle of his back, the rain streaming off it giving it a lovely shine. His skin was smooth and unmarred. She realized she was clenching her hands into tight fists, fighting the strong urge to touch all that faintly golden skin. She also realized that she was very nearly panting.

Even as she struggled to calm herself, she had to marvel over how the mere sight of this man's backside was making her feel. She felt warm, as if all the blood in her veins had become heated despite the chill, damp air. Her heart was racing and it was proving very difficult to control her breathing. This was lust, she decided, astonished by the strength of it.

"Lass, could ye hand me the blanket I set down just inside the cave?" he asked.

"How did ye ken I was standing here?" she asked, silently cursing the blushes heating her cheeks and very glad that he could not see them.

"I heard ye wake up. The blanket, lass? Or, I could just turn round and fetch it myself."

"I will fetch it."

The lilt of laughter in his deep voice irritated her, and she had to smother the urge to slap his very attractive backside. Most of her irritation came from the fear that if he had heard her wake up, he might have also heard all that panting she had done. Worse, she had actually considered letting him carry out his threat. She had wanted to see the front of him. Silently scolding herself for such wanton thoughts and keeping her gaze averted, she thrust the blanket at him. She listened to him as he rubbed himself dry with the blanket, and fought to hide her embarrassment before they faced each other again. And hide her lust, she mused, and grimaced. It would not be wise to let him see how deeply she was attracted to him. He might well try to use it to pull her into a marriage she was not sure she wanted.

"'Tis safe now, lass," he said.

Kenna turned around and scowled at him. It was not easy to continue to look so cross when he looked so handsome. He wore a clean linen shirt and his plaid that was a mix of deep blues crossed with black and a touch of golden yellow that almost matched his eyes. Although it was still raining, the sky was bright enough to see him clearly. The firelight had not deceived her. Sir Bothan MacNachton was a very beautiful man. His was the sort of beauty that caused a woman to act like a fool, and Kenna feared she was very close to doing so.

It took Kenna a moment to notice that Bothan was staring at her as hard as she was staring at him. Feeling herself start to blush, she dashed out of the cave, murmuring something about needing privacy. She was pleased to find that the rain was easing as she sought out a place that was sheltered and convenient, a place where she could try to recoup her obviously scattered wits.

Bothan grinned as she hurried away. He was not vain but he knew women liked the way he looked and Kenna had just gotten a very good look indeed. There had been the glint of interest in her eyes. He was absolutely sure of it. It was odd, but he felt more flattered by that hint of interest in

Kenna's brilliant green eyes than he had by any other woman's far more blatant admiration, something he had had more than his share of.

Suddenly he wondered if it had been wise to allow her to leave, and then he shook his head. Her horse and all of her belongings were still there in the cave. She would not try to flee without them. There was a part of him that felt very confident she would not leave him anyway, but he struggled against heeding it.

"Ah, Moonracer, my stalwart companion," he said as he walked toward his mount, "I think I may actually have to work hard to woo this lass into my arms." He stroked the gelding's strong neck and grinned. "Weel, mayhap I am a wee bit vain after all. Aye, and spoiled. The lasses have always come too easily to me. This is one I shall have to fight to win, but I begin to think she will be worth it."

Moonracer snorted and shifted closer to Kenna's sleek, black mare.

"She *will* marry me. 'Tis in her best interest to do so. Aye, and mine. I shall be a laird." Bothan grunted softly when Moonracer butted him lightly in the stomach. "Aye, 'tis her rightful place, but fair or nay, the clan willnae easily accept a wee lass as its laird. I will share the honor with her, ne'er fear, but her people will be more at ease if there is a mon at her side. I intend to be that mon."

Bothan took two apples from his saddle packs and held them out for the horses to eat. "She has hair the color of ripe chestnuts, deep brown but with a strong hint of red. It looks to be both verra long and thick. A fine pelt I am eager to get my hands into. And her eyes are as green as spring buds with a ring of darker green around the lighter color. That is why they appeared so odd in the firelight. Unusual but beautiful. A seer's eyes, ones that see far beyond what others can. I can foresee myself willing to look into them for many, many years." The apples now gone, Bothan returned to stroking his horse's neck. "We will be settled soon, Moonracer. Mayhap I have a touch of the seer in me, for I truly believe my hunt for my enemy and for my future will end at Bantulach. I but pray that it ends weel."

Kenna shivered as she washed herself in the rain. She was not as bold as Sir Bothan, or as shameless, and could not bring herself to stand naked in the rain. Instead, she huddled in a small hollow in the hillside, dampening a piece of linen with rain and wiping her body clean as best she could without removing all her clothes. The first inn she came to she was going to demand a hot bath and no one best give her any trouble about it, or about being a woman traveling alone.

She shivered more fiercely and pressed back up against the stone, the very word *alone* causing her an even greater chill than the rain. Because of her gift she had been very much alone for all of her life, she sternly reminded herself. But not like this, a small voice whispered in her mind. Not without a home or a clan to claim or turn to in times of need. Kenna knew she did not even have a chosen destination yet or a faraway kinsman to turn to.

"Oh, *Maman*," she whispered, fleetingly thinking of how her habit of speaking to her long dead mother only proved just how utterly alone she was, "I dinnae ken what to do. Do I go on alone and pray I can find some safe haven where I may live out the rest of my days or do I wed a mon I have just met, one who holds fast to some verra dark secrets? Oh, and who is called a demon by some, a creature spit up out of hell to feed upon the souls of innocent maids and wee bairns."

Shaking her head, Kenna laughed softly. "'Tis all utter nonsense, of course. Just as I am no witch, he is no demon. He is a beautiful mon who is verra different in ways he seeks to hide, but I truly dinnae think he is evil.

"Oh, how I wish Florrie was here. I need to make a verra important decision, *Maman*, and I am so deeply afraid I will make the wrong one. I want to go home and 'twould be best to do so with a strong mon at my side. I *was* willing to marry to hold fast to Bantulach, but I was planning to choose a mon from my clan, one I have kenned all my life, nay some mon who steps into a cave from out of the rain. Aye, and one who has been merrily skipping through my dreams for far too long and not in a way that had a lass thinking of marriage. I dinnae e'en ken why I am considering it."

That was a lie, she decided a moment later. Kenna forced herself to be honest. She had been considering it from the moment he had suggested it. In truth, she had decided on it when she had seen him naked. What she was doing now was trying to convince herself that she was not being led along by blind lust for a beautiful man.

"'Tis shameful," she muttered. "A lass shouldnae think of marrying a mon just because he has a handsome backside." She felt herself blush. "Verra shameful indeed, *Maman,* for when he said he would turn around, I had to force myself to fetch him that cursed blanket ere he did so. I wanted to see *all* of him. 'Struth, I wanted to touch all that lovely golden skin of his. I have ne'er thought such things about any mon, ne'er felt such a wild longing. But, that isnae a good reason to marry him, is it, *Maman?* I think lusting can be a verra fickle feeling and marriage is for life."

Kenna experienced a tickle of superstitious fear when she felt something brush against her cheek. It felt like a kiss. Even stranger and more frightening was the whisper that passed through her mind. It told her to think, to look very hard at her choices, for there was more than lust there. Much more. It told her to think about Bantulach. It was not her own inner voice. Her memories of her mother were faint, for she had been only eleven when the woman had died bearing a stillborn son, but Kenna could not shake the feeling that the voice in her head was her mother's.

"Och, nay. Nay! The dreams are quite enough, thank ye verra much. I willnae start hearing spirits as weel."

Even as Kenna raced back to the shelter of the cave, she wondered why she did so. If she truly was being haunted by her own mother, there was no place she could hide. But, despite her efforts to quell it, panic ruled her now. The very last thing she needed or wanted was another *gift*.

Bothan stared at Kenna in surprise as she burst back into the cave, stumbling to a halt just inside the opening. Then he tensed, for she looked pale, her eyes wide with alarm. He put his hand on his sword as he approached her while she stood there struggling to catch her breath.

"What has frightened ye?" he asked.

Kenna grabbed him by the arm, tugged him in to the cave opening, and pointed toward where she had been when she had heard the voice in her head. "Do ye see anything there?"

After looking carefully in that direction and then in all other directions, Bothan slowly shook his head. "Nay, I see nothing. I hear nothing as weel. There is naught out there but rain and rock. What did ye think ye saw?"

"Naught." She was suddenly embarrassed by her blatant display of fear. "I saw naught. I am nay accustomed to being all alone out in the middle of nowhere, 'tis all." Then she suddenly had the thought that if Bothan believed she was a madwoman he would lose all interest in marrying her. "I just thought I heard my mother's voice."

"Oh. Do ye think she may have followed you?"

"Nay. She has been dead for nearly ten years."

"I see. Ye fear ye are being haunted." Kenna looked so cross now that Bothan had to smile.

"'Tisnae something to laugh about, sir. I was talking to her as I sometimes do and she answered."

"Do ye often speak with the dead?"

He was supposed to be alarmed, not amused, Kenna thought, feeling sorely tempted to hit him. "Nay. 'Tis mostly that, weel, sometimes I need to talk out my thoughts and problems, and if I cannae find anyone else, I talk to *Maman*." She shrugged. "Foolish, I suspect, but it often helps. Except, this time, I heard her answer me. It was *her* voice in *my* head." Kenna touched her cheek and whispered, "I e'en felt something akin to a kiss upon my cheek."

Bothan put his arm around her shoulders, and ignoring

the way she tensed over this familiarity, urged her back to the fire. As she sat down and stared into the flames, he fetched his wineskin. He handed it to her as he sat down beside her.

After a few deep drinks of wine, Kenna began to feel more irritated than afraid. She had spent most of her life trying to either hide her gift or get people to accept it. Was she now to be cursed with yet another gift that would cause people to shun her or, worse and far more dangerous, think she was a witch? Would people see her ability to converse with the dead as better or worse than her portent-laden dreams? Even more important—if her mother could speak to her from beyond the grave, why had the woman not done so before now?

"Aye, why now?" Kenna muttered.

Because ye need me now, said the voice.

"I needed ye before," she snapped.

Nay, my child, ye just wanted me.

"I dinnae see such a great difference atween the two."

Kenna suddenly realized she was carrying on a conversation with a voice in her head. It was only a soft whisper in her mind, but she was speaking out loud. She looked at Bothan and blushed slightly. Although she had considered that Bothan might decide he did not really wish to marry her if he thought she was mad, she was no longer so certain that would be a good thing.

"Ye cannae hear the voice, can ye?" she asked him and sighed when he shook his head. "I didnae think so. Mayhap I truly *am* going mad."

"Ah, and so I shall cease to want to marry ye because I fear ye may pass this insanity on to whate'er children we are blessed with?"

Kenna slowly nodded, bemused by the thought of bearing children with Bothan's fine looks.

Bothan gently but firmly grasped her by the chin and gave her a swift, hard kiss. "Nay, ye most certainly arenae mad and I still intend to marry ye."

Say aye, lass, whispered the voice. *Say aye.*

Ignoring the voice and struggling to calm her racing heart, Kenna also ignored the urge to demand Bothan give her another, longer kiss and forced herself to frown sternly at him. "Why? I am already feared because of my dreams. If I can now talk to the dead, that fear will only grow stronger and I cannae be sure I can hide this gift any better than I have done the other. Ye have some verra dark rumors swirling about you. The two of us joined together would probably turn those fears into a real danger. Nay, not probably. Certainly. As I said before, all our marriage will bring about is a race to see who can build the biggest, hottest pyre to cook us on."

"Nay, I dinnae think that will happen. As to why I wish to marry you? Many reasons. Ere I met ye I searched for a bride who could bring some land to our union. Ye will bring Bantulach to the marriage. Howbeit, unlike those other women, ye have a true need for a strong mon to help ye regain your rightful inheritance and to protect ye from your uncle. That will be me. There is also an attraction between us." He ignored her gasp, for her sudden blush disputed that sound of denial and outrage. "That will serve us weel. I think your uncle is one of a group of men who begin to band together to hunt my clan, thus he is my enemy as he is yours. We shall be working together to defeat a common enemy. Another bond between us. We both suffer from the sting of superstition. Yet another bond. I begin to think the hand of fate led me here. Oh, and I will be a faithful husband and am willing to share the lairdship of Bantulach with you. So, I say again—marry me."

She looked so disgruntled Bothan had to struggle hard not to laugh. He knew exactly what troubled her now. There had been not one single word of romance in his speech. It was far too early in their relationship for such things and he had no doubt that she knew it. She had none to offer him, either. He wondered why that thought stung, but shrugged aside that puzzle as he waited less than patiently for her answer.

Say aye, said the voice, loudly and with the sharp snap of command.

Startled, Kenna said, "Aye."

Before she had even fully realized what she had just done, she was being heartily kissed by Bothan. Her last clear thought was that she hoped her mother could not see as well as speak.

Five

Married, Kenna thought as she stared at the thick ring Bothan had stuck upon her finger. It had required a lot of ribbon wrapped around it before it had settled securely on her much smaller finger. The band was lovely, etched all around with intricate swirls such as she had once seen upon an old cairn stone. She supposed the ring's stone could also be called pretty, but that beauty would take some time for her to fully appreciate. She wondered where Bothan had found a stone that so closely resembled a large drop of blood. It was not a ring that would do much to still all the dark rumors about him, she decided.

She felt dazed, as if she had fallen and hit her head too hard upon a stone. From the moment she had said aye, the man had moved with astonishing speed. She had not even caught her breath, had still been reeling from the power of his kiss, when she had found herself on her horse, her belongings all packed. Kenna had assumed there would be some time to discuss the matter with Bothan, a time to come to some agreements, but that time had never come. He had kept them moving along at a steady pace until they had reached a small village, a kirk, and a priest. In no time at all, she was married. She had no doubt in her mind that he had done so purposely.

And this Father James bore a close resemblance to her new husband, she realized, frowning toward where Bothan and Father James stood near the altar having a very intense conversation. Bothan held his cloak over his arm and Kenna found herself studying it very closely. He had kept that cloak on, the hood pulled up, even after the rain had ceased to fall and the sun had begun to occasionally peek out from behind the lingering clouds. It looked to be very thick, made up of several layers, and she suspected it was very heavy. As he had ridden along just in front of her, shrouded in that dark cloak from head to foot, she had been strongly reminded of a picture she had once seen in a book. It had been a depiction of Death. A fanciful thought, but one that had begun to make her seriously question her decision to marry Sir Bothan MacNachton. It was too late now. Unless, she suddenly thought, the marriage remained unconsummated. If there was no bedding, the marriage could be annulled. Kenna wondered why such a perfect solution to her dilemma should make her heart ache so. Temptation had obviously disordered her wits.

"Your bride isnae blushing, Bothan," murmured James. "She isnae smiling, either. Are ye certain this is what ye want to do?"

Glancing toward Kenna, Bothan smiled faintly. "She just feels that she has lost control and that sits ill with her. And, aye, I am certain about this. More so with every passing moment."

"E'en though she was sent out to kill a MacNachton?"

"Aye, for I feel increasingly certain she could ne'er have done so. She told me she had plans to find someplace safe and spend the rest of her life plotting ways to make her uncle pay dearly for all his sins."

"Yet she left her home and kinsmen and set out on the quest he demanded of her."

"She left her home because she had the wit to ken that

refusing the bloody quest he set for her would only buy her a little more time, that her uncle would simply look for another way to be rid of her, although she is verra reluctant to admit to that verra often. Just as she kens that succeeding in that quest will also buy her naught." Bothan shrugged. "I do remain wary, but I dinnae think I truly need to be. She is no killer."

James nodded slowly, silently agreeing with that assessment. "She is an Outsider, however. She doesnae ken what we are."

"Nay, but I have hope that it willnae matter to her. Aye, she is an Outsider, but she isnae fully welcomed by her own kind. She has dreams, ye ken. Foretellings and warnings." Bothan suddenly grinned. "And it appears that her mother, who has been dead for these last ten years, has decided to talk to her now."

"She can speak to the dead as our cousin Berawald can?" James asked, his voice taut with curiosity.

"Only her mother, and Kenna isnae too happy about it for all that I suspect she loved and missed the woman. Her dreams have caused her enough trouble in her life. She doesnae want to have another strange gift. She kens that I have some secrets but she hasnae pressed me to tell her what they are. In her dreams she saw me as a mon with the heart of a wolf and an ancient, dark soul."

"So close to the truth," James whispered. "She is a true seer."

"She doesnae think she is, although I do. All she told me about her dreams concerning me were verra clear and easy for me to understand the meaning of. Howbeit, what matters now is reaching Bantulach safely and seeing just how great a danger her uncle is, to her and to the MacNachtons."

"Do ye really believe the mon may be one of those hunters ye have heard about?"

"I do, and, as concerns those hunters, I am verra certain

they are out there. All I am nay sure of is how many of them there are, and if they have found each other and begun to band together. Alone they are only a small danger, an irritant. As an organized band of men they are a far greater one if only because a group of men who believe the rumors about us can make others start to heed them as weel."

"And thus continue to increase their numbers and their strength."

"Exactly. This needs to be stopped ere it grows too great a threat to be handled quietly. If naught else, this uncle of Kenna's gives me many a good reason to kill him, so what he may believe about us or has told anyone about us wouldnae be seen as the reason I killed him. In truth, what he may have said about us will all be seen as just another way he sought to destroy the mon who had taken what he was trying to steal."

"Ye *have* thought this out verra carefully, havenae ye."

"Verra carefully. I think this uncle isnae only one of the hunters I have been seeking but may e'en be one of the ones who is trying to bring them all together to act as a united force against us. Kenna believes her uncle has long been obsessed about the MacNachtons."

"And the fact that ye gain a bonnie wee bride and lands of your own make the coming victory all the sweeter, aye?"

"Of course. I would be a liar if I claimed elsewise. Dinnae fret, James. 'Twill all right itself in the end."

"I pray ye are right. Now, are ye verra certain ye dinnae want any of us to be at your side or watch your back? Not e'en your twin?"

"Nay. It would be best if the people at Bantulach werenae confronted with too many MacNachtons at once. Her uncle has been speaking too freely about us and I shall need to calm those fears he has roused. Dinnae frown, cousin. If I feel I cannae solve this trouble alone, I am nay so proud that I will hesitate to ask for aid from my kinsmen." He clapped his cousin on the back. "Now, I intend to go to the inn and show my fair bride what a fine mon I am and make her smile."

"But nay to truly make her your mate?"

"'Tis too early for that." Bothan grimaced. "Aye, much too early in the game to expect that great an understanding of my new bride. Who can say? I may nay feel the urge, anyway. Not all of us born of two worlds do feel it. The mix of bloods is different in each of us. My own twin is different from me in what he took from our mother and our father. Our eldest brother, born whilst our own mother was nay more than a glint in her father's eyes, is more Outsider than either of us. Ye, too, are different."

"I ken it. Just step carefully, Bothan. Verra, verra carefully."

"I will. Take care yourself, James. I will have need of ye to christen all my bairns." He winked at his cousin, donned his cloak, and then walked over to where Kenna waited for him near the kirk door.

"He is a kinsmon of yours, isnae he?" Kenna said as Bothan took her by the hand and led her out of the tiny, stone church.

"Aye," replied Bothan. "A cousin, in fact. I was intending to visit with him ere I returned home to Cambrun."

As they approached the small inn where Bothan had already stabled their horses and gained them a room, Kenna began to feel increasingly nervous. They had still had no chance to talk about this, something she knew Bothan had worked hard to accomplish. She had not even been able to speak of her recent decision to leave the marriage unconsummated, at least until they had had time to become more to each other than strangers. Have pity, she thought—she was already trying to weaken her own decision.

"We have to talk, Sir Bothan," she said as they entered the inn, and then she squeaked in surprise when he stopped and gave her a quick, hard kiss.

"I see I shouldnae have left ye alone for so long," he

murmured as he pushed back the hood of his cloak. "Ye have been thinking, havenae ye? Talking wasnae one of the things I planned to do on my wedding night, ye ken."

She decided to ignore the remark concerning the danger of her thinking. "'Tis about the wedding night," she began, feeling herself blush at the mere mention of it, much to her annoyance.

"Ah. Mistress Kerr, there you are," Bothan said, slipping into Gaelic and smiling ever so sweetly at the plump innkeeper's wife. "Is my wife's bath prepared?" he asked.

"That it is, sir, and yours as well." The woman blushed and giggled when Bothan kissed her work-roughened hand. "Yours is ready back in the kitchens, sir. I will take your bride up to your room, shall I?"

"You are most kind, my dear woman."

Kenna was fighting the urge to roll her eyes over Bothan's flirtation with the older woman when he abruptly pulled her into his arms and soundly kissed her. By the time she had recovered her wits and her breath he was gone, and a chuckling Mistress Kerr was leading her up a narrow stairway. It was not until she was standing in the bedchamber she and Bothan were intended to share that Kenna realized Mistress Kerr had asked her a question and was awaiting an answer, a knowing smile upon her round face.

"I am very sorry, mistress," she said in Gaelic, "but I fear I did not hear what you just said." She sighed with resignation when Mistress Kerr laughed heartily and patted her on the shoulder.

"He is a fine man, fine enough to turn any woman's wits to warm gruel, that he is. I asked if you needed any help with your bath."

"Ah, no, thank you most kindly."

"Good enough. I will see that the food your man asked for is readied for you. Ah, lass, such a very fortunate woman you are," said Mistress Kerr, sighing heavily. "I have only seen a few MacNachtons but each and every one of them is a fine sight."

"And you are not troubled by the rumors that stick to them and their clan like burrs?"

"About them being demons and all that?" When Kenna nodded, the woman shook her head. "No. Their cousin is a priest, is he not?"

Which obviously absolved the entire clan of all possible taint, Kenna thought as the woman left. Eager to get into the bath before the water began to cool, Kenna hurried to shed her clothing. A hot bath was a luxury she had sorely missed. After stepping into the large wooden tub, she sighed with pure delight as she slowly sank her whole travel-wearied body into the hot water. She quickly washed her hair and then relaxed, resting her head against the rim of the tub and wondering how long the peace she now enjoyed would last. Somehow she just knew that Bothan was savoring his bath as much as she was hers and that gave her some time to stiffen her backbone and plan what she had to do next.

Unfortunately, thinking of Bothan in his bath filled her mind with the memory of his very handsome, very naked backside. Kenna suddenly felt so warm she was a little surprised that the water did not begin to boil. The way Mistress Kerr had fawned so over Bothan only confirmed Kenna's opinion that the man was dangerously handsome. He could also be nauseatingly charming when he chose to be. Of course, Mistress Kerr had never been at the wrong end of his dagger, she thought crossly as she began to bathe. At that moment Bothan might still have been as handsome as a summer's day was long, but he had been very far from charming.

And that was the man who would soon be joining her in this bedchamber, expecting to bed his bride. Kenna could not decide which she felt more strongly—fear or anticipation. Any woman with blood in her veins would appreciate having such a handsome man climb into her bed. Many women would also know what to do with him when he got there and therein lay the cause of her unease. She only had a very vague knowledge of what occurred between a man and his wife. As the laird's only surviving child, the only female of any rank at Bantulach, she had led a very sheltered life. Kenna knew what animals did when they mated, but she truly hoped what she and Bothan were about to do was different.

She cursed softly as she scrubbed her feet. The man had dragged her into this marriage for reasons that seemed to be all to his benefit. Now, even though they were still strangers, he intended to help himself to one of those benefits.

"Weel, I willnae do it," she muttered.

Aye, ye will.

Kenna stared at the water she sat in and wondered if sticking her head under it would drown out her mother's voice.

He is your husband now, child, and that gives him the right.

"He is a stranger."

Nay, not completely, and weel ye ken it. Your dreams—

"Said naught to me about marrying him."

Oh, aye, I think they did. When a mon appears in a lass's dreams as often as he appeared in yours, 'tis just what it means.

"Mayhap it meant that he would help me defeat Uncle Kelvyn and naught else. Mayhap it meant that I should beware bonnie men in caves."

Such a stubborn lass. Ye take that from your father.

"I think Uncle Kelvyn murdered him."

I think he did, too.

There was something in the tone of the voice in her head that told Kenna her mother did not think it; she knew it. Kenna felt the sting of a still-raw grief. Her father had been a gruff man and little given to displays of paternal affection, but she had loved him. When she had stood at his graveside, she had been forced to face the hard, cold fact that, aside from a few distant cousins, her uncle was her only surviving family. The thought had left her feeling painfully alone. The clan should have been her family, but it had never fully accepted her, and her uncle had swiftly widened the chasm that had always existed between her and the clan.

Shivering as much from that memory as from the cooling water, Kenna stepped out of her bath and began to dry herself. "Is Papa with ye now, *Maman*?"

Aye, but nay here. This is my job to do, nay his.

"What do ye mean?"

I am here to make sure ye take the right path. 'Twas clear to see that ye were uncertain of which way to turn.

"Of course I was, and am. This mon is a complete stranger to me. How can I e'en be sure I can trust him? And Bantulach was to have been mine, yet he will sit in the laird's chair." She pulled her night shift out of her packs and yanked it on over her head.

Bury that resentment, child, or it will sour ye and your marriage. Aye, 'tis unfair but sulking willnae change anything. The mon has said he will share that seat with ye. Few men would do that.

That was true, but Kenna had no way of knowing how much trust she could place in Sir Bothan MacNachton's promises.

A lot. He is a mon of his word.

Kenna gasped. "Can ye read my mind?"

Nay, just your expression.

"Ye can see me?"

Aye, in a way, but 'twould be difficult to explain. Ah, my child, try to have faith.

"Weel, if I could have some time to learn a wee bit more about the mon—"

Nay, there is no time to play that game. Few lasses ken their husbands weel ere they are wed, and some men think wooing a lass is naught but some game. They tell a lass what they think she needs to hear and 'tis naught but lies. A heavy sigh wafted through Kenna's mind. *That isnae important now. This mon isnae lying to ye.*

"Nay? He holds fast to his secrets. Is that nay lying in a way?"

'Tis, but he has good reason to do so and ye will learn all the truth of it in time. All ye need to ken now is that ye need that mon to defeat Kelvyn and Kelvyn must *be defeated, nay just for your sake, but for Sir Bothan's, for his clan, and for the people of Bantulach. Ye must enter Bantulach as mon and wife, truly united against Kelvyn.*

"And for that I must allow him into my bed?" Kenna did not know if she was more outraged than resigned, or an equal measure of both. "Are ye saying that for the sake of the people of Bantulach, people who turned their backs on me and believe all the rumors about the MacNachtons, that I must share my bed with a mon I met but yestereve?"

Aye.

A soft trill of laughter rippled through Kenna's mind and she almost smiled in response to it. It was as if her mother's humor touched her heart in some odd way.

Come, come, my child, he is such a bonnie laddie any lass would welcome him into her arms. Why so hesitant?

"I dinnae ken what to do," Kenna whispered. "I was kept verra sheltered, ye ken. All I do ken is that the bedding is verra important to a mon and I fear I shall fail in that, fail miserably, and make an utter fool of myself." She trembled faintly when she felt that ghostly kiss upon her cheek again.

Be at ease, love. Such a bonnie mon has undoubtedly kenned many women and he will guide ye in this. Now, I must go, for your new husband stands at the door.

Kenna just grunted and looked at Bothan. Her nervousness faded away beneath a surge of annoyance born of jealousy. Why she should feel so angered and hurt by the thought of all the women he had probably bedded she did not know, but there was no denying the feeling. Now she had to fear more than his many secrets and her own ignorance of the world. Now she had to worry about becoming just one more amongst so many for this man. She could just spit.

Six

She was talking with her mother again, Bothan mused as he entered the bedchamber and then shut and bolted the door. The look upon Kenna's face was far from welcoming. He wondered just what she and her mother had been discussing, for it had obviously put Kenna into such a temper her eyes glittered with it and that anger was directed right at him.

"Was your bathing water nay warmed to your satisfaction?" he asked, and watched her clench her fists.

"'Twas a lovely bath," she said with forced civility.

"Ah, weel, then something else had annoyed ye. Shouldnae a bride greet her new husband with a smile, mayhap with a wee blush of shyness? Ye look verra inclined to break my nose," he said as he set his saddle pack, sword, and cloak near the fireplace.

Kenna took a deep, slow breath to calm herself down. It was foolish to be so jealous. It was also puzzling. Even if she counted the times he had walked through her dreams, she had not known the man long enough to care for him or care much about who he had frolicked with in the past. She told herself that she was simply righteously annoyed that while he would be her first and only lover, she would just be one more in a long list of women for him.

"Ye have given me no time to talk about this with ye," she said finally.

"What do ye think we need to talk about?" he asked as he slowly approached her.

Kenna resisted the urge to back up and keep some distance between them. "This marriage."

"Ye said aye, lass. I heard ye quite clearly."

"I ken it and am nay trying to dispute that, but, mayhap, if we dinnae consummate it—"

"So that is what ye have been pondering all this time, is it?" He took her into his arms, ignoring the way she grew tense as he held her close. "Banish such thoughts from your head, wife." He began to follow the lines of her face with soft kisses. "We are wed, made mon and wife through the blessings of the church. Ye belong in your mon's bed. Are ye afraid of the bedding, then? Is that it? Ye dinnae need to be. I cannae promise it will be painless. I have ne'er bedded a virgin—"

"Missed one, did ye?" she mumbled against his shirt.

He ignored that interruption and had to fight against a smile, for he knew she would feel it against her skin. Now he knew what had put her into such an ill mood. In her talk with her mother something must have been said about the experience he had undoubtedly gained over the years. Kenna was jealous. Even if that jealousy was born of something as shallow as pride or irritation over the ways of men, it was a good thing.

"But," he continued as if Kenna had never spoken, "I have heard that there can be some discomfort. Ye need not worry about that. I intend to stir your passion to such heights that ye willnae be troubled by any of it."

He gently nipped her neck close to where the blood pumped through the life-giving vein there. Bothan was a little surprised at how strongly he could sense its presence, its heat. He could almost smell it. Kenna's skin was soft and sweet, but he still felt the stirring of that dark hunger the members of his clan had been cursed with for so many years, a hunger he had never felt when with any other woman. It worried and intrigued him. Why her? Why a tiny woman who wore night shifts large enough to house an army? Yet the feeling was definitely stirring inside of him. Satisfying that urge would have to wait, however. It would require an understanding and acceptance from Kenna that he could not be certain she had or would ever acquire. She had to be beyond suffering the fear that he was the predator and she the prey, and his clan had long ago discovered that Outsiders were very slow to release that fear.

Kenna heard a rap at the door and quickly pulled free of Bothan's embrace. Realizing that she wore only her night shift, she grabbed her cloak and put it on as Bothan moved to answer the knock upon the door. The smell of food helped Kenna shake free of the spell Bothan's words had put on her. As she moved to sit at a small table set near the fire, she decided her husband was not only experienced, he was skilled. There was no doubt in her mind that he had wooed many a woman into his bed.

After thanking Mistress Kerr for the food and watching her two burly sons remove the tub of water, Bothan joined Kenna at the table. He smiled at her as he poured them each some wine. By the look upon her face, Kenna was still struggling to subdue her jealousy.

"To our marriage," he said, tapping his wooden goblet against hers and watching her over the rim of his goblet as he drank.

Since Kenna could see no way to escape her fate now, especially not with both Bothan and her mother shoving her along this path, she drank her wine. She would need all the good wishes and high hopes she could grasp hold of. Feeling a little warm beneath his steady gaze, she shed her cloak. Her night shift was not, and never would be, the spur to making a man act rashly, so she felt no unease in appearing in it before Bothan. As she began to eat the mutton stew

Mistress Kerr had brought her, Kenna tried to think of something to talk about in the hope of easing the growing tension between her and the man who expected to share her bed tonight. It was then that she noticed that, along with the mutton stew, Bothan had been given a thick piece of beef, a very scantily cooked piece of beef.

"Ye should send that back to Mistress Kerr, Sir Bothan," she said. " 'Tis almost as if the woman forgot to cook it."

Bothan inwardly grimaced even as he continued to eat his meal. Mistress Kerr had been meeting and serving MacNachtons for many years and knew their likes and dislikes very well. After having exposed himself to the sun for so much of the day as he rushed to get Kenna to a priest before she changed her mind, he was sorely in need of something to renew his strength. Even the thick cloak his mother had made for him had not been enough to fully dim the dangerous effects of too much sun. Mistress Kerr asked no questions, but it was obvious that Kenna Brodie, now MacNachton, suffered from no such restraints. He decided to tell his wife the same thing he had told Mistress Kerr.

"'Tis done just as I requested it done—barely seared." He shrugged in response to her look of surprise. "'Tis a cure for a weakness in the blood. A wise woman told me that I must eat barely cooked meat if I am to strengthen my blood."

There was a look of doubt in her lovely eyes, but Kenna then smiled faintly and returned her attention to her meal. Bothan breathed an inner sigh of relief, for he really had no wish to lie to her. What he had already told her was very nearly the truth, but it was far too soon to tell her all about the dark hunger the MacNachtons were cursed with.

He shook aside that concern and turned his thoughts to planning the best, and speediest, way to get his bride into bed. She was obviously feeling shy and reluctant. Fortunately, Kenna seemed gratifyingly dazed whenever he kissed her and he had every intention of making full use of that. Bothan did wonder if even he had the skill to unwrap her from the yards and yards of white linen she called a night shift. Well, he mused with an inner smile, he had never been the sort of man to shy away from a challenge. Getting his little wife naked certainly looked to be the greatest challenge he had faced in a very long time.

The moment the food was gone, Bothan set the tray outside the door and bolted it shut again. He kept only the wine and the goblets in the room, for either he or Kenna might have need of a drink later. As he approached Kenna where she still sat at the table, he had to smile. In that large white night shift, with her hair braided and her hands clenched tightly in her lap, Kenna Brodie looked like a child, a child ready to bolt if he made one wrong move.

Standing behind the chair she sat in, he slowly unbraided her hair. He was surprised at how long and thick her hair was as he combed his fingers through it. Bothan could all too easily imagine the feel of it brushing over his skin as they made love and it felt as if his whole body tightened in anticipation. Holding fast to the patience he would need to teach his new wife the pleasures they could share might prove difficult.

Bothan moved to Kenna's side, grasped her by the hand, and tugged her up onto her feet. "And now, my wee bonnie wife, 'tis time to pledge ourselves with our bodies."

Kenna blushed but did not resist as he led her toward their bed. "I havenae done this before."

"I ken it, love," Bothan said, smiling gently as he pulled back the covers on the bed, grasped her around the waist, and then set her down in the middle of it.

"Nay, what I meant is that I dinnae ken what to do. Weel, I have seen animals mate, but—" she stuttered to a halt when he leaned over and lightly kissed her.

"'Tis nay so verra complicated, Kenna. I will teach ye. First we get naked."

That was one of the things that worried her, Kenna

thought, but she started to unlace her night shift. As she loosened the last of her laces, she glanced toward where Bothan stood by the side of the bed and gasped so sharply that she coughed. Bothan stood there with his hands on his lean hips, watching her and wearing only a crooked smile. The one part of him she had not yet seen was there to view in all its glory, all its very large glory. As she stared at it, it appeared to grow even larger. Kenna quickly looked up at Bothan's face and was surprised to see the hint of a blush upon his cheeks. A swift glance up and down his body was enough to smother the sudden warmth that sight brought to her heart.

"This isnae going to work, Bothan," she said, clutching the front of her night shift closed. "I am a small woman, ye ken? I think ye need someone bigger. Much, much bigger."

Sensing Kenna's growing urge to bolt, Bothan quickly got into bed and pulled her into his arms. "Dinnae fret, my bonnie wee wife, 'twill work weel between us. Aye, better than weel. All is just as it should be."

Before Kenna could argue that, he kissed her. The feel of his lips against hers quickly banished her fears. She wrapped her arms around his neck and held him close, enjoying the feel of his heat. Just as she was becoming thoroughly lost in the pleasure of his kiss, he nipped at her bottom lip. She gasped in surprise at the gentle assault and, suddenly, his tongue was inside her mouth.

Startled, Kenna tensed and placed her hands upon his broad shoulders. Then he began to stroke the inside of her mouth with his tongue and she lost all urge to push him away. She felt both weak and exhilarated, a strange, needy heat spreading throughout her body from the point where their mouths were joined. Realizing that she could now freely touch the body she had so admired, Kenna quickly took advantage of that, stroking his smooth, warm skin from his shoulders to every other part of him she could reach. The sounds he made told her that he welcomed her touch.

When he stopped kissing her, it took her a moment to realize that he had removed her shift. He was crouched over her, staring at her body. Kenna felt as if her whole body was blushing. She could count on the fingers of one hand the number of people who had seen her naked since the day she had left her infancy, and they had all been women. They were also not people she had had any inclination to please with her body. Then she looked at Bothan's face and the heat in his gaze burned away all of her doubt and embarrassment. For the first time in her life she actually felt pretty.

Bothan fought the urge to immediately bury himself in Kenna. The sight of her pale body cushioned by the long waves of her glorious hair had made him feel ravenous. She was not fulsome like the women he had known in the past, but he thought she looked beautiful. She was sleek and strong, her skin like pale silk and unmarred. Her breasts were not large, but they were plump and round, the nipples a dark rose and invitingly long. Her hips were gently curved and her legs were surprisingly long, considering her lack of height. And her nether hair was a neat little vee of dark red hair shielding that part of her he so ached to enter.

"Ye are beautiful, Kenna," he whispered as he brushed his lips over hers.

"I am small," she whispered back.

"Aye, but ye are sleek and strong like some creature of the forest."

Kenna was still savoring that bit of flattery when Bothan bent his head and kissed her right breast. Shock over such an intimacy briefly caused her to stiffen, but only briefly. As he slowly covered that breast with kisses he stroked the other with his hand. Kenna felt as if her breasts were swelling and they began to ache. When he took the tip of her breast into his mouth, suckling her like a babe, she clutched at him, holding him closer, and ceased to think at all. It no longer mattered what he did, what he saw, touched, or kissed, so long as he did not stop.

The way Kenna turned to fire beneath his touch severely

strained the control Bothan had always prided himself on. He had to keep reminding himself that she was a virgin. The soft, breathy noises she made as her passion flared hot drove him wild. The feel of her small hands moving over his body with an obvious greed stirred his desire to heights he had never known. When he slipped his hand between her slender legs she barely flinched and the hot, damp feel of her beneath his fingers actually had him panting. Knowing he had to be inside her soon or he would utterly disgrace himself by spending upon the bed linens, he slid a finger inside of her and began to ready her as best he could for his entry.

When the pleasurable feel of Bothan's finger was replaced by something a great deal larger, Kenna felt some of passion's haze clear from her mind. She clung to him, fighting the urge to tense and pull away from this strange invasion of her body as he ever so slowly pushed his way inside. A flash of stinging pain rippled through her and her eyes widened. She was no longer a virgin. She was now truly Bothan's wife. That thought restored the desire that had begun to lessen and she savored the return of its heat. When he pushed her legs up she wrapped them around his lean body and gasped with delight as he pushed even deeper inside her. Despite the lingering sting where their bodies were linked together, Kenna felt a pleasure she knew she would never be able to adequately describe. She even enjoyed the feel of his hot breath against her neck as he lay still in her arms. After a moment, however, she began to feel the urge for more, although she was not sure what that more was.

"Has the pain eased, lass?" he asked, his words humming against her neck in a way that sent shivers through her body.

"Oh, aye," she replied in a near whisper.

Then he began to move and Kenna knew that this was the more her body had been clamoring for. She clung to him and quickly caught the rhythm he set, greedily meeting his every thrust as she tried to pull him even deeper. Something began to tighten and ache inside her belly, an ache that grew even more demanding when he again began to suckle at her breast. Kenna was just about to demand that Bothan do something about that when the tight knot inside of her snapped and she felt herself flung into a blinding, mindless well of pure pleasure. Her last clear thought was that she hoped the door was thick enough to muffle that very loud noise she had just made. A small part of her dazed mind also took note of Bothan shouting her name a heartbeat later and she decided that sounded very nice indeed. She did not complain when he collapsed on top of her, just held him closer.

Bothan blinked and realized he was sprawled on top of his much smaller wife. He shifted to the side a little and felt a pang of loss when his now soft manhood slipped free of her body. Although he had never tasted a passion as sweet or as fierce before, and fully intended to taste it as often as Kenna would allow him to, he was a little concerned about his loss of control. Bothan glanced at her neck, saw no sign of a mark there, and breathed an inner sigh of relief. The need to mark her was there, raging inside him, but he had obviously retained enough of his wits not to indulge that craving. He knew he would not be able to ignore it for very long, but he still had time to prepare Kenna, to try to gain her full acceptance of what he was. Bothan just hoped that did not take too long.

He brushed a kiss over her mouth and caught his breath when she opened her eyes. They looked to be solid green and that color was as tumultuous as their lovemaking had been. Then he noticed the white around the green and wondered if he just imagined the change in her eyes. Kenna smiled shyly and he shrugged that puzzle aside to smile back at her.

"There now, lass, that wasnae so bad, was it?" he asked.

"Nay, my cocksure Sir Bothan, it was tolerable," she

replied and then suddenly thought of how what had been so wondrous for her was merely just another bedding for him.

Seeing the sudden shadow that entered her eyes, Bothan strongly suspected she was thinking about his amorous past again. "Nay, wife, it isnae the same."

Kenna eyed him warily. "Ye can read my mind?"

"Nay, just your bonnie, sweet face. And, aye, I have bedded my share of women, and although it would have been verra fine to have come to your arms as innocent of another's touch as ye came to mine, I make no apologies for my past. I was unwed, unpromised, and as eager as all young men are. I didnae bed innocent maids or other men's wives, which is more than many another mon can claim. Howbeit, nary a one of those women, nay e'en the first, gave me the pleasure ye have just done. On my word of honor, I swear it. Nary a one. And, from the moment we exchanged our vows, all such frolics ended for me. Yours is the only bed I will crawl into now."

Even though she smiled and kissed him, Bothan could tell that she had a few doubts about his claims. Arguing about it would not soothe those doubts, however, so he kissed her, tugged her close, and settled his head upon her breasts. "I have ne'er slept the night with another lass, either," he added softly and touched a kiss to her breast before he closed his eyes.

Kenna smiled faintly and stared at the ceiling as she idly stroked her husband's thick hair and, occasionally, his broad back. It was pleasant to think that she gave him something no other woman had, but she suspected she would be a long time in believing that. What she needed to settle firmly in her mind and heart was the fact that she and Bothan were truly married now and there was no going back. She felt a rush of warmth as she thought of all the nights they would share together from now on. Perhaps all the benefits of this relationship were not his alone.

Then her now sleeping husband began to make a noise

she recalled from their lovemaking. Kenna glanced at his face to reassure herself that he was really asleep. She softly rubbed the spot behind his ear and he made the sound again. There was indeed something very different about Sir Bothan MacNachton. He purred.

Seven

The sun would set soon and Kenna expected to see her new husband emerge from the tiny stone hut they had sheltered in for much of the day. They had known each other for four days and been wed for three, yet Kenna could not think of one single time where Bothan stood out in the full light of day, at least not without that cloak he was so fond of. He always found someplace dark to shelter in when the sun was high, and flattering and pleasurable though it was to think otherwise, she was beginning to believe his claims of an unbridled lust for her were but excuses to get out of the sun.

Just as her dreams had foretold, her husband was a creature of the shadows. Kenna sighed, crossed her arms over her chest, and leaned against the wall of the small, windowless hut they had sought shelter in. When she had roused from the stupor Bothan's lovemaking had put her into, she had had to get outside. This shelter reminded her far too much of a tomb. Now that she was outside, however, she rather missed being held in his strong arms and listening to him breathe. She was a sad, pathetic woman, she decided, and smiled faintly. Kenna had to admit that Bothan was not the only one who was benefiting from the marriage, for despite her doubts and concerns, she felt content in many ways.

Now that she was alone and not distracted by his looks or his kisses, however, Kenna tried to fix her mind on solving the puzzle that was her husband. To be fair, she had to admit that Bothan was not exactly a creature of the night, for he seemed at ease in the early hours of the day and at dusk. It was only when the sun was fully risen and at its full strength that he seemed very eager to find some shadowy place to go to, and he clearly knew where every one was along the route they took to Bantulach. He ate the same foods she did, although his enjoyment of that severely undercooked piece of beef Mistress Kerr had served him still troubled Kenna a little. She was not sure she really believed his explanation about a weakness in the blood. Even stranger and more difficult to describe, even to herself, was how, although Bothan was obviously strong and healthy, he had seemed even more so after devouring that nearly raw meat. She blushed when she recalled how thoroughly he had proven his vigor that night.

Get your mind out of the bed, Kenna Brodie MacNachton, she scolded herself. That was not easy to do, however. She was discovering that she had a very greedy appetite for the pleasure Bothan could give her. She was greedy for that fine body of his as well. She loved the feel of his skin, the smell of him, even the taste of him. She had become a complete wanton and she felt no guilt or shame about it.

It was probably why she was so slow to look long and hard at the very odd habits of her new husband. Yet, a wife could not ignore everything. Her husband had fangs. He was careful in how he smiled, laughed, or spoke, and she had begun to think she had imagined seeing them that time he had attacked her. Then, this very morning, she had been awakened by a most inelegant noise coming from her husband. Bothan had been sprawled on his back, his mouth open as he loudly snored, and she had gotten a very good look at his teeth before she had kicked him, causing him to snort a few times and roll onto his side. He definitely had fangs. Although she had heard of how a few men would file their teeth into points to add a fearsomeness to their looks, she could not make herself believe that was why Bothan had such long, sharp teeth. The other reasons a man would have fangs were not ones she wished to consider.

Her big, strong, manly husband purred. Kenna smiled, for it was rather endearing, not frightening at all, but there was no denying the fact that it was an odd thing for a man to do. The first time she had heard it, she had convinced herself that it was just a sound born of the pleasure he was feeling. It took her a few more times of listening to it before she could no longer deny what the sound was. Bothan purred like a big, beautiful cat.

Being rather fond of cats, Kenna had begun to notice other similarities between her braw husband and a cat. He moved like one, silently and gracefully. He even stretched very like a cat did. He could see very well in the dark, which was probably very useful to him since he seemed inclined to spend so much of his time lurking in the shadows. She had a strong suspicion that his hearing and his sense of smell were equally as keen. Thinking on such things strongly reminded her of how, when he had attacked her that first night, she had seen something very cat-like in his face. It was puzzling, for she could not really see how such abilities matched with what she had seen in her dreams—that Bothan had the heart of a wolf. Some of those feral qualities could belong to cats or wolves, she supposed. Kenna cursed softly and rubbed at her temples, trying to soothe the growing pinch of a headache.

"Poor lass, does your head ache?"

Kenna jumped in surprise when that familiar, deep voice spoke near her ear, for she had not heard a sound to announce Bothan's arrival. She looked at him, liking that look of concern upon his handsome face, yet annoyed by the way he so often startled her. Then he smiled at her, that sweet, well controlled smile that hid those very sharp teeth, and she frowned at him.

"Ye dinnae have to be so careful, so verra precise, in the way ye smile," she said. "I have seen them." And felt them, too, she suddenly thought, but decided not to mention that, for it had been when he had been giving her little love bites. At least she hoped that was what they were.

Bothan felt a tickle of unease but fought to subdue it. Kenna did not look particularly frightened or uneasy. It was probably for the best if he began to tell her a few things about himself, feed her the truth little by little to lessen whatever shock she might suffer when the full truth was made known to her. Despite that decision, he donned a look of confusion.

"Seen what?" he asked.

"Your teeth. Nay, your fangs. Ye were snoring—"

"I never snore."

She ignored that interruption. "Ye had your mouth wide open and there they were. Fangs. I had thought I had seen them before when ye attacked me in the cave, but I convinced myself that I was wrong. Weel, I wasnae. Did ye file them to be that way?"

"Nay. Many of my clan have such teeth. They arenae so verra strange. Ye have a pair of pointed teeth."

"Bothan, I am your wife, true enough, and thus I am with ye night and day. Howbeit, I doubt I am the only one who has noticed how ye avoid being out in the sun, how ye prefer the shadows, and how ye appear only in the verra early morn or at dusk. I suspect there are others who have e'en noticed those teeth. If naught else, ye should give me an answer, an explanation of some sort, so that I might use it when others ask why this or that is."

"Ah, there is that to consider."

"Aye, there is."

"It isnae verra monly, but the truth is that I cannae abide

the sunlight when it grows strong. It makes me ill. And, nay, my clan hasnae been able to fully breed that out, either, although I and my brothers are less sensitive to it than my father." He shrugged. "As I said, it isnae a verra monly affliction."

"Sunlight makes ye ill?"

"Aye. Why do ye still frown so? I have told ye the truth."

"Oh, aye, I believe ye have. I also think that ye havenae told me *all* of the truth, but it doesnae matter. What ye have told me will serve weel enough." She glanced toward where the sun was rapidly disappearing beneath the horizon and then looked back at him. "We will be leaving soon, aye?"

"Aye. There will be a full, bright moon tonight and that will light our way. We should reach Bantulach soon."

She nodded. "If we have no trouble 'tis but a day's ride away, mayhap a day and a wee bit."

"And then our wee honeymoon will be at an end."

Kenna eyed him with suspicion when he moved to stand in front of her, placing his hands against the stone wall on either side of her. He had that glint in his fine golden eyes, the one that made her go a little weak in the knees. Her husband was proving to be a very greedy man.

"Should we nay collect our belongings?" she asked, unable to silence a murmur of pleasure when he kissed her neck.

"Soon." Bothan tugged up her skirts and caressed her bottom. Her very naked bottom, he thought, and frowned. "Where are those wee braies ye always wear?"

"When I woke up I felt a need to get out of that wee tomb verra quickly and so I just yanked on my shift and gown and hurried outside." Kenna gasped with a mixture of shock and delight when he slipped his hand between her thighs and began to stroke her in that way that made her crazed with desire.

"Ah, my bonnie wee delight, ye already weep for me."

Before she could foolishly try to deny how swiftly he could rouse her need for him, he was planted firmly inside her. He wrapped his arm around her waist and lifted her up a little so that he could stand straight and thrust himself in even deeper. Kenna knew she ought to protest this abrupt, somewhat rough, lovemaking and the fact that they were outside. Instead she wrapped her arms and legs around him and kissed him with all the greed she could not hide as he took them both to their own private paradise.

Bothan grinned as he watched Kenna fuss with her skirts and pat at her hair, both actions clearly revealing her embarrassment. He should probably be embarrassed as well, but he was not. Their lovemaking had been rough, fierce, and lacking any practiced skills at all, and he had loved every brief minute of it. Kenna might still blush and suffer the sting of embarrassment, but she was a fiercely passionate woman and he was eager for the time when the latter smothered the former. When Kenna finally recognized her power, accepted her passionate nature and reveled in it, she would probably kill him, he thought and grinned.

Kenna scowled at him. "How can ye smile so? We are outside! I cannae believe we just did that," she muttered and shook her head.

"There was no helping it, lass," he said. "I could smell me on ye and ye on me. That got me to thinking on why I could smell that, about how that scent got there, and I had to have ye. The need came o'er me too swiftly and fiercely to ignore."

Taking a swift sniff of her arm, Kenna frowned with suspicion. There was a faint aroma of lovemaking in the air, but she could smell nothing on her skin. In truth, what troubled her the most was not how, when, or where they made love, but how quickly she succumbed to the man. The smug, satisfied look on his handsome face irritated her as well.

"Then I had best go and bathe in the burn," she said. "We wouldnae want ye to be overcome with such urges once we begin our journey, would we. It could frighten the horses."

He laughed as she hurried inside to get a few things she would need to bathe in the burn, but then frowned when she came out and started to walk toward the thick growth of trees blocking all sight of the water. "Mayhap I should come with ye." Bothan came to an abrupt halt when she held her hand out toward him, the palm facing him.

"Nay. I am a grown woman who likes privacy when she bathes."

"Lass, we just—"

"I ken verra weel what we just did."

"And I have seen ye naked."

"I ken that, too, but seeing me naked when we are doing, er, that is different. I am nay thinking about being naked then." The way he cocked his eyebrow told her he was thinking that explanation was a foolish one, but he had the good sense not to say so. "I will still be close enough that ye will have no trouble hearing me if I scream for help."

"Ye had best be quick," he said as she started to walk away again.

"Considering how cold the water will be, I have nay doubt at all that I will be verra quick about it."

Bothan watched her until she disappeared into the trees. He could not shake the feeling that it was a very bad idea to let her out of his sight or go anywhere alone, yet she wanted her privacy and he knew he ought to allow her to have some. After a moment he decided he would also have a brisk wash down at the burn. Not far from where Kenna was headed, there was a bend in the little river where he could be near to her yet out of her sight. He got what he needed to bathe and headed toward the burn, careful to stay out of her line of sight in case she happened to look back.

Kenna stuck her fingers in the clear water of the burn and grimaced. It was cold and she was tempted to forgo a complete bath, just washing a few particular spots instead. Then she sighed and began to take off her gown. She might not be able to smell Bothan on her skin, but she was sure she could smell other things she would prefer to be rid of such as horses and sweat. Lovemaking was a very vigorous business, she mused.

After a moment of thought, Kenna decided to keep her shift on. It also needed washing and she could not really bring herself to bathe naked in the open air. It would be just her luck to be caught at it by some passing raiding party. Taking a deep breath to prepare herself, she plunged into the water and yelped softly as the chill of it hit her full force. This was definitely going to be a very, very short bath.

As she vigorously scrubbed herself clean, Kenna thought about what she had just done with Bothan. Her embarrassment was gone, but she remained somewhat concerned. She had no control over her desire when he touched her. Or kissed her. Or looked at her with that glint in his feral eyes. In truth, she had absolutely no control over her own desires at all. Her passion for her husband appeared to lurk just under her skin, ready to flare to life at a smile from him. Rather like a particularly nasty rash, she thought crossly. She was his whenever the mood took him, and he knew it. Her only consolation was that he appeared to desire her with an equal ferocity. Although, she knew she was too ignorant of such things to know if that was really because of her or because men were always eager and lusty. There were all those jests she had heard about men and sheep that she only now understood fully to confirm that opinion. Still, there was a chance that she could affect him as strongly as he did her. She simply needed to learn a lot more about the business of lovemaking.

Kenna sighed, finally admitting to herself just why she felt almost desperate to prove that Bothan needed her as much as she needed him. She was in love with the man. There were still a lot of secrets he held fast to, but she no longer really cared what they were. They would make no difference to what she felt for the man. She was just not sure how he felt about her aside from the desire he made no effort to hide. That was fine, very fine indeed, but she needed so much more from him.

"So now what do I do?" she muttered.

Run!

"*Maman?*"

Run, my child! Run now!

Without asking why, or where her mother had been since leaving her alone on her wedding night, Kenna hurried out of the water. She was just reaching for her clothes when six men burst out of the surrounding wood. They grinned as they stepped closer, hemming her in on three sides with the water at her back. Kenna shivered and she knew it was not just because she stood in a soaking wet shift in the cool evening air.

"Ye were a lot easier to find than he thought ye would be," said the tall, pale man directly facing her, his grin revealing that what few teeth he had in his head were rotting.

"Than *who* said I would be?" she asked, desperately trying to think of some way to escape these men. At the moment it appeared that leaping back into the water was her only choice, but she would not be able to stay in that cold water for long, and one of these men just might be able to swim.

"Your uncle."

Kenna heard her mother curse and nearly echoed it. Her uncle had obviously wanted to make very sure that she never returned to Bantulach. Even though it was not the great shock it should have been, since she had already guessed at his murderous tendencies, it still hurt. People of your own blood, your closest relatives, were supposed to be the ones you could turn to in a time of need. They were not supposed to turn on you, to try to kill you, and to try to steal what was rightfully yours.

"And ye have sought me out for what reason?" she asked, crossing her arms over her chest to try to hide her breasts, which the men were staring at a little too intently.

"Come, ye look to be a lass with a little wit, eh? To kill ye, of course."

"I see. He has hired ye to do what he is too cowardly to do himself."

"Aye," the man replied with no hesitation, and his compatriots snickered. "He was afeart ye might find a way to come home." He nodded to his men as he and they drew their daggers. "'Tis a sad business and all of that, but the mon pays weel."

"How nice for ye. And what about my husband?"

"Is that what ye are calling your braw lover, eh? Wheesht, dinnae think to threaten us with that bonnie laddie. Two of my men are—"

"Dead. As, I promise, ye soon will be."

Kenna watched the man in front of her pale as he realized that Bothan had somehow managed to drop from the sky and now stood behind him. Somehow Bothan had crept up behind the man and none of them had noticed him. She winced as her husband grabbed the man by the head and sharply twisted it, loudly snapping his neck, and then let the body fall to the ground. Bothan had that feral look upon his face again and, as he grabbed the dead man's dagger, she did not think he had ever looked so beautiful to her as he did right now. She did wonder, however, just how Bothan expected to defeat so many men armed with only a dagger.

"Can ye swim, lass?" he asked.

"Aye, like a fish," she replied.

"Good. Take a deep breath right now."

Eight

Her husband threw her into the water. Kenna was several feet under the water before she fully accepted the fact that, with one hand, her husband had flung her into the water as if she was a child's toy he no longer wanted. Then she recalled the men with their knives, and she used all her strength to swim to the surface as fast as she could. How dare he toss her aside when he faced such terrible odds. She should be at his side helping him in any way she could.

The first sight she got of her husband as her head cleared the surface of the water told her that he did not really need anyone's help. In the short time he had been out of her sight, he had killed two more men. The remaining three looked ready to bolt, torn between a need to survive this confrontation and a pride that rebelled at the thought of such an ignominious retreat from one man, especially since that man was once again unarmed. Kenna could see Bothan's mouth moving and suspected he was taunting the men. She tried to get the water out of her ears so that she could hear as well as see what was happening.

Suddenly all three men lunged at Bothan, and Kenna cried out in alarm as she watched her husband disappear beneath three cursing, knife-wielding men. She hurried to reach the bank, not sure what she could do, but feeling a desperate need to help Bothan. When she was barely a foot away from the bank, she stopped and gaped at the sight before her. The three men attacking Bothan slowly began to rise up. Bothan was getting to his feet despite the weight of three-full grown men still clinging to his body. It was impossible, and yet she could not deny the proof of her own eyes.

A strange noise escaped her husband. It strongly reminded her of the sound a cat makes while fighting. The man who had been clinging to Bothan's right arm suddenly went flying through the air. Kenna winced and felt a little ill when his body slammed into a tree and she heard the cracking of bones. The way he fell to the ground and did not move told her that he, too, was dead. She looked back at Bothan as she slowly crept that last, short distance to the bank. The two surviving attackers now looked absolutely terrified and she could not blame them.

There was a man clinging to Bothan's back and Bothan used his now free right arm to reach around and tear the man off, then toss him aside. Although she was shocked and fear was a tight knot in her belly, Kenna thought Bothan looked magnificent. He was like some great beast lashing out at the ones who had dared to corner him in his lair.

"What are ye?" asked the third man even as he released Bothan's left arm and took a step back.

A good question, Kenna thought.

"Your executioner," Bothan replied.

He moved so quickly, Kenna did not realize what he was doing until she heard the ominous snap of bone. Her uncle's hireling fell to the ground, his head at the odd angle that told her his neck had been broken. It had all been done with such swift, cold precision that Kenna felt torn between admiration and revulsion. Throughout most of the battle, Bothan had had no weapon and yet he had killed five men. She suddenly recalled mention of men who had been sent to kill Bothan. After seeing what her husband was capable of, Kenna had no doubt that those two men were dead as well.

Then, without a hint of warning, the man Bothan had tossed from his back stood up, his dagger in his hand. Kenna heard herself cry out a warning as the man thrust his dagger toward Bothan's chest. The two men grappled with each other for a moment and she could not see if the attacker's blade had struck home. A moment later she watched her husband duck his head a little and the man with the dagger released a strange, watery scream. Kenna felt close to fainting when she realized Bothan had just bitten the man's neck, had used his sharp teeth as a weapon. He was very slow to release the man, but, when he did, she felt her stomach turn. The final one of her uncle's men was dead, his throat torn open.

Bothan slowly fell to his knees and hung his head. Kenna could see his broad back heaving as he fought to catch his breath. She felt torn between the urge to rush to his side and one to run away from him as fast as she could. The one thing that puzzled her also added to her fears. Why was there so little blood coming from the fatal wound upon that last man's throat? Kenna did not really think she wanted that question answered.

Go to him, child.

"*Maman,*" she whispered, "did ye nay see what he just did?"

Aye, he saved your life. Now, go to him. He needs ye and did ye nay just decide that ye love him?

She had, she thought as she slowly crept out of the water. Of course, that was when she had thought he was just a little different. However, a man who is just a little different does not kill eight men with his bare hands. He does not toss people around as if they weigh little or nothing. He does not rip open a man's throat with his teeth. He does not yowl like an enraged cat. He also does not survive, apparently unharmed, when three men with drawn daggers leap on top of him.

Suddenly realizing that Bothan could actually be wounded, even mortally so, Kenna rushed to his side. She slowly knelt down by his side as she saw the blood upon his shirt and how it was ripped in several places. Looking more closely, she could see that some of those tears had been caused by the thrusts of daggers. She could see blood all around those cuts in his shirt, but none was flowing now. That made no sense to her, but then little of what she had just witnessed made any sense, either.

Wary about startling him, she resisted the urge to touch him and softly asked, "Are ye wounded, Bothan?"

When he finally looked at her, Kenna had to swiftly smother a gasp of shock and surprise. He still had blood upon his mouth. Despite the battle he had just been in, he looked hale and strong. In fact, he looked as if it had all invigorated him. There was also the shadow of something dark and feral lingering in his expression. Just who was this man she was now bound to for life?

Bothan saw the wariness in Kenna's eyes, that glint of fear, and inwardly cursed. He wiped his face with the sleeve of his shirt and silently cursed again when he saw the new bloodstains that had appeared. Instinct and the need to survive had driven him to feed upon that last man. Bleeding from several wounds, he had been rapidly weakening and had blindly sought out the quickest, surest way to recover his lost strength. He was not sure how much of that his wife had seen, but he suspected the way he had fought and killed her attackers was more than enough to stir that unease he could see reflected in her face.

"I am fine," he said, pleased when she did not flinch as he lightly caressed her cheek with his fingers. "Did they hurt ye?"

"Nay." She sighed. "My uncle sent them to kill me."

"Aye, I suspected it. I should have watched for just such an attack more closely." He saw her shiver. "Ye are cold, lass. Wrap yourself in a blanket, collect up your things, and return to the bothy."

"Alone?" she asked, even as she moved to do what he said.

"I will be along shortly. I must wash away this blood first," he added softly.

Kenna nodded as she collected her things and walked away. Bothan watched until she was out of sight and then got to his feet. Looking around at the bodies scattered along the riverbank, he grimaced. He had saved her life but it might have cost him very dearly. Caught in a fight for her life and his own, all that made him his father's son had burst forth and she had seen it. As he moved to search the bodies for anything of value, such as the proof of just who had hired them, Bothan tried to find some consolation in the fact that she had rushed to his side to offer aid and she had not shrunk from his touch. There might still be hope that he had found the woman who would not flee from what he was. He now knew that he needed that acceptance from Kenna, needed it as he had never needed anything else.

Ye are thinking on it all far too much, child.

Sighing as she packed her things, Kenna was not really surprised to hear her mother's voice again. For some reason her mother was determined that Kenna stay with Bothan. The woman had pushed her into this marriage and was now making sure that she did not falter.

"*Maman,* the mon isnae merely different. I begin to fear that he isnae e'en human."

He is human, lass, just a different breed of human. Are ye nay different from others?

"Aye, but I dinnae toss grown men about as if they weigh naught and I dinnae rip their throats open with my teeth. And where did the blood from that gruesome wound go? Nay, dinnae answer that. I dinnae want to ken the answer."

He isnae a demon, love. Do ye really think I would be here urging ye to stay with him if he was?

"Nay." Kenna finished lacing up her gown and then

began to braid her still-damp hair. "Ye dinnae need to lecture me. I am still here, aye? I will stay with him. I just need time and ye cannae fault me for that. What he did today was more than enough to send anyone else running for the hills. Aye, I do feel a wee touch of fear, but I also ken that he willnae hurt me. I can see now that he could have killed me in a heartbeat back in the cave, but he didnae. I also see that all he just did was done to save me. 'Twill just take me a wee while to understand, to accept it all."

He will explain it all to ye soon, my child.

"How soon?"

There was no reply, and Kenna cursed. A moment later Bothan arrived. For the first time in days she felt uneasy around her husband. There was a look in his eyes that told her he knew it and it hurt him. Kenna felt bad about that, but knew she could do little to change how she felt. She still loved him, but she now saw that he was still mostly a stranger to her, a somewhat frightening stranger as well.

"Your uncle was fool enough to put his order to those men in writing, though it surprises me that any of them could read," Bothan said as he handed her the missive he had found in one of the dead men's packs. "He also paid them weel with money that is rightfully yours." He tossed her the purse of coins he had found and was a little surprised at how neatly she caught it, but then he moved away to collect up his belongings. "He could hang for that alone."

He could, Kenna thought as she tucked both items into her pack, but she would be the one who would have to order it done. Unlike her uncle, she did not really have the stomach to order someone's death even when it was a just punishment, especially when that someone was such a close kinsman. It appeared that she did lack some of what was needed to be a strong laird. That thought made her feel sad and she sighed.

"The mon wanted ye dead, lass," Bothan said quietly as he picked up her belongings.

"I ken it. I ken he is a threat to me, but I fear I am nay such a great threat to him. At first I was hurt and insulted by my father's command to get a strong mon to stand at my side, but now I think he kenned me better than I did myself. My uncle *should* be hanged, but I am nay sure I can order it done."

"Then I will see to it for ye."

"That would certainly solve my problem," she said carefully.

"But ye are nay sure ye have the stomach for that, either. Weel then, we banish him from Bantulach the moment we get there."

Bothan watched her face as she considered that solution. He would feel much better if the man was immediately killed, but he could understand her hesitation. If she chose banishment he would abide by her wishes, but he would keep a verra close watch on her and her uncle. He doubted the mon would give up easily. Kelvyn Brodie had been willing to kill his own brother and niece for Bantulach. The mon would not be defeated by mere banishment.

What interested him far more at the moment was that she was talking to him. More than that, she was still including him in her plans, her decisions, and her future. Despite the wariness he sensed in her, she had not decided to turn her back on him yet. He needed to take her to bed and taste her passion for him again. That would help to still his fears, but it was far too soon for that.

"Aye, banishing him might work," she said at last, not sounding at all confident of that.

"If he doesnae stay banished, lass, if he still tries to harm ye, I *will* kill him."

Kenna slowly nodded. "I understand. We cannae allow my weakness to harm us."

Us she said, and Bothan felt something inside of him relax a little as he took their belongings out to the horses. It might be a long, hard road ahead to soothe her concerns and gain her full acceptance, but he still had hope of doing so. If, after all she had seen today, she could still say *us*, there was most definitely hope for him.

The fact that her acceptance of him was so important to him was only a little disconcerting. Kenna was, after all, his wife. They were bound together for life by vows given before God, vows witnessed by his own cousin, no less. They were also bound together in the spirit and the flesh. He was as certain of that as he was of his own name. She was his mate. That urge he felt to mark her so, an urge that grew stronger each time he held her in his arms, was all the proof he needed.

That acceptance had to come first, however. He was not really starved for such acceptance, as both sides of his very large family accepted him for all that he was. He even had a few carefully chosen Outsiders as friends who did so. Yet Kenna's acceptance was truly vital to him, if only because she would be the mother of his children. And, he thought with a grimace, if he was truly honest with himself, a very large part of his heart ached for it.

When Kenna joined him by the horses, he helped her mount and kept his hands upon her waist for a little longer than necessary. She could already be carrying his child. The MacNachtons might be poor breeders, but the Callans, his mother's family, were very fertile. It was a gift from her ancestress, the Celtic shape-shifter. He had enough of those catlike qualities peculiar to the Callans to be hopeful that he was fertile as well.

As he mounted Moonracer, he decided he was going to have to tell Kenna everything very soon. If he was as fertile as a Callan, Kenna needed to know what to expect in any child they bred together. He would allow himself a month, mayhap even two, to win that acceptance he so deeply craved. After that he would simply tell her the whole truth and pray that he had won enough of her heart not to lose her.

* * *

"There lies Bantulach," said Kenna, pointing to the large stone keep set upon a knoll. Bothan nodded.

She quickly covered a big yawn with her hand as she nudged her mare to follow Bothan's gelding toward the gates of her home. They had ridden as hard as they had dared, and the moon was only beginning to fade in the sky as the sun crept up over the horizon. She ached for a bath and a nice, soft bed. After she ate a very hearty meal, of course, she decided when her stomach loudly reminded her of how long it had been since she had eaten.

Glancing at Bothan, she could see how tensely he sat in the saddle as they rode toward the slowly opening gates. He was preparing himself for the confrontation with her uncle. Kenna realized she had given that little thought, for her mind had been filled with the puzzle of Sir Bothan MacNachton and just what she should do about him. A part of her was pleased that they had not discussed what had occurred near the burn, for she feared she might have said something that could have hurt his feelings. Another part of her wished they had, for she needed to talk about it with someone, and her mother was gone again. Her friend Florrie would be no help, either. One thing Kenna was sure of was that most of the people at Bantulach could not know the truth about her husband, for they were too deeply mired in superstition, and Florrie had never been good at keeping a secret.

As they rode through the gates of Bantulach, Kenna became aware of how hard everyone was staring at her. It was rather obvious that many of them were stunned to see her alive. To her surprise, it looked as if many were truly pleased to see her return home safe and sound. Perhaps things would be a little different now.

"Is that your uncle, lass?" Bothan asked as he reined in Moonracer and Kenna reined in her mare at his side.

Kenna looked at the tall, thin man walking toward them. "Aye, 'tis my dear Uncle Kelvyn."

"I thought it might be, as, for just a moment when he first stepped out of the keep, there was a look of shock and anger upon his face. He is most displeased to see that you have come home."

"He will be even more displeased in just a moment."

"I dinnae trust him, lass."

"Neither do I."

"Banishment might not be enough to stop him."

"After giving it some thought as we rode, I came to that conclusion myself, but I have to at least try it."

"Agreed."

"Greetings, Kenna," said her uncle as he reached them and stood in front of their horses. "I didnae expect ye to return so soon. Have ye accomplished your quest, then?"

"In a way, Uncle," she replied. "I considered the matter verra carefully as I rode about the countryside, all alone and unprotected, and I decided that returning with only a few bits of a mon was foolish. After all, didnae Papa say that I should marry a strong mon?" Kenna saw her uncle's jaw tighten as the people around them murmured their agreement to her words. "So, instead of the hand, head, and heart of a MacNachton, I decided to bring all of one home. I really couldnae decide which bit to wed, anyway." She ignored Bothan's grunt of disgust at that poor humor and nodded toward him. "Allow me to present to ye Sir Bothan MacNachton, my husband."

The look upon her uncle's face was worth every sore muscle she had collected in her long night of riding.

Nine

"Are ye certain we should have banished Kelvyn from Bantulach so quickly?" Kenna asked, absently smiling her gratitude to the young boy who set the fruit on the table in front of her and Bothan.

"Ye seemed to think it was wiser than killing him," Bothan replied. "He is your kinsmon, after all."

He spoke of killing her uncle so calmly, almost pleasantly, and Kenna felt a slight chill ripple through her. Yet, she understood why he would think it a proper judgment on the man. Bothan also had the safety of his own clan to consider. She had no proof that her uncle had killed her father, but there was no doubt at all that he had tried to kill her. From the moment she had seen the proof that her own uncle had hired men to kill her, she had wavered back and forth between killing him as the law allowed or just making him go away. The man had been gone for two days and she still wavered over her decision.

"I am not usually so indecisive," she murmured and smiled faintly at Bothan when he set a peeled, cored, and neatly cut-up apple before her. "At first I thought it was because I was so verra tired, but I am weel rested now."

"Aye, ye have done little but sleep since we arrived."

There was a tone to his voice that told her he was growing weary of using their bed only for sleeping. She was sure he knew she was not playing at being so weary in some attempt to avoid him, but such a passionate man had to be growing tired of lying next to a woman who probably could not have been awakened if two dozen pipers stomped through the bedchamber. Kenna found that she really had no hesitation, no doubts or reservations, about indulging in the passion they shared, although she still had some uneasiness concerning what he was. That was a puzzle she really needed to take some time to figure out. And she would. Soon.

In some ways her long rest had dimmed the shock she had suffered that day by the burn. Most of her fear had fled as well, conquered by her confidence that Bothan would never hurt her. Questions crowded her mind, however, but she could not bring herself to ask them. Part of her was afraid of the truth and part of her was afraid he would not tell her the truth. Kenna felt certain that what little he had told her was not really a lie, but it was not the whole truth, either. At some point they were going to have to end this dance, but she was not sure she was ready to do so yet.

One thing did continue to haunt her. In that vision she had had in the cave she had seen Bothan with blood on his lips, but not as she had seen him by the burn. In her vision it had been her blood. She was certain of it. What she was not certain of, and what continued to trouble her, was the meaning of that vision. Did it mean that Bothan had a taste for blood, something that had already been revealed, or did it mean that at some time in the future he would be sinking those very sharp teeth into her neck? And, if so, why?

"Ye are looking troubled again, lass," he said quietly.

"There is a lot to be troubled about. And, I am sorry I have left ye to deal with the people of Bantulach all alone, especially since my uncle has poisoned their minds against ye with all he has said about the MacNachtons."

"There has been no trouble. 'Struth, the people mostly do their best to avoid me."

"Oh, dear. They are obviously going to put us to the test. Does no one welcome ye?"

"A few. Simon, your friend Florrie, who has been asking after ye, Ellar in the stables, who has decided that any mon with a horse like Moonracer cannae be a demon," he smiled briefly when she laughed, "Fergie the Lame, Agnes in the kitchens, Mungo the blacksmith, and Alban. Oh, and Freja, the swineherd's sister."

"What of Ian the swineherd?"

"He isnae sure, I think."

"Actually, Bothan, I fear Ian is a mon who is ne'er sure of anything. Freja has e'er been the strong one in that family. But 'tis a start. Of course, each of the ones ye have mentioned are the same ones who were always good to me. 'Tis a fine group of fair-minded people who dinnae let foolish superstition rule them. The others used to avoid me as weel, but that must change now. I am just nay sure how to do it," she added quietly, knowing that changing the habits and beliefs of years would be a great challenge.

Bothan reached out, took her hand in his, and kissed the inside of her wrist. The faint tremor that went up her arm at the touch of his lips encouraged him. Tonight he would put their passion to the test just as he had been wanting to since that day by the burn. He felt himself harden at the mere thought of making love to her again and forced his mind back to the matter of her visit with her people.

"Just be what ye are, lass," he said. "I havenae sensed any rejection of ye as the rightful heir. In fact, most seem relieved that your uncle is gone e'en if they havenae openly and cheerfully welcomed ye as the laird."

"That is something to be pleased about, aye?" She smiled when he nodded. "Weel, I shall have to see how the wind blows as soon as I finish this apple. I will walk about and talk to the people."

"Do ye wish me to go with ye?" Bothan was not sure that would be a good idea, but was willing to go if she wanted him to.

She kissed his hand before slipping hers free of his grasp and reached for a piece of apple. "I would like that, but I think this time 'tis best if I wander about alone." She was relieved when he nodded, for she had feared insulting him or even hurting his feelings with her refusal. "And, it *is* a verra bright, sunny day," she murmured, and grinned at the narrow-eyed look he gave her. "Nay, I will go about as I always have. No one at Bantulach has e'er held their tongue round me, so I may gain a truer idea of how everyone feels than if ye were there standing next to me."

"Agreed. Just remember that ye are your father's heir, that together we are their laird. Use that knowledge to stiffen your backbone." He had to smile when she sat up straighter. "Aye, listen to what they have to say, as 'tis your duty to do so, but ye are now the one who makes the final decision and that is what ye must impress upon them."

Finishing the last of her apple, Kenna stood up and kissed him on the cheek. "*We* are the ones who make the final decisions," she said.

As she walked out of the great hall, Bothan slowly unclenched his hands. It had been hard to resist the urge to pull her into his arms, but it had been a wise decision. She needed to see and be seen by her people, needed to hear what they had to say about him and about her marriage. Even if her uncle had not stirred up a lot of fear and superstition against the MacNachtons, the people of Bantulach would still be reluctant to speak to him. In Bantulach, *he* was the Outsider.

The kiss she had given him and her words before she had walked away had nearly broken his restraint upon his need for her, however. He had hoped that her long and much-needed rest would dim the memory of that time beside the burn, but he had also feared it could strengthen her wariness because the memories of that time had plagued her in her dreams. It was clear that he had come out on the winning side this time. He just prayed that his good luck would continue.

* * *

"Kenna!"

Pulled from her thoughts about what to do about Mistress Anna the alewife, Kenna looked to see who had hailed her. She smiled when she saw Florrie racing toward her and opened her arms just in time to return her friend's hearty embrace. Slightly taller and a great deal more buxom, the fair-haired Florrie tended to smother Kenna when she hugged her, but Kenna did not complain. It felt good to find someone happy to see her.

"I feared ye were sick," Florrie said as she stepped back and carefully looked Kenna over. "Ye look fine."

"I am fine. I was but verra, verra tired," replied Kenna as she hooked her arm through Florrie's and they started to walk along the road back toward the keep.

"Aye, it must have been an ordeal to leave here and come back with such a verra, verra handsome mon." Florrie laughed along with Kenna, but then grew serious and asked quietly, "He isnae really a demon, is he?'

"Of course he isnae, Florrie. Do ye really think I would marry a demon? Or that a demon would have a priest for a cousin?"

"He has a priest for a cousin?"

"He does and 'twas the cousin who married us in a wee stone kirk."

"Ye will have such bonnie bairns."

"Aye, and I hope they have his bonnie golden eyes," Kenna said and realized that she truly meant it. "But, that isnae of importance just yet. I have been walking about, talking with everyone I can, just to see how much trouble Bothan and I shall have being accepted."

"It willnae be easy, I fear. I saw ye talking with Anna. She is the worst and is most outspoken about her feelings. She isnae really changing anyone's mind, but she does keep those who feel as she does all afire with fear and indignation. The things your uncle said about the MacNachtons truly frightened some people, Kenna. 'Tis verra odd, but I begin to think the fact that he is such a verra handsome lad has only added fuel to that fire."

"The devil would send us a beautiful mon, or woman, to tempt us, wouldnae he?"

"Ah, aye. I hadnae thought of that. It does make sense. Still, I dinnae understand what they are all complaining about. No one liked your uncle and most people think he had a hand in your father's death."

"So do I, but I have no proof. I did have proof that he tried to have me killed."

Florrie nodded. "Simon told me. Your husband showed it to him and a few others when some gathered the courage to go to him to complain about how rudely your uncle was tossed out of the keep. Tossed out and told to keep on going until he was no longer on Bantulach lands." Florrie shook her head. "To kill his own kin just to lay claim to a place where he has always been free to live anyway, and to live verra weel, is pure madness."

"Ah, but he wasnae the laird. He didnae rule, did he? He was naught but the laird's younger brother and that wasnae good enough for Uncle Kelvyn."

"Ye dinnae think he will give up, do ye?"

"Nay, I dinnae. Banishing him was chosen because I couldnae stomach ordering the death of my kinsmon, but I think he will force me to see him killed. I but pray he doesnae take me or Bothan with him."

Kenna sat before the looking glass her father had given her on her sixteenth birthday and idly combed out her still-damp hair. She had pampered herself with a long, hot bath and felt quite relaxed now. Even the events of the day could be looked upon with calm. It was not as bad as it could be. No one was collecting the kindling for a pyre yet. She and Bothan had only a few allies, but they also only had a few serious enemies. Most everyone else at Bantulach could not decide one way or the other and simply waited to see what would happen.

When Bothan entered their bedchamber, Kenna struggled not to blush and was not sure she was completely successful. Tonight she was wide awake and he would be expecting, wanting, to make love to her. She wanted to make love to him, too. The fact that they both expected to do that made it all seem so planned, and she suspected that was why she felt a little embarrassed and shy.

Bothan stepped up behind her and took the brush from her hands. He began to slowly brush out her hair, running his fingers through it almost as often as he pulled the brush through it. He had been patient throughout the long meal shared with Simon and Florrie. It had been informative and they had had a very good discussion about how to still the fears Kelvyn had roused in the people, but he had been eager for it to end. Finding the patience to wait as Kenna had her bath had been hard.

"I think it will be a verra long time ere we are fully accepted by e'en most of the people of Bantulach," Kenna said.

"Aye, but we will do it. One thing that will help is the fact that we will soon be more prosperous, for your uncle, I fear, was stealing from you and from your father."

"I should nay be shocked by that, but I am. He took a lot?"

"Aye. Now it will stay where it belongs and can be used to make life better for the people of Bantulach. The better their lives are, the better ours will be."

Kenna nodded and then tensed slightly when he leaned forward to set her brush down on the little table she sat in front of. That tension fled in a heartbeat when he kissed her neck. Just the touch of his lips against her skin made her hungry for him. When he reached down and slowly began to unlace her night shift, she felt her earlier attack of shyness swiftly replaced by a need to feel his hands upon her skin.

"I am a verra hungry mon tonight, my wee wife," he

murmured against the side of her neck. "It has been a long time."

"It has been but two days," she said, laughter tinting her voice.

"It has felt more like two years."

She gasped softly with pleasure and closed her eyes when he slid his hands inside of her shift and caressed her breasts. Even though she had needed her rest and would not have given it up, she had missed his touch. Kenna knew this hunger for him ought to tell her something about the validity of the unease she still suffered from at times, but she would have to think about that later. Her passion was flaring so quickly and hotly now, she doubted she would be able to recall her own name soon.

Bothan suddenly pulled her to her feet and yanked off her night shift. Kenna did not even have time to blush over her nakedness before he picked her up and almost threw her onto the bed. She watched as he hastily tossed aside his clothes and then joined her on the bed. The eagerness he was revealing was very flattering, but he looked a little disconcerted by it.

"I was going to love ye slowly, make ye so crazed with passion your eyes rolled back into your head," he muttered against her left breast, "but I cannae wait. Sleeping next to ye and nay touching ye has shredded whate'er control I have."

Kenna slid her hand slowly down his spine and caressed his taut backside. "Who asked ye to exercise any control, husband?"

That was obviously invitation enough. Kenna was briefly surprised at the ferocity of his lovemaking, but she quickly got caught up in the same fever infecting him. She wrapped her body around his and gave herself over to this fierce, unquenchable desire they shared.

Bothan slowly turned onto his back and dragged Kenna's limp body close to his side. So much for his plans to use her passion to soothe the unease she still felt. He had just shown all the restraint and finesse of a boy with his first woman. His only consolation, and it was actually a very fine one, was that Kenna had been as crazed with need as he had been. It might not have been the way he had planned to see if her passion for him still ran hot, but it would serve.

"That wasnae exactly how I had planned this reunion," he murmured and felt Kenna smile against his skin.

"Ye mean my eyes didnae roll back into my head?" she asked and laughed softly when he grunted. "Does it really matter how we get to that place of bliss?"

"Nay, although leaping upon ye like a mad fool isnae the best way."

"It felt like the best to me."

He smiled, absurdly flattered by that remark. "Weel, as soon as I have rested and recouped my strength, I will try again."

"How nice," she murmured in a sleepy voice. "Wake me when ye decide ye are ready to give me this fine show of all your ill-gotten skills."

"Actually, I had plans to practice a few new skills, to try a few things I have ne'er done before."

"Are these things accepted by the church?"

He laughed softly. "If they arenae, I will just get my cousin to give us both absolution."

"How nice to have a priest in the family to take care of all those wee difficulties. Do ye ken, telling some people that ye have a cousin who is a priest seems to be enough to make them think ye couldnae possibly be a demon. 'Tis the strangest thing," she whispered.

Bothan felt her go limp against him and grinned again. He had exhausted his wife. Considering how much she had slept over the last two days, that was definitely an accomplishment to take pride in.

He suddenly thought hard about her exhaustion. It was true that she had probably been worn to the bone by her experiences since her uncle had sent her away from Bantulach, yet all that sleeping she had done should have cured that. Now, after one bout of lovemaking, she was tired again. It had been a vigorous bout, but he was usually the one who slept a little after such a thing. He felt sure that Kenna was not ailing from some strange malady. That left only one other thing that could make a woman sleep so often and feel so tired all the time. Kenna was already carrying his child.

Since they had been married for only a week, he found it hard to believe she would already be showing such symptoms, but he could not shake the feeling that that was exactly what ailed her. He sternly reminded himself of the inability of MacNachtons to breed children, their seed weakened by decades of inbreeding. Unfortunately, his mind quickly reminded him of the excellent ability of the Callans to breed children, lots of children, and quite often in pairs. For all he knew, Kenna was a woman whose body immediately reacted to the planting of a seed. He would have to keep a very close watch on her.

After indulging in a huge yawn, Bothan closed his eyes. Kenna may have gotten a lot of sleep over the last two days, but he had gotten very little. He had fretted over the chance that her passion had cooled toward him and his inability to test that. He had fretted over the possibility that Kelvyn Brodie would keep trying to kill her. He had even fretted over the possibility that he and Kenna would never gain the acceptance of her clan and what that could mean to their future at Bantulach. He had, in short, fretted much of the night away for the past two nights and he was tired. He would sleep for just a little while and then he would make love to his wife again.

Ten

Kenna awoke feeling so hot she almost checked to see if someone had set the bed on fire. Then she realized she was being kissed. Between her legs. Shocked even as desire continued to run hot through her body, she dared a glance in that direction. Bothan was sprawled between her legs, his mouth upon that part of her body she had no decent name for.

"Bothan," she gasped.

"Hush, my wee wife," he said, gently nipping her thigh when she tried to clamp her legs together. "Ye will like this."

Like was a mild word for what she felt. That moment of clarity caused by her shock faded as she succumbed to her own desire. All modesty and restraint left her as he teased and stroked her with his tongue, loving her with his mouth. When she felt that bliss approaching, she called out his name, but he ignored her urgings for him to join with her, taking her to that sweet paradise with his mouth instead of his body.

The moment her senses cleared, Kenna began to feel embarrassed. She sternly told herself that although Bothan was different in many ways, he was still a man and had not shown any tendency toward perversion. Yet, the deep intimacy of that kiss was difficult to accept calmly. She slowly opened one eye and saw him grinning at her.

"I kenned ye would like that," he said, and playfully kissed her nose.

"Did ye, now. And how would ye ken that?" She silently cursed for asking the question, knowing it revealed her lingering jealousy over all the women in his past.

"I have been assured by men who have indulged that it can drive a woman mad with desire."

Kenna frowned. "Assured by men?"

"Aye. Men talk about such things, ye ken. I decided to put their claims to the test." He began to trail little kisses down her throat.

"Do ye mean ye have ne'er—"

"Aye, 'tis just what I do mean." He teased her hardened nipples with his tongue. "I ne'er felt inclined to be that intimate with women who carried the scent of other men. Ye carry only my scent."

"Ye mean they didnae bathe much?"

"Nay. I always insisted upon their cleanliness, but a bath couldnae take away that scent. I have a verra keen sense of smell."

Very keen indeed, she mused. She idly stroked his back and he lightly kissed and caressed her breasts. With her desires already well fed, she was able to simply enjoy his idle attentions so she tried to think of how keen a sense of smell had to be to detect that a woman had known another man, even after she had bathed. Inwardly she shook her head, for she simply could not understand how that would work. It was probably all part of what gave him the heart of a wolf.

Instead she turned her thoughts to what he had just done and felt only a tiny twinge of lingering embarrassment. Judging from the hard length she could feel gently moving against her thigh, it was obvious Bothan had been stirred by the way he had loved her. She realized he had not yet achieved his satisfaction, that the loving had been all for her enjoyment this time.

An idea popped into her head that made her blush, but she could not shake it. If she liked such intimate attentions, and he apparently liked giving them, then surely he would like it if she gave him the same sort of intimate kisses. Knowing that if she thought about it too long she would turn cowardly, she lightly pinched him on his side. He muttered a curse and turned onto his side to frown at her. Kenna shoved him onto his back and sprawled on top of him. When he cocked one brow at her, she grinned at him, suddenly feeling very daring. After giving him a brief kiss on the mouth, she began to kiss her way down his long, strong body. She hoped the way his body tensed beneath her attentions was a sign of rising passion and not revulsion at her boldness.

"Kenna, what are ye doing?" Bothan asked, struggling to keep his voice calm.

"Guess."

"I am guessing, but I am nay sure what I am thinking is right."

Having reached her goal, Kenna slowly dragged her tongue up and down his manhood and heard him groan. "Was it this?"

"Aye," he managed to gasp, almost afraid of speaking in case it made her stop what she was doing.

"And this?"

"Oh, sweet Jesu."

He threaded his fingers through her hair and fought to stem the rising tide of his desire as she took him into her mouth. That his wife would so freely give him this delight was almost enough to send him over the edge, but he gritted his teeth and tried to control his need so that he could enjoy this pleasure for as long as possible. That control lasted only a few moments and he knew he could not last much longer.

"Mount me, Kenna," he said, his voice a hoarse, raspy whisper. "Now, lass. Now."

It took Kenna a moment to realize what he was saying.

Loving him that way had proven as intoxicating as all the other ways they made love. She gathered what few wits she could and mounted him, shivering with delight as he filled her. As she stroked his broad chest, she rode him slowly, savoring the way it felt to control the lovemaking this way. Then he growled, grasped her by the hips and urged her to move with a greater speed. Soon she was as eager to reach those pleasurable heights as he was, and she needed no more of his urging to make her take them both there.

Bothan opened his eyes and looked down at the woman sprawled on his chest. He grinned. She looked as wrung-out as he felt. They were good together, and he felt sure she was beginning to accept that passionate side of herself. It had been unusually bold of her to do what she had done for him. And she had done it very well indeed, he mused, and grinned again.

Only once had he enjoyed that pleasure, and the enjoyment had not lasted long. As he had looked down at the woman pleasuring him so, he had suddenly understood the Outsiders' fear of being prey, and all his pleasure had fled. He was not sure if it had just been some strange whim of the moment or something about the woman herself that had put such an idea in his head, but he had never done that again. With Kenna, however, he had felt only pleasure—blinding, sweet, overwhelming pleasure. It was going to be hard not to ask her to do it again and again and again.

A knock on the door startled him out of a pleasant dream concerning him sitting in a chair sipping wine while his wife loved him with her mouth. "Dinnae come in. Just tell me what ye want," he called out, smiling a little when Kenna squeaked and hastily ducked beneath the covers.

"'Tis Simon, m'laird. Someone says they have seen Kelvyn."

Bothan was out of bed and pulling on his shirt so quickly that Kenna had not even finished gasping in shock over that news. As he donned his plaid, she scrambled to put on her night shift, for she knew that as soon as he yanked on his boots he would be opening that door. His thoughts at the moment were fixed solely on the chance to catch her uncle. She was still lacing up her shift when Bothan grabbed his sword, gave her a quick kiss, and rushed out of the door.

Kenna sighed as she leaned out of the door and called for Jean. After telling the young girl to fetch her some hot water to wash with, Kenna turned to the matter of sorting out what she would wear. It was a rather abrupt way to start the day, and she wished she could believe that Bothan would be successful, but she found she simply did not think Kelvyn would be caught today. There was more trouble ahead, of that she was certain. She could only hope that she and Bothan would survive it.

Kenna frowned at the papers spread out in front of her. After breaking her fast she had come into her father's ledger room. She had suddenly felt a need to see just how much her uncle had stolen from Bantulach and, perhaps, find a way to recoup those losses. Bantulach was not a rich place, although there had been very few truly hard times, and it would be nice to have that money back. Instead she had come across a large collection of letters.

As she sorted them by date as best she could, she realized they went back three years and came from men scattered all around Scotland. Satisfied that they were as organized as possible, she picked up the first one and began to read. She had read only a few sentences before she felt chilled. The letter concerned the MacNachtons and was filled with all the same rumors and superstitious nonsense her uncle had spouted. By the time she reached for the second letter, she was truly alarmed. Her uncle had been a very busy man and his goal had been the utter annihilation of the clan MacNachton. These letters were apparently the result of his attempts to find like-minded people and, if the number of letters before her was any indication, he had been very successful. She poured herself a glass of wine and began to read more carefully, even making notes of names and dates and what she considered important facts. Bothan would need to know about this.

By the time she set aside the last letter, Kenna was cold with fear for her husband. She had also read a few things that might just be the truth she was still waiting for him to tell her, but she could not be troubled by that now. Bothan had said he was hunting for men who were hunting for his clansmen and she had found them. A lot of them. Worse, these men fully intended to bring more into their fold.

Just as she was about to go and do a little hunting herself, eager to find Bothan and put this all before him, he walked into the room. His face told her he had not found her uncle, but she suspected that would seem a minor irritation soon. As he approached her, she struggled to think of the best, clearest way to present the news of all she had learned.

"Ye didnae find him, did ye?" she said.

"Nay. I believe Anna is helping him," he answered as he bent down and kissed her. "I think we should banish her, too."

"Aye, we should. There is one small problem with that verra wise idea. She is our only alewife and she makes verra fine ale."

Bothan only needed a moment to consider the consequences of banishing the clan's only alewife and he grimaced. "Then we must try to keep a verra close watch on her to see just how she is helping your uncle. What do ye have here?" he asked, touching the stack of letters.

She looked at the letters and looked at him. There really was no soft, gentle way to tell him this news. Kenna reminded herself that Bothan had already learned that there were men who hunted his clansmen and that they might be trying to gather together to make themselves stronger, so this would not come as a shock to him.

"These are letters my uncle has saved. They go back about three years. They are your hunters, Bothan."

Bothan stared at her for a moment and then looked at the large pile of letters. "Where did ye find them?"

"In a little chest tucked under the floorboard o'er by the window." She blushed when he looked at her in surprise. "I was trying to find the money he stole. I thought he might have hidden some of it away." She touched the letters and then handed him the papers she had made her notes on. "It isnae good, Bothan."

He sat on the edge of the large, heavy table and slowly read her notes. They were neat and precise and she had selected only the most important things. He doubted he could have done better himself. He also doubted he had ever read anything that had caused him to feel so cold with apprehension.

"It is as bad as I had feared," he said when he was finished. "Nay, 'tis worse."

"They are already organized."

"Aye, but worse than that, they arenae planning some honorable acre fight or direct attack. They mean to use stealth, to pick us off one by one."

She sighed and nodded. "That was what I thought, although 'tis best if ye read the letters so that ye can decide for yourself. Have ye lost any of your clan lately?"

"Last year my cousin Egidia was killed."

Kenna sorted through the letters until she found the one she wanted and handed it to Bothan. She was not surprised at the anger that was soon revealed on his face. His cousin had suffered greatly before she had died. The men had even raped her repeatedly out of some strange belief that it would make them stronger.

"This mon will be the first to die," Bothan said softly.

That was definitely a promise that would be kept, Kenna thought, but found that she had no sympathy for the man who had led the attack upon that poor woman. "Will ye be the one to go after him?" she asked, suddenly afraid that she was about to lose him to this fight.

"Nay, her brother will want the honor. Now I understand why she was so easy to find. They wanted us to see her body, to see what they had done. However, the signs were not as clear as they had thought they would be, and we were unable to discern how she had died. We just kenned that it hadnae been a natural death." Bothan looked at the letters and then at Kenna. "Were there others?"

"Two were mentioned. 'Tis best if ye read the letters, Bothan. If naught else, there may be things ye think important that I havenae made note of."

He stood up, grasped her by the hand, and pulled her up and into his arms. "Thank ye."

"What for? 'Tis but chance that allowed me to find them."

"Aye, but I thank ye for showing them to me."

"Why wouldnae I? These men wish to kill ye, and as one of those letters said, clear all MacNachtons from the face of the earth."

"I ken that more than threats are in those letters, that they say things about MacNachtons that could have frightened ye or repulsed ye."

"Ah, ye are thanking me because I didnae think it might be best if these men were allowed to carry out their bloody plot?" She pushed him away and glared at him. "I may occasionally feel a strong urge to beat ye about the head with a stick, but I dinnae believe I have e'er given ye reason to think I want ye dead."

Bothan quickly pulled her back into his arms, ignoring her tension. "I beg your forgiveness. Nay, ye have given me no reason to think such a thing. I was still infected with the filth and hate I had just read in that letter. I fear I lashed out at ye because ye are one of them, 'tis all. And that doesnae make all that much sense as ye arenae really one of them, either. I am sorry, wife."

Feeling her relax, he sighed and rested his chin on the top of her head. "Just kenning that there is a group of men out there with the intention of killing all MacNachtons made me a little crazed. I suddenly felt cornered and alone and ye took the brunt of that. 'Twas wrong and I dinnae really think it of ye." He smiled fleetingly when he felt her stroke his back as if she tried to comfort him. "I think I must take ye to our bedchamber and apologize with greater vigor."

Kenna looked at him. "I think ye had best read those letters and get word of this threat to your clan."

"If I sit down and read those letters I will be enraged, probably for several hours. I cannae come to ye when I am enraged and feeling as if all Outsiders are the enemy. It will take me time to calm myself and be reasonable again."

"When will ye read them?"

"As soon as I have made love to my wife."

"And had a wee nap afterward?" she asked as he picked her up in his arms and started out of the room.

"And a feast after that. With my body happily sated, a good rest, and a full belly, I will be better able to face that filth and ken how to tell my family."

Kenna idly waved at a gaping Agnes as Bothan started up the stairs and the woman giggled. "'Tis difficult to understand such hatred."

"'Tis born of fear, love. I am different so I am to be feared. Most of my clan is different, and thus they have always been feared. Superstition feeds that fear and, sad to say, so does the church at times. James says some of the church fathers feel it is necessary to stir up such superstitious fears to keep people coming to the church. There is naught like a deep fear of the devil and the safety of the sanctity of one's soul to bring a mon to the church and open his purse."

"What a cynical thing for a priest to say." She sighed as they entered their bedchamber and he kicked the door shut behind him. "E'en sadder is that it might weel be true."

Bothan stood by the edge of their bed and looked down at her. For a brief moment, after reading all his cousin had suffered before her death, he had looked at his wife and seen the enemy. She was an Outsider, was all he had been thinking. He felt deeply ashamed of that and knew he had allowed her lingering uneasiness to make him uncertain of her. She might still have a few doubts, but a woman did not make love to a man as she made love to him if she was truly afraid of him or repulsed by what she feared he was.

He did wonder what she had read in those letters. In the one he had read there had been a lot of the usual nonsense but also a lot of hard, cold fact about his clan. Bothan wondered how much she had believed and how much she had simply thought were the rantings of a deeply superstitious man. He was tempted to just ask her, but he fought that temptation. Now was not the time to get into a discussion of what he was and what his clansmen were. If Kenna reacted badly to the full truth, he could too easily toss her back into that group he saw as his enemy and he knew in his heart that she was not and never would be.

"Ye are looking at me verra strangely," Kenna murmured.

"Am I? I am just trying to decide if we should get naked first or during."

"Lecherous swine," she said sweetly.

He set her down on her feet. "I think I can get naked before ye can."

"Aye, ye probably can as ye are wearing less clothing," she said, even as she began to unlace her gown.

Kenna was laughing by the time Bothan had removed all his clothes. He rapidly helped her off with the rest of hers and tossed her onto the bed. As he sprawled on top of her, she suddenly recalled something he had called her, something he said he had seen her as in the heat of his anger.

"Bothan, what did ye mean by an Outsider?"

He kissed her in reply and she quickly forgot the question.

Eleven

There was trouble brewing. Bothan could almost smell it upon the light morning breeze as he walked to the stables. Discontent and fear had tightened its hold upon the people of Bantulach. This was Kelvyn's doing, he mused as he entered the stables, pleased to be out of the sun. He should never have just banished the man. He should have just killed him and dealt with Kenna's dismay later. Unfortunately, he had wanted to please Kenna, and although Kelvyn Brodie had no qualms about killing off his closest relatives, Kenna did. Bothan feared they might soon pay very dearly for that show of mercy. Somehow Kelvyn was slipping back onto Bantulach lands and stirring up those superstitious fears he and Kenna were trying so hard to put an end to. Keeping a close watch on the alewife was gaining him nothing. It looked very much as if he was going to have to hunt the man down and silence him. Considering what the man had planned to do to the MacNachtons, Bothan found that thought a very pleasant one. Too pleasant. He turned his mind to all the other problems he faced.

Appearing around Bantulach in the daylight had obviously not succeeded in ending the dark and dangerous suspicions Kelvyn had roused in the people and was obviously still feeding. Bothan had suffered for all his efforts to appear a normal man, and it annoyed him to discover that it had all been for nothing. Less than nothing. The people of Bantulach still eyed him with fear and he had made himself dangerously weak. Worse, it was difficult to get what he needed to restore that lost strength. Instead he spent far too much of the night sleeping next to his bride. Although it may have helped ease the fear that he would be creeping about every night seeking virgins and bairns to devour, sleeping a lot was the very last thing he wanted to do when in bed with Kenna.

Kenna still remained wary. It was not as strong as it had been shortly after he had killed those men, but it was still there. He kept telling himself that it had only been a fortnight since the fight by the burn, and that she needed time, but he was beginning to lose his patience. He was also beginning to get the feeling that the unease he glimpsed in her on occasion had to do with something other than what he had done there. Soon he would have to confront her about it. Cowardice held him back, for he did worry over what she must have seen when she read those letters, but he was slowly conquering it. He might not wish to hear what she had to say, might even find it painful, but something had to be done. They had been growing so close before that day at the burn and now he feared they might be growing apart. The only thing he was still certain of was her passion, but if the distance remained between them for too long, that, too, could just fade away. It chilled him to the bone to even think about that possibility.

As he fed apples to Moonracer, Bothan wondered where Ellar was. That man had remained a strong ally. He was also not one to leave his beloved horses alone for too long. A little concerned that something had happened to the man, Bothan moved to the rear of the stables and rapped on the door of the tiny room Ellar called his own. Hearing an odd muffled sound, he opened the door and nearly gaped. Ellar was tied and gagged and lying on the floor. Just as he bent to undo the man's bonds, something slammed into the back of his head.

"Hurry, lads, he is waking up."

Bothan winced at the sound of that voice as he slowly opened his eyes. He was a little surprised that he had actually fallen unconscious, for a blow to the head did not usually do much more than irritate him. Whoever had hit him had obviously wielded his club with great strength and caught him in just the right place. Feeling an ache there, he moved to rub it and tensed when his hand did not obey his mind's instructions.

Glancing down at himself, Bothan discovered that he was spread out on the ground, his wrists and ankles lashed to stakes driven into the ground. His first instinct was to simply break free, but when he subtly tested his bonds he realized that might not be as easy as he had thought. The stakes were either driven into the ground very deeply or driven into solid rock. He could do it, but he would need to recover from his head wound first. He also had to consider what such an action would make the men standing around him think. It certainly would do little to ease the superstitious fears that had caused them to stake him out like this in the first place.

Then he felt the warmth of the sun on his face and inwardly cursed, long and profanely. This could prove to be very dangerous. It also explained why he found his bonds so tight and hard to move. By the time his head wound began to heal, he would already be badly weakened by lying in the sun. He glared at the men who stared down at him as if they expected him to suddenly change into some horrible beast and devour them all.

A skinny man with red hair and a bad complexion stepped forward and dropped something onto his chest. Bothan looked down and nearly rolled his eyes. It was a cross. All the men stared hard at it and then began to frown.

"A verra nice bit of carving," Bothan drawled.

"Naught is happening to him, Georgie," said the skinny man who Bothan now recalled was named Ian the herder.

Georgie, a big man with a soft belly and the manners of a bully, stepped a little closer and emptied a vial of liquid on Bothan's face. "That will do it. I told ye that Holy Water is what is needed. Ye just wait and see."

"That is my mother's cross," said Ian the herder, "and it has been blessed by the Pope hisself."

"Who told ye that?"

"My mother."

"And just when would your old mother have seen the pope?"

"She hasnae, but she bought it from a mon who was selling all manner of things that had come from Italy and were blessed by the pope."

Before the argument between Ian the herder and Georgie could grow more heated, Bothan gently cleared his throat. The moment all five men were looking at him, he slowly licked up all the water on his face that he could reach and then smiled. If death was not so close in the form of that bright orb hanging in the sky, Bothan knew he would have found the astonished looks upon their faces very amusing.

"And for your next trick?" he asked calmly.

"We could cut out your heart," snapped Georgie.

He should not have asked, mused Bothan.

"Nay," said Ian the herder. "That would be murder, and what if he isnae what Sir Kelvyn says he is, eh? Then we would have killed an innocent mon and our own laird. That would get us all hanged right quick."

After glaring at Ian, Georgie nudged one of the stakes with his foot and sneered at Bothan. "Then this is our next trick. This will kill ye and take ye straight back to hell where ye came from. Demons cannae abide the sun."

"How odd," Bothan murmured. "Considering demons live in hell—a rather warm place, from all the church tells us—ye would think the heat of the sun would be nay threat at all, wouldnae ye?" Although Georgie kept right on sneering, his compatriots frowned in thought and exchanged worried looks.

Bothan subtly tested his bonds again and felt a tickle of alarm. They felt even stronger to him than they had before. He was already weakening and it would only get worse. He was strongly tempted to bellow for his wife, but he decided to try a little longer to talk these men out of this plan. It somehow seemed undignified for a laird to call for his tiny, delicate wife to get him out of trouble.

Kenna frowned as she looked into the ledger room and did not find Bothan. He was always inside by this time of the day, yet she could not find him anywhere inside the keep. She sternly told herself that there was no cause to worry, that they could simply be missing each other as they both went from room to room, but she could not shake the feeling that something was wrong.

She went to the great hall and found only the boy, Jamie. "Jamie, have ye seen my husband?"

"Nay," Jamie said quickly and tried to hurry past her.

She caught the boy by the back of his shirt and forced him to face her. The look on his freckled face told her that he was hiding something and she felt her worry for Bothan grow even stronger. "Where is Sir Bothan, Jamie?"

"He went out to the stable," the boy hastily replied and took quick advantage of Kenna's suddenly loosened hold to break free and run away.

Since there was nothing wrong with her husband going to the stables, Kenna had to wonder why the boy had seemed so afraid to tell her where Bothan was. Deciding that she had to see for herself that he was in the stables and safe, she went outside. As she walked toward the stables, she noticed a group of men staring at something on the ground. A few more steps and she saw what that something was. They had staked her husband out on the ground, in the full light of the sun.

Kenna's first impulse was to race over there and rescue her husband, but she fought that urge. These men believed the sun would kill him because he was a demon. If she rushed to Bothan's side in a panic, she would only fuel those beliefs. Taking a deep breath to steady herself, she strolled over to them and looked down at Bothan. Seeing that he had no gaping wounds and only looked a little pale, she then looked at the men.

"Might I ask what ye are doing?" she asked the men.

"We are saving your soul, m'lady," said Ian the herder.

"By staking my husband out like a deer hide to be tanned?"

"We are proving that he is a demon, a spawn of the devil. The sun will kill a demon, ye ken."

"Why would the sun kill a demon? They must be quite accustomed to heat." She idly wondered why Bothan chuckled to himself.

"That is just what the laird said," murmured Ian the herder in surprise, and the other men grunted in agreement.

She looked down at Bothan. "Great minds think alike and all that." She looked at the men again. "He is your laird and my husband. I think it would be verra wise to give me a knife so that I might cut him free."

"But, m'lady," began Georgie.

"Now."

Bothan was astonished by the hard command in his wife's voice and even more astonished by how quickly the men obeyed. All five of them thrust their daggers toward her. She very delicately took Ian the herder's, knelt by his side, and proceeded to cut his bonds. The only problem he could see now was that he needed to get these men to go away or have their attention diverted for a moment before she freed him as he was now too weak to stand without help.

"Someone has left poor Ellar tied up in the stables," he said.

Kenna looked up at the five men, who all looked very

guilty. "I would strongly suggest that one of ye go and free poor Ellar."

All five men ran toward the stables. Kenna shook her head and cut Bothan's last bond. This nonsense had to stop. She realized she had lost the last of her hesitation to have her uncle killed. He was too great a danger to allow him to run free any more.

"Ye will have to help me up, love," Bothan said quietly.

Alarmed by the fact that he had to ask for her help, Kenna hurried to pull Bothan onto his feet. He swayed, draping his arm around her shoulders to steady himself, and she wrapped her arm around his waist just as the five men who had staked him out came running back out of the stables, pursued by a furious Ellar wielding a pitchfork. Kenna shook her head and continued to help her husband get back into the keep.

"Mayhap if we look a wee bit amorous, no one will think it strange that we have our arms wrapped about each other," Bothan said.

"My uncle prompted this, didnae he?" she said as she tried to look like they were speaking love words to each other.

"Aye. First a cross was placed against my skin and then holy water was splashed on my face. Georgie suggested they take out my heart but Ian the herder didnae think they ought to do that."

"I should have them all soundly whipped," Kenna muttered, horrified by what could have happened to her husband.

"I will think of some suitable punishment." He breathed a hearty sigh of relief when they entered the keep but knew it did not really mean that he was completely out of danger.

"I hope Ellar catches up with them and pokes a few holes in them with his pitchfork."

Catching sight of one of the laundry women peering around a corner at them, Kenna kissed Bothan on the neck.

She could tell that he, too, had seen the woman as he let his arm slide slowly down her back and wrapped it tightly around her waist as he rubbed his cheek against her hair. It was difficult going up the stairs, for with each step he seemed to lean more heavily on her, but she finally got him to the door of their room. Once she closed the door behind him, he wrested free of her and staggered toward the bed. He fell on top of it and she hurried to remove his boots and make him more comfortable.

"Bothan?" she called softly when she saw that his eyes were closed. "Is it bad?"

"Aye, 'tis bad. I need," he grimaced as he tried to think of a way to tell her what he needed that would not send her running from the room.

"Raw meat," Kenna said, the hint of a question in her voice.

"That would help a little."

"Oh." Kenna suddenly recalled one of the things she had read in those letters. "I ken what ye need. I will be right back."

Bothan opened one eye and watched his wife disappear out the door. What he needed was his father's doctored wine—a very large bottle of it. Somehow he did not think Kenna understood that this time he couldnae get the strength he needed from a slab of uncooked meat. He needed blood. For a moment he cherished the thought of having her bring him Georgie so that he could feed on that man, but he quickly shook that thought aside. They had handled the trouble just as they should have. Those men were left with the feeling that a lot of what Kelvyn had told them was wrong and that their laird's daughter was very angry with them.

He closed his eyes and hoped she at least brought him the meat. It would help, for he knew he was dangerously weak. Even what little nourishment he could get from the meat might be enough to keep him from growing even weaker.

* * *

Kenna cursed when she found Agnes in the kitchen. It was not going to be easy to get Bothan what he needed with the woman right there. She smiled at Agnes and then began to search the kitchen for what she needed. When she found it, she was suddenly struck with an idea for the perfect explanation and she grabbed the bowl.

"Here now, lass, what are ye meaning to do with that?" asked Agnes. "I was to be making the black pudding tonight."

"I ken it, but I need this, Agnes." She leaned closer to the woman and spoke softly. "My husband has a weakness of the blood, ye ken. 'Tis a verra closely guarded secret, now. Ye must nay speak of it."

"Och, nay, lass, I would ne'er do so. What ails him?"

"Weel, do ye ken how some folk burn in the sun and can e'en feel unweel if they stay out in it too long?"

"Aye, I most certainly do. My uncle was once burnt so bad that he was covered in blisters and sick for weeks."

"Just so. Weel, Sir Bothan just gets ill. Ye see, he doesnae burn, doesnae e'en sweat much, whilst in the sun. 'Tis as if his body doesnae ken what to do when he gets hot. Nay like all the rest of us do. So, he gets verra ill. Georgie, Ian the herder, and a few others have listened too much to my uncle's tales and they staked my husband out in the sun."

"The bastards."

"My thoughts exactly. Howbeit, he is now verra ill, but ye see why we cannae tell anyone."

"Och, nay, of course we cannae. Those fools will think it proof that that bonnie, sweet lad is a demon." She frowned at the bowl Kenna held. "And that will help?"

"Disgusting, isnae it, but a wise woman told him that this is what he needs. 'Struth, raw meat on occasion is enough, but he has been sorely abused by this and I dinnae think it will help much at all now."

"Weel, he cannae stomach that." Agnes took the bowl and started to sprinkle a few herbs and spices into it. She then topped it up nearly to the rim with the hearty wine she used for her cooking. "Here, 'tis the best I can do. What ye must do, lass, and I will help ye with it, is fortify his wine. Then he can but have himself a wee glass of wine when he needs what the wise woman told him he needs and none will be the wiser."

Kenna kissed Agnes on the cheek, and after the woman draped a piece of cloth over the top of the bowl, she hurried back to her bedchamber. As she approached the bed, she feared she was too late as Bothan was lying very still, his breathing shallow. It was hard to believe that someone could be hurt by such little exposure to the sun, but it was very clear that Bothan was in a dangerously weakened state.

"Bothan?" she called softly and felt nearly faint with relief when he opened his eyes.

"Ye brought the meat?" he asked, frowning when he saw that she held a cloth-covered bowl.

"Nay." She set the bowl down on the table by the bed and helped him sit up against the pillows. Taking the cloth off the top of the bowl, she sat at his side. "I brought ye this instead. Can ye hold it yourself or do ye need me to help ye?"

Bothan stared at the bowl of blood, obviously mixed with spices and some wine, and then looked at her. She started to frown and look nervous, but he did not know what to say. He was also not sure he wanted her to see him feed his hunger.

"Was I wrong? I read of it in the letters and, since ye have eaten that nearly raw meat, it made sense. But . . ."

"Nay, ye are not wrong. I just wasnae sure I wanted to do this in front of ye as I will need your help."

"And if ye dinnae drink this?"

"There is a good chance I could die. I am nay getting stronger. That means I was in the sun for too long and have passed the point where I can just rest and regain my lost strength."

"Weel, then, 'tis nay much more revolting than any other potion healers try to pour down unwilling throats."

He drank it and then slumped back against the pillows. In moments he felt his strength begin to return. When Kenna settled herself beside him on the bed, he wrapped his arm around her and kissed the top of her head. Now she knew one more truth about him and she still stayed.

"Agnes suggested that we fortify your wine so that ye can take your medicine without anyone getting all afeared and superstitious," said Kenna.

"Agnes kens that ye brought me that?"

"Agnes is the one who added the spices and the wine. She was verra touched by your affliction, ye poor, sweet, bonnie laddie, you."

He laughed. "Weel, that is one hurdle cleared."

"Aye. She is an ally in this and will hold fast to the secret. Now we must clear another hurdle. What happened today has convinced me of it."

"And what is that hurdle?"

"We must find my uncle and shut him up—for good."

Since that was exactly what he needed to do, ached to do, Bothan just nodded and kissed her cheek. As soon as he regained all his strength he would begin to hunt down Kelvyn Brodie.

Twelve

Kenna smiled to herself as she made her daisy chain. It was something she used to do when her mother had been alive and it stirred up some very pleasant memories. It was also an extremely irresponsible way to spend the morning, but she had seen the daisies in bloom from the parapets and had been unable to resist. There was a lot of work she needed to do, but it would still be there when she returned to the keep after her frolic in the sun.

She glanced up at the bright sun and felt a pang of regret. Her husband could never share this pleasure with her. He could probably join her for a short time, but then he would have to return to the shadows, and perhaps even gnaw on a slab of red meat.

A giggle escaped her, surprising her. When had that particular need of Bothan's ceased to trouble her? When he had nearly died after some of her clansmen had staked him out in the sun? At some point over the last month, as they had struggled together to be accepted at Bantulach, she had obviously lost the last of her lingering fears. She carefully searched her heart and mind and found not even the smallest twinge of fear or distaste remaining. He was what he was, she thought, and she loved him.

There really was no doubt in her mind that he would

never hurt her or the innocent. In many ways he needed her protection, needed her to stand between him and a world that would never fully accept what he was. He was a good man, but no one would see that if they ever found out the full truth about him. From the beginning it had been her duty to soothe any unrest and calm any fear, and she had been doing that without even realizing it. She had even calmed her own.

Unfortunately, her uncle had been stirring the people up as fast as she calmed them down. A few more had drifted into her camp, accepting her and Bothan. Most of the ones who had seemed content to just wait to see who won this battle were still just waiting. It was people like Anna who kept the fires of superstition burning hot. Both she and Bothan were sure it was people like Anna who were helping her uncle come and go as he pleased, but they had not caught anyone at it yet. As laird, she or Bothan had the right to put a stop to Anna's talk, but they had hesitated to take any harsh measures against the woman. Soon, Kenna feared, the woman would force them to act against her.

Espying one of the sheep struggling to free its thick wool from a briar, Kenna walked over to help it, moving closer to the wood. It was not until she was right next to the animal that she realized something was not right. The animal's wool was not caught tightly, yet the beast seemed unable to move away from the briars. Even as she looked down and espied the rope leashing the animal to the bush, she heard someone move up behind her. Before she could turn around, something hit her hard on the head and she fell into blackness.

"Ah, there ye are, m'laird," said Florrie. "Have ye seen Kenna about?"

Bothan looked up from his work to see Florrie standing in the doorway of his ledger room. He forced himself to smile in welcome, even though he was ill-pleased to be disturbed. He had been carefully going through all the letters

Kenna had found and they always made him angry. Florrie was a friend, however, and did not deserve to suffer from it.

"Nay, I have been working here most of the day," he replied and then frowned. "Was she supposed to be meeting with ye?"

"Aye." Florrie blushed. "She was to help me with my wedding gown, aye? I am to be wed in a week and it still needs a wee bit of work. She was supposed to be at my cottage by noon, but 'tis near two now and I havenae seen and cannae find her."

That sounded ominous to Bothan and he immediately forgot the letters. "Have ye asked Agnes in the kitchens?"

"Aye, and she hasnae seen Kenna, either, nay since this morning. One of the men said he saw her go out to a wee field just this side of the wood to pick daisies."

"But did he see her come back?"

"Nay, m'laird. No one has seen her since then."

Florrie jumped as he leapt up and strode toward her, but Bothan ignored that sign of nervousness. Kenna was always wandering around the keep or the lands, but one could always find someone who had just seen her. To have Florrie say that no one had seen Kenna since the morning was definitely cause for alarm.

"We had best go and find her then, hadnae we?" he said, trying to speak gently to Kenna's friend even though he felt an urge to start running through the keep, bellowing Kenna's name.

"I dinnae like this," Florrie muttered as she struggled to keep pace with Bothan as he strode toward the great hall.

"It is worrisome," he agreed.

Kelvyn has her.

Bothan looked at Florrie, who was frowning into the great hall as if the severity of her expression would suddenly make Kenna appear. "Did ye just say something, Florrie?"

"Nay, m'laird. I will just go speak to wee Jamie," she said and hurried over to where the boy was sweeping the ashes from the fireplace.

Kelvyn has her.

The voice was in his head and it was most definitely not his own. It was a woman's. Bothan suddenly felt a great deal of sympathy for Kenna. Having some strange voice in your head was a very unpleasant feeling.

"*Maman?*" he asked in a whisper, even as he wondered why he should suddenly be able to hear Kenna's mother.

Aye, lad, 'tis Kenna's mother. Kelvyn has her. The fool lass was out in the field all on her own and he grabbed her. Hit my poor lass right o'er the head.

"I should have killed him the day we returned to Bantulach."

Aye, ye should have, but regrets willnae save my wee lass. Ye will have to let go of some of your secrets, lad, for I fear ye willnae be able to save her on your own. Kelvyn kens all your weaknesses.

"But who can I trust? Kenna and I have just spent a month trying to get everyone to believe that I am just another mon, one of them."

Weel, I dinnae think e'en those who are on your side think that. Ye can trust the ones ye felt ye could trust soon after ye arrived.

"Who are ye talking to, m'laird?" asked Florrie as she rejoined him.

"Myself. Just muttering my concerns aloud. Did Jamie ken anything?"

"Nay, he hasnae seen her since this morning, either."

"My laird!"

Bothan turned to face Ian the herder as the man stumbled to a halt just behind him. Obviously feeling guilty for having been part of the group who had staked Bothan to the ground, Ian had become a bit of a nuisance with all his efforts to ingratiate himself to his new laird. The man thrust a dirty scrap of paper at Bothan.

"A lad just brought this," Ian said.

"Who was the boy?" asked Bothan as he read the note and felt his blood run cold.

"I think he was one of the Monroes, for he was bowlegged. He thrust that into my hand and ran away."

"I need ye to fetch me Simon, Ellar, Fergie the lame, Mungo the blacksmith, and Alban."

"Is there trouble?"

"Aye, Sir Kelvyn has stolen my wife and this missive holds his demands. Go."

Ye can trust him, ye ken.

Glancing around and realizing that Florrie had disappeared, Bothan said, "He is one of the ones who was sure I was a demon and he helped stake me to the ground."

But he doesnae believe it now. He wouldnae let Georgie cut out your heart because he didnae fully believe it then, either. Do as ye like, but I really think ye can trust him.

Bothan idly wondered if a spirit's assurances should carry more weight than anyone else's. He glanced at the letter in his hand. This was going to require help, for Kelvyn had made a demand that put Bothan at a great disadvantage. He wanted Bothan to meet with him, in the open, in one hour. The sun would still be at its full strength and he knew that was why Kelvyn had demanded such a meeting. There was also no doubt in Bothan's mind that the man intended to hold him there until he was too weak to defend himself. Yet, with Kerra's life at stake, what choice did he have?

"She is still alive?"

Aye, for now.

Those ominous words kept echoing inside Bothan's head as he went to the ledger room and paced while he waited for the men he had sent Ian to find. They had not really needed to be said. He knew Kelvyn could not allow him or Kenna to survive this confrontation. Only their deaths could secure the man's hold on Bantulach. Bothan also knew that if he did not plan his every step very carefully, Kelvyn would win. Timing was vitally important, for he would grow weaker with each minute he was forced to stand out in the sun.

When the men he had sent for hurried into the room,

Bothan had to resist the mad urge to lead them on a charge to find Kenna and kill Kelvyn. He needed to let them know that he might well prove to be the weak link in any plan they made. Seeing how Ian lingered in the doorway, Bothan sighed and decided to trust in Kenna's mother.

"Step in here, Ian, and shut the door," he said.

"Ian says Kelvyn has taken Kenna," said Simon, his dark eyes hard with anger. "What is your plan?"

"My plan is to meet with him as he has commanded," Bothan replied. "In an hour, unarmed, in an open field. 'Tis less than an hour now."

"And what do ye want us to do?"

"Find Kenna."

"Willnae Kelvyn bring her with him?"

"He may, but he may not. Kelvyn needs me to stand in that open field under that lovely, bright sun. He willnae bring Kenna within my reach, at least nay until I begin to weaken."

"Weaken?"

Bothan prayed Kenna's mother was right and that he was not about to lose what few allies he had at Bantulach. "Sunlight weakens me." Bothan nodded at Ian when the man gasped. "Aye, ye were verra nearly successful that day. 'Tis a weakness in the blood that has long plagued my clan. Married too often within the clan, perhaps. Who can say? All that doesnae matter now. I tell ye this in confidence." All six men nodded their agreement to keep what he was saying a secret, and Bothan began to relax. " 'Tis something our enemies have long used against us e'en if only to stir up superstitious fears. Kelvyn now uses it against me. 'Struth, I think he begins to believe his own tales."

"He has been spinning them for a verra long time," said Simon, and the other men murmured their agreement to those words. "Are we to try to find some way to protect ye from the sun?"

"Nay, ye are only to try to find Kenna," Bothan replied.

"I will keep Kelvyn with me. I dinnae think she is too far away from the meeting place Kelvyn has chosen. He will want her close at hand in case he feels inclined to taunt me. Or her."

"Anna isnae home," said Ian abruptly and blushed when everyone looked at him. "Thought it might be important." He shrugged. "She was Kelvyn's lover, and she ne'er leaves her home."

"If that is true, then it means she is with Kelvyn," Bothan said. "She may be the one guarding Kenna. I need ye to find her as Kelvyn wants her dead and that is what he plans for the ending to this confrontation."

"Shouldnae ye have someone to watch your back?" asked Fergie the lame, the concern upon his boyish face making him look far younger than his nineteen years.

"Nay, he says I must meet with him alone," replied Bothan. "I just needed ye to ken that once I meet the mon, once I stand there in the sun, there is a verra good chance that I willnae be much use to anyone. Kelvyn kens it. That doesnae mean he hasnae set some of his allies round the meeting place to watch for any men I might try to bring with me. If when I first meet with him I could ken that my wife was safe, I could kill him and end this. Howbeit, with each minute that passes, that chance slips away. Do ye think ye can search for Kenna without alerting Kelvyn?"

"Aye, we can," said Simon, "and when we find her we will bring her to the meeting place so that ye can ken it." When Bothan handed him the note from Kelvyn, Simon quickly read it and handed it back. "I ken where that is. Ye will need to leave soon, for 'tis at least a ten-to-fifteen-minute ride. Since that, too, will put ye out in the sun, do ye think ye can get there?"

Bothan nodded. "I will wear my cloak and it will help. 'Tis several layers thick, ye ken, and made to protect me. I will already be growing weak, however, and thus will already be at a disadvantage when I meet with Kelvyn. 'Tis nay doubt why he has set the meeting where he has. The faster ye find Kenna, the greater chance I will have of still being strong enough to deal with the bastard."

"But the mon says ye must come unarmed and he will be weel armed."

"If I havenae grown too weak, I willnae need a sword or dagger to kill him. I need but my hands."

The men all stared at him for one long moment and then nodded. Bothan could see that they were now aware that not all of the tales about his clan were lies. It was clear that it did not matter to them, however, and he breathed a silent sigh of relief. They still did not know everything, but he began to think it would not matter if they did. It was acceptance of a sort and he welcomed it, especially now.

When the men left, Bothan sat at the table and stared at the letters he had spent so much time studying. He had found his enemy and warned his clan, but he began to think he had not heeded his own warnings. In a short while he would be facing his enemy unarmed and exposed to the sun, one of the few things that could kill even a Pureblood. The only ally he might have at that time was the voice of Kenna's mother in his head. Very bad odds. For Kenna's sake, he would do it, but he had never felt so helpless.

"M'laird?"

He looked toward the door to see the plump, graying Agnes staggering toward him carrying his heavy cloak and three bottles of wine. "What is it, Agnes?" he asked as he quickly moved to her side to relieve her of the weight of his cloak.

"Your horse is saddled and ready and I have brought ye these for the journey."

He frowned at the bottles she held out. "I thank ye but I dinnae think I need wine."

"'Tisnae just wine."

"Oh." He suddenly smiled, seeing a glimmer of hope. "I see."

When he took the bottles and set them on the worktable, she folded her arms over her chest. "Kill the bastard, m'laird, and bring our wee Kenna home."

"I intend to. I hadnae realized ye had heard the news of her kidnapping."

"Young Fergie told me." Agnes blushed. "As ye are aware, I ken about your affliction and suddenly thought that, weel, if ye had these to drink on the way, ye may at least start out as strong as can be hoped for. And, 'tis the oddest thing, but the thought just popped into my head, and 'twas as if something ordered me to do it and do it quickly."

Kenna's mother, Bothan suspected. She was a very busy spirit. "These could prove my saving grace, Agnes. I am most grateful."

"And I am glad ye let Ian help. He is my nephew, ye ken. 'Tis a secret, and I ken I can trust ye to keep it, but the lad was born of Sir Kelvyn's raping of me sister when she was but twelve. The old laird ne'er kenned all the evil his brother was up to, but when ye just banished the mon, I did think it wasnae the best plan. Still, I ken that wee Kenna hadnae the stomach to order the death of her kinsmon, nay matter that he had tried to kill her. And, he may have had the wit to stay banished. But, ye will kill him now, aye?"

"Oh, aye, Agnes. I will kill him."

Agnes nodded and started to leave, but paused in the doorway and looked back. "And Laird?"

"Aye, Agnes?"

" 'Tis most unkind of me, I ken, but, weel—will ye let the bastard ken that he has lost e'er ye end his miserable life?"

"Ye can be verra sure that Sir Kelvyn will ken it ere I send him to hell."

Bothan finished the second bottle of Agnes's fortified wine as he reached the meeting place. The wine had proven as helpful as he could have hoped for. He looked at Sir

Kelvyn, who stood in the clearing flanked by two men and smiling with the confidence of victory. Bothan prayed he would have the chance to wipe that smug look off his face.

"Weel come, Sir Bothan," said Kelvyn. "If ye would be so kind as to dismount and remove your cloak?"

As he did as the man commanded, Bothan looked all around as subtly as he could. It appeared that Kelvyn only had the two men with him. There was a chance that he and Kenna had been more successful than they had realized in winning over the people of Bantulach, slowly robbing Kelvyn of his allies. That could well be one of the reasons Kelvyn had acted so boldly now. Bothan walked into the center of the clearing and stood, smiling faintly when he caught the scent of fear on the three men facing him. Kelvyn was not as confident as he looked. There could actually be some advantage to being thought a demon, he mused.

"Where is my wife, Kelvyn?" he demanded.

"Ye will see her soon," the man replied.

"I think I would prefer to see her now."

"Weel, ye arenae in a position to make demands, are ye? Ye will soon be dying, and ye face three armed, strong men without e'en a dagger. Ye will see her when I want ye to see her."

Bothan was about to make a sharp retort when a very familiar scent caressed his nose. Kenna. He looked around but could not see anything, yet he knew she was near. She had to be or he would not be able to smell that sweet skin touched with lavender.

She is here.

"I ken it," he said. "I can smell her."

"Who are ye talking to?" demanded Kelvyn after briefly looking around.

Tell him Meggie is here to watch him go to hell.

"Meggie. She says she is here to watch ye go to hell and I intend to give her that gift."

Kelvyn turned white and Bothan smiled.

Thirteen

The way Anna smiled at her made Kenna want to kick her in the face. She resisted the urge, for in her current precarious position, that could prove fatal. When she had begun to wake from the knock on her head, she had found herself tied at the wrist and ankles. Before she had even had time to react to that, a large, hairy man had hoisted her up onto this rock she now balanced so precariously on, and a rope had been tied around her neck. She glanced up at the tree branch the rope hung from and cursed silently. It looked very securely tied. If she slipped from the rock, she could not hope that the rope would miraculously unravel and let her fall to the ground. She would slowly strangle.

Kenna looked at her uncle. "Ye would kill your nearest blood kin?"

"I have done it before," he drawled and smiled.

"Aye, I had rather thought ye had."

"Such a clever wee lass," he sneered.

"My husband will kill ye for this."

"Your husband will soon be coming to meet with me, aye, but all he will accomplish is to be a witness to your hanging. I ken what he is, ye see. I ken that he will die if he is out in the sun for too long. And, when he is too weak to fight, I will bring him here to watch ye die."

"What my husband is, Uncle Kelvyn, is a far better mon than ye will e'er be." She tensed when he took a step toward her, afraid that he was about to push her off the stone, but he visibly controlled himself.

"Your husband is naught but a beast born of the devil and his whore. Ye ken it, but ye are too beguiled by his bonnie face to understand what a threat to all of us he is."

"The only one my husband is a threat to is ye, the mon who feels no guilt o'er killing his own brother and stealing all that belongs to me."

"What I am, niece, is the mon who is going to watch him die."

Kenna cursed as her uncle kissed Anna and then walked away with his two men. Bothan was in as much danger as she was, Kenna realized. The sun would quickly rob him of his strength and his ability to put an end to her uncle's plots. There appeared to be no escape from this, and yet she simply could not believe that it would all end this way, with her uncle gaining from his sins.

"Why are ye a part of this, Anna?"

"Why?" Anna patted her thick auburn hair that was well sprinkled with gray. "I will be the laird's wife as I should have been years ago. But, nay, your father wed that wretched Meggie instead. Weel, his brother wasnae so blind. He sees me for the fine, strong woman I am and has long loved me."

"Then why hasnae he married ye?"

"Because your father wouldnae let him!"

That was a lie but Kenna decided it would be best not to argue the matter. There was a tense uneasiness in Anna that made Kenna sure the woman could be pushed too far very quickly. She had learned all she needed to know. There would be no help from Anna.

Bothan has come.

Although it was strangely comforting to hear her mother's voice, Kenna rather wished her mother's spirit had the ability to take shape and cut her ropes. She also wished there had been better news to hear. The sun was high and bright today and that would be a slow poison to her husband. She could not think of what he could do to defeat Kelvyn.

He has help and they will soon be here to tend to this fat cow.

Obviously spirits could be snappish, Kenna mused, and almost smiled. All her husband would need is a little help and he would end all their troubles with her uncle today. The quicker that help arrived, the better the chance that Bothan would survive this confrontation.

A little white dog suddenly trotted up to Anna. Since it was Anna's dog, Kenna was a little surprised at how pale the woman got. A moment later, she understood as six men stepped forward and surrounded the woman.

"I thought he would find ye, Anna," said Ian as he picked up the dog and scratched its ears. "Dinnae worry, I will care for him after ye are gone."

Anna made a soft, strangled noise and bolted toward Kenna. Before anyone could stop the woman, she pushed Kenna off the rock. As Kenna fought to swing her bound feet back on the rock while the rope tightened painfully around her neck, she heard a soft grunt. A heartbeat later, she was being held up by Mungo the blacksmith as Fergie the lame climbed the tree with amazing agility and cut the hanging rope.

Once set on her feet by Mungo, Kenna saw who had made that grunting noise. Anna was sprawled on the ground with a dagger protruding from her back. Feeling no sympathy at all, Kenna turned her attention to getting some feeling back into her hands and feet as Mungo and Simon cut her bonds.

"Where is Bothan?" she asked, as, with Simon's help, she stood up.

"Meeting with your uncle. We were sent to find ye," said Simon. "The laird said he couldnae act against your uncle until he kenned where ye were and that ye were safe."

"Then we had best let him ken it as quickly as possible."

"Aye, 'tisnae good for him to be in the sun too long."

Kenna stared at the men in shock and realized that they

knew about Bothan, at least about his inability to endure sunlight for long. Yet, not one of them looked very troubled by that. Perhaps she and Bothan had been more successful at making a place for themselves than she thought. It would be something to think about after she got him home. He might be doing well enough now, but she had seen how desperately weak he had gotten before and did not wish to risk wasting another moment.

"Where is he?" she asked.

"Just beyond those trees," said Mungo. "There are two men with him and Kelvyn. Kelvyn and his men are armed. The laird isnae."

"Of course, my uncle wouldnae wish to actually fight for what he wants to steal," she muttered as she started toward the trees. "But three armed men will be no trouble for Bothan if he hasnae gotten too weak. He killed eight when we were attacked by Uncle's hirelings at the burn as we traveled here."

"Are ye sure he isnae a demon?" murmured Ian.

"Nay, Ian, he isnae," she said a little sharply. "He is just a wee bit different." She ignored Simon's muffled laughter. "He is of an old line, one that goes way back to before there was the church or priests, and the clan has remained much alone since those dark times. The gifts of their ancestors have remained strong, is all." Kenna frowned briefly, for she had the strongest feeling that what she had just said was actually the truth, even though she had meant it as a tale to still any rising fear in the men.

Kenna stopped and stared when she reached the edge of the clearing where Bothan stood facing her uncle and his two men. "The only demon I see there is the mon who killed his own brother and wanted to kill his own niece."

"Verra true," murmured Simon. "Laird," he called out, "we have found her."

Bothan looked toward the edge of the clearing and saw Kenna standing with his men. He nodded slowly to them, idly wondering why Ian was holding a little white dog, and then looked at Kelvyn and his men. Even as those three men looked around for a way to escape, Bothan's six men began to encircle the clearing.

For a brief moment, Bothan feared he was already too weak to defeat these men, but quickly shook aside that doubt. He could and he would. Knowing he could quickly return to the keep, seek nourishment and rest, gave him strength. So did rage.

"Now we will end this, Kelvyn," he said quietly.

Kelvyn's two men rushed him. Bothan easily dodged the swing of their swords. One got past him, but he grabbed the other by the arm and flung him aside. The other then came back at him and, after a brief struggle, Bothan snapped his neck. The one he had tossed aside saw that there was no route of escape for him and rushed Bothan a second time. Bothan quickly gave him the same swift death he had given the other man. He then turned to smile at a pale, sweating Kelvyn.

" 'Tis time to die, Kelvyn," he said, knowing the almost cheerful tone of his voice added to Kelvyn's fear.

Kelvyn looked all round and realized there was no way for him to escape, either. He turned his full attention back to Bothan and held out his sword. "Ye should be dead! Ye have been out in the sun."

"Did ye expect some fine show? Thought I would become some growling creature or burst into flame? I have seen the letters from your compatriots and ye are all victims of your own superstitious nonsense. Aye, I willnae deny that the sun weakens me, but it takes a while, fool, especially when I have had Agnes's fine wine to bolster my strength and the cloak my mother made for me to shelter me as I rode here.

"Now, I intend to fulfill a few promises I have made. Meggie wants ye to be sent to hell, possibly for murdering her husband, and Agnes wants ye to clearly see that ye have lost ere ye die. Shall we have at it?"

Kelvyn screamed in rage and charged Bothan. For just a

little while, Bothan taunted the man, keeping out of the reach of Kelvyn's sword and tossing the man aside time and time again. Then he felt his rage ease and the weakness begin to creep over him and decided it was time to end it. The next time Kelvyn charged, Bothan grabbed him by the arm, swung him around until his back was up against a tree, and then held him there.

"But, I stabbed ye," whispered Kelvyn.

Bothan glanced down at the wound high up on his right shoulder. "Why, so ye did. Ah, weel, 'twill heal. Ye, I fear, will not."

"What are ye?"

"A mon, ye fool. Just a mon with a few wee differences. I dinnae drink souls, either." He slowly smiled, revealing his fangs and watched Kelvyn's eyes widen. "I drink blood," he whispered and sank his teeth into the man's throat.

Knowing what Bothan was about to do, Kenna tried to cover the eyes of the men who had regrouped around her. Instead she found her whole face covered by six hands. Cursing softly, she shoved them aside.

"I have seen it before," she snapped.

She looked at the men watching her husband and frowned. They looked more curious than frightened. It was as if they were not surprised at all. Yet, if they believed all that her uncle had said about the MacNachtons, why were they so apparently accepting?

"Ye shouldnae be seeing this," she said quietly.

"Och, weel, 'tis a wee bit disgusting," agreed Mungo. "I feel no pity for your uncle, though, and at least the laird isnae the soul-taker your uncle accused him of being."

"Your uncle tried to use the laird's weakness to kill him and you, lass," said Simon. "If ye think we fear the mon will make a habit of this, we dinnae." Simon smiled. "Each to their own, eh?"

Kenna wondered if her eyes were as wide as they felt to be. It was the first time she had ever seen Simon smile so widely and now she knew why. Simon had fangs.

"Ye are a MacNachton?"

"In part. My grandmother had a lover. He died around thirty years ago. Came to her village to see her and they slaughtered him. My mother always said that her mother's heart broke that day and she died soon afterward. My mother wed my father and they came here."

"Why havenae ye told him? He thinks he is all alone here."

"Nay, he has ye, lass. I but needed to see what sort of mon he was. I kenned little or naught about my grandfather except that he gave my mother life as weel as a few of his strengths and weaknesses. I needed to see if there was a reason they were so feared, a reason other than superstition. I ken what it is now. They are stronger."

"Unless they are left out in the sun too long," Kenna muttered as she rushed to her husband's side as he took several steps away from Kelvyn's body and simply sat down on the ground.

The moment Kenna knelt beside him, Bothan took her into his arms. He smiled his gratitude when Simon fetched him his cloak. Releasing Kenna only long enough to shelter himself with it, he pulled her back into his embrace. He stroked her hair as the men told him how they had found her and what her uncle had planned for her.

"I need to get back to the keep," he said.

"But," Kenna took a quick peek at her uncle, "I thought ye, weel . . ."

"Feasted? Nay. I promised Agnes that I would make him ken all he has lost. I think she wanted him to die trembling in fear. In a way, he did. I had barely sunk my teeth into the fool's neck when his heart stopped." He kissed her ear and whispered, "I got but just enough to get me home without collapsing. Agnes's potions will do the rest."

"This should help, then," said Simon as he crouched before Bothan and held out the last bottle of doctored wine.

Bothan took it, had a deep drink, and then looked carefully at Simon. "Ye ken what is in here, dinnae ye?"

"Aye. I ken exactly who and what ye are. Or would like to."

"Simon has a verra bonnie smile," Kenna murmured and met her husband's frown with a smile as they stood up together.

"Wheesht, Simon, just tell the mon," grumbled Fergus.

Simon grinned at Bothan, a wide, fang-bearing grin. Bothan gaped at the man. "A kinsmon?"

"Aye, from my grandmother's lover."

"Who?"

"I fear I dinnae ken the name, only the village where they met, where they bred my mother, and where he was killed."

"My father will ken it. He will only need the name of the village."

Bothan suddenly embraced Simon and the man laughingly returned it. All good humor fled, however, when as Bothan stood back from Simon, he swayed a little. With Mungo's strong assistance he was mounted on Moonracer. Even though he would have preferred to ride with his wife, Bothan did not complain as Simon mounted behind him. He was weak and might be in need of a strong man's support before they reached the keep.

Kenna sat on the bed next to her sleeping husband and idly stroked his hair. She would soon curl up at his side and go to sleep, too, but she needed a little more time to assure herself that he was well. They had come too close to dying today and it still chilled her.

She thought about how he had killed her uncle and sighed. In a way, she pitied her uncle, for he had not died a very glorious death and now lay in an unmarked, unconsecrated grave with Anna. In the end, he had not even been able to give her husband back the strength he had lost while standing in the sun.

There was no denying it, no making little excuses for what she had seen at the burn that day. Her husband could not only rip open a man's throat with his teeth, he drank their blood. She waited for that to appall or frighten her, but it did neither. He only did it when he was in battle for his life, or hers. Dead was dead, as far as she could see, and if, in the man's last miserable moments, he could give her husband back his lost strength, so be it. She did wonder, however, why it was that Bothan never seemed to have any wounds even though his shirt had shown the evidence of one both times.

Placing her hand over her still-flat stomach, she also wondered if these things would be passed on to the child she was sure she carried. It was troubling to think of her bairn having fangs, needing shelter from the sun, and having a taste for blood. There was no turning back now, but she knew she needed some time to think about everything she had learned about her husband and about all the things she knew he had yet to tell her. When she told him about the child, she wanted to do so without any shadows in her eyes, without any fear of just what they may have bred together.

Fourteen

Bothan frowned as he got dressed. He had recovered quickly enough, needing only one long night of sleep. What troubled him was that his wife had not been at his side when he had woken up. There had been a worrisome look in her eyes as she and Agnes had fed him what he needed and made him comfortable in bed. What he feared was that this time she had seen what he could do all too clearly.

Determined not to let her hide away or think too long on what she had seen, he set out to find her. He finally located her in her solar. She sat in the window with the little white dog on her lap. As he walked closer, she turned and smiled at him, but it was not a particularly warm smile. It was as if he had disturbed her very deep thoughts. Since that was what he had wanted to do, he wondered why he did not feel better about it.

"Ye look weel rested," she said.

Taking her by the hand, he tugged her to her feet, ignoring the whined complaint of the dog as he was dislodged from her lap. He led her over to the chairs set before the fireplace and gently urged her to sit down. As she watched him with curiosity glinting in her eyes, he turned the other chair and sat down facing her. It was time to tell her everything.

"Is something wrong?" she asked

"Nay, but it isnae exactly right, either," he said. "Ye have seen me at my worst," he began, and held up a silencing hand when she began to protest. "Aye, ye have. Twice ye have seen me in battle and that is indeed when a MacNachton is at his worst, his most frightening. I think it is time to explain exactly what sort of mon ye have married."

Kenna tensed, eager yet afraid. She had just talked herself into accepting whatever sort of child they had. She was not sure she wanted to hear that there was even more she would have to learn to accept. Yet, she knew they could not continue with all these secrets between them, not when they would soon be parents.

"It isnae so verra bad, love," he said gently when he saw her frown. "My clan is an ancient one. We arenae e'en sure how far back into the mists of time we go. In the distant past we were nay such a good lot of men and women. I fear we saw people as little more than cattle to feed on. We were called the Nightriders by the villagers who had the misfortune to live near us. But that changed long ago. About thirty years ago our laird decided we needed to change again."

"Change how?"

"He is a mon born of both worlds, of a Pureblood and an Outsider. There was a lot of trouble about it, worries about weakening the blood and all that, but he prevailed when he decided that was what we must all do. We must marry Outsiders whene'er we can and slowly breed out the things that have kept us confined to Cambrun. The world was inching closer and it would soon be too difficult to hide away."

"What things? The fangs and the way ye cannae go out into the sun?"

"Aye, those and a few others." He sighed and dragged his hand through his hair. "We are verra strong, even the ones like our laird. If we get too weak, we need blood. These teeth are to enable us to get that when we need it. We also live a verra long time."

"How long?"

"We arenae sure, but a verra long time if ye are a Pureblood. I am not. I am the son of a mon who is almost a Pureblood and a woman of the Callan clan. My aunt is the laird's wife. My father married the sister three years later. They brought e'en more, er, gifts to the bloodline. They are descendants of a Celtic shape-shifter, a woman who is said to have been able to change into a big cat."

"She is why ye purr," Kenna murmured.

"I dinnae purr."

"Aye, ye do, but go on. Unless there is something verra strange about the Callan blood, ye dinnae need to tell me all about that now. I have seen those catlike qualities and have ne'er heard a whisper of superstition about the clan."

Bothan nodded, relaxing a little, for she appeared very calm despite what he was telling her. "There isnae all that much more to say. Strong, long-lived, no sun, need blood, have fangs. I believe that is all."

"What about when ye are wounded?"

"Oh. We do heal weel and verra fast."

"Especially if ye can get some blood."

"Aye. It isnae like it says in all those letters," he began.

"I ken it," she interrupted. "I didnae heed those vicious words. I was most particular about what I kept in mind to think about. I just dinnae ken what difference any of it makes. I have guessed at most of it, but am most pleased that ye finally have told me the truth."

"There is one other truth—MacNachtons rarely have bairns. 'Tis why our laird demanded that some of us marry Outsiders. Purebloods hadnae bred a child amongst themselves for over forty years. We were dying as a clan. I am of both worlds, but I cannae be sure if I can give ye a child. Aye, the Callans are as fertile as the cat they have in their blood, but—why are ye smiling?"

"Because ye had best send your mother a verra fine gift of thanks, as 'tis her blood ye have to be grateful for."

Bothan slowly stood up and then knelt before her, his hand lightly resting on her stomach. "Ye are with child?"

"Aye. I suspected a little while ago, but I waited to be sure. I am sure now."

"Then my laird was right."

"Aye, he was. Why did ye think he might not be?"

"Because he and my father married Callan women. As my mother likes to say, Callan women can find themselves with child if their mon just winks at them." He smiled when she laughed and then pulled her into his arms and held her close. "Ye dinnae care what I am, do ye?"

"Nay. Ye are the mon I love. 'Tis all I need to ken."

Bothan took her face in between his hands and touched a kiss to her mouth. "Ye love me?"

"Aye, Bothan. I think I have almost from the moment we met."

"I think I kenned it, too," he whispered, and frowned when her eyes filled with tears. "I thought ye would be happy that I love ye as weel."

"Och, I am." She dabbed at the corners of her eyes with her fingers. "'Tis the bairn. Nay, 'tis just happiness."

As he stroked her hair, Bothan stiffened his backbone to tell her one more thing. "There is one other thing that we havenae quite bred out. Some of us born of both worlds suffer the need, some of us dinnae. 'Tis a need to mark one's mate. I had thought I hadnae been given that need, but I was wrong. I felt it the verra first time I held ye in my arms."

"Mark me? How?"

He touched her throat. "Here. One bite."

For just a moment, Kenna hesitated and felt a twinge of fear. Then the thought of being marked as his settled into her mind and heart and that tickle of fear faded away. The only thing she did wonder about was whether or not it marked him in some way as well. That would seem only fair.

"And are ye marked, too?"

Bothan nearly cheered, for in that soft question, he heard the acceptance he had been so hungry for. "I am marked in that I am all yours. As ye saw in your dream, I have the heart of a wolf. 'Tis said they mate for life. 'Tis one reason we always tended to marry within the clan, for we kenned they would live as long as we did. There are only a few ways to kill a Pureblood, and most of the half-breeds. The sun, too many wounds and too much blood lost, beheading, and a knife thrust directly into the heart."

"Except for the sun, most of those would kill any mon."

"Aye, 'tis just verra difficult to give a MacNachton that many wounds."

"So I saw. So, one bite?"

"Aye, one bite and, as my mother says, a wee sip." When she reached to undo her laces, he grasped her hand in his. "While we make love. In truth, 'tis just at that moment that I spill my seed inside of ye. As I give ye my essence, I take back a wee bit of yours."

"A blending," she whispered.

"Aye, a blending."

"When shall we do this?"

"'Struth, m'love, I am feeling verra eager to do it now."

"'Struth, my laird, so am I."

They were in their bedchamber, stripped and in bed in minutes. Kenna was still giggling about their haste when he kissed her. She felt her passion rapidly soar and knew it was because he was about to join with her in a way few others could.

A wildness grew inside her as he kissed her breasts, and a wantonness she had never felt before flowed through her. She arched brazenly beneath his kisses and caresses, showing no hesitation even at the most intimate of kisses he gave her. She returned each one until, almost violently, he pushed her down onto her back and joined their bodies. The fact that she had driven him to such a point of need, fired his passion to such mindless heights, only heightened her own.

When he suddenly stilled in her arms, she looked up at him and caught her breath. He looked gloriously feral. Kenna knew it should frighten her but it did not. He kissed her once more and then bent his head toward her neck. She heard herself cry out softly as he bit her, but there was no pain. Instead, wave after wave of pleasure swept over her until she could take no more.

Bothan slowly regained his senses and eased his body off Kenna's. He had never felt such a deep, searing pleasure as he had when he had marked her as his mate. The lovemaking had been fierce and fast, and that, too, had seemed perfect. He lifted his head from her breasts and felt a moment of alarm when he saw that she appeared unconscious. He had never heard that the marking would seriously hurt a woman.

"Kenna?"

Kenna slowly opened her eyes and smiled at her husband. "What?"

"I had thought I had hurt ye—badly."

"Och, nay." She touched her neck. "'Twas the strangest thing, Bothan. 'Twas painful for about a heartbeat, and then," she blushed, "there was naught but pleasure. A great deal of pleasure. I think I must have swooned from the strength of it."

He grinned and brushed a kiss over her mouth. "I made ye swoon from pleasure, did I?"

"Cocksure fool." She could feel only the smallest of marks beneath her fingers. "I dinnae seem to have a wound that will need tending."

"Nay." He kissed the mark. "'Tis but a wee bit red and that will fade as weel. Still, there will always be a mark there."

"Weel, we can tell people that it was caused by the rope my uncle put around my neck."

"A verra clever explanation." He rolled onto his back and pulled her into his arms. "I still feel the cold touch of fear when I think about what he planned for ye."

"Mayhap ye should worry about my side of this union, about the touch of madness."

"Nay, 'twas just blind greed." He idly stroked her slim

back. "I heard your mother just before that ransom note was delivered."

Kenna raised her head from his chest and stared at him. "My mother spoke to ye?"

"She did. She was the one who told me ye were alive and ye were close at hand. It gave me strength. Do ye think she has left ye now?"

"Nay, I was talking to her in the solar. It appears that she likes flitting by and will keep doing it from time to time." She grimaced. "She did leave with me a warning, however."

"A warning about what?"

"A warning about others trying to speak to me. It seems that, now that the word is out that I can hear the dead, there are others who wish to intrude." She slapped him lightly on the chest when he laughed. "'Tisnae funny. I hate hearing strange voices in my head."

"Aye, I got a wee taste of what it feels like when your mother snuck inside of mine and I can sympathize." He shrugged. "There really isnae anything ye can do about it, I fear."

"Nay, I will become accustomed if it happens." She brushed a kiss over his lips. "Ye love me e'en if I have voices in my head?"

"Aye, lass, I love ye e'en when ye have voices in your head, when ye are scowling at me, when ye smell bad, when ye are—" he chuckled when she clapped a hand over his mouth.

"Thank ye for loving me," she said quietly.

"'Tis my pleasure. The true gift is your love for me."

"To settle this argument, I declare that the true gift is the child I carry."

He reached up to stroke her cheek. "That, my love, is indeed the real truth."

Kenna settled herself against his chest and sighed with contentment. "I hope the bairn has your eyes."

"Ah, and here I was hoping she has yours."

"Bothan, we will be happy, willnae we?"

"Aye, m'love, we will be. I did fret o'er that, but there are many at Bantulach who accept me as I am. I willnae flaunt my differences, but I dinnae need to fear that they will get me killed. Having a kinsmon here also helps. Simon is obviously weel trusted and liked and he will be standing at my side. Aye, I think we can be at ease. We will be happy and our bairn will be accepted nay matter which side of the family he or she takes after."

"And that really is all anyone can ask for in life—love and acceptance for all that ye are."

"I couldnae have put it better, my love."

"Weel, my handsome neck-biter, I think we are verra lucky indeed."

And for that comment, Bothan decided he had to make love to his wife all over again.

THE RESCUE

Lynsay Sands

One

It was a shriek that startled Calum MacNachton from sleep. Eyes shooting open, he sat up abruptly and cursed as his head slammed into solid rock. It didn't slow him much. Ignoring the pain in his head, he rolled out from under the overhang where he'd nested and gained his feet.

Calum was moving the moment his feet hit the ground, inching along the narrow space between his horse and the cave wall, hand pressed to his stallion's flank to help keep his balance in the narrow confines.

The shriek that had awoken him was still carrying on and seemed to echo around the dark cave, bouncing off the stone walls and eating into his still-groggy mind. Dear God, the suffering was painful to listen to. Eyes squinted shut and expression a grimace, Calum stumbled past his horse to the bend in the cave.

The stygian darkness eased the moment he turned the corner into the small, open alcove that looked out onto the clearing. Bright sunlight was creeping around the bush that concealed the entrance to the cave. That light made his footsteps slow as he approached.

Calum had a natural aversion to sunlight, as did the rest of his people. Most of his kind couldn't bear it at all. He could, but not much, and hesitated at the bush, peering out into the clearing in search of the death scene that had awakened him.

What he found was a peaceful scene. A mare stood munching at the grass that ran along the river, apparently unconcerned by the shrieking. At first, the horse appeared to be the only presence in the clearing, but then the animal lifted its head, twitched its ears and shifted, moving to the water's edge to drink of the clear, cool stream. Calum immediately spotted the woman in the water. She was still shrieking, but it wasn't a death cry, he realized. The woman was attempting to sing. *Attempting* being the key word. The creature was warbling in the most god-awful, off-tune manner he'd ever heard.

Calum's concern immediately gave way to irritation. He'd almost have been more pleased had murder been taking place as he'd first thought. At least then it would have meant an eventual end to this horrendous sound. As it was, the woman could warble away endlessly in this painful fashion.

Sagging with disgust that his sleep had been disturbed thusly, Calum glared at the girl. For one moment, he considered shouting out or scaring her in some other manner that might send her running, but then his better judgment kicked in and he decided against it. The chit would just run to her village and send men back. His resting spot would be discovered and he'd have to move on. It had been a relatively comfortable spot until now. The cave was dry, cool, and dark, conducive to a good day's sleep. He supposed he'd just have to suffer her presence and her horrid attempt at singing until—

Calum blinked as the girl suddenly stood up in the stream. Water rushed down her naked skin, leaving small droplets behind to glitter on her pale flesh like diamonds under the bright afternoon sun.

Dear God, the woman was completely naked!

Calum supposed he shouldn't be surprised—she was bathing, after all—but judging by the quality of her mare, the woman was a lady. Most ladies bathed in their chemises for modesty's sake. A ridiculous practice, he'd always thought. Apparently, this young woman agreed with him.

His gaze slid over her again, this time with more interest. Her hair was piled on her head—long, honey-gold tresses trapped in a haphazard bun that he noted was threatening to fall. Afraid it would do so and cloak her beauty before he'd fully explored it, Calum let his gaze drop. His eyes slid over the hollows and planes of her back, then to the soft, round curves of her hips before his view was finally obscured. However, it wasn't her hair that blocked his view—it was the back of a man suddenly stepping in the way that hid the little blonde from him.

Calum shifted to the side a bit in the hopes of catching a glimpse of the girl again, but the man was still in the way. He scowled at the unknowing man's back for destroying his view and wondered where he'd come from. The clearing had been empty of anything but the mare when he'd first peered out, and Calum hadn't heard the sound of hoofbeats to warn of anyone's approach.

He supposed the man must be with the girl. He must have ridden in with her on the one horse and been off relieving himself in the bushes when Calum first glanced out.

His thoughts scattered as the man suddenly shifted and the girl was again revealed. Calum had a very brief glimpse of her creamy perfection; then her hair finally escaped its bindings and fell around her shoulders, cloaking her in golden tresses. The horrible warbling promptly ended as she "*tsked*" her displeasure and reached up to catch the wayward hair at the nape of her neck. She performed the maneuvers necessary to return it to the top of her head.

Calum stared with fascination at the curve of breast revealed by her raised arms and wished she'd turn in the water so that he could see all of that breast. Luck wasn't with him, however, and she didn't. The girl had just finished with her hair when the man spoke.

"*Lady* DeCourcey." The greeting was filled with a sly

amusement Calum didn't care for. He watched as the girl stiffened with surprise, then dropped her hands to cover herself and sank back into the water as she turned to face shore. Her wide, alarmed eyes told Calum at once that he'd misjudged the situation. The man *wasn't* with her. He supposed that meant the other three men who suddenly moved into view in the clearing weren't, either.

Calum heaved a small sigh, his hand moving down to clasp the grip of his sword as he listened to the exchange.

"Jocks." The woman sounded confused and wary. "What do you want?"

"Lord d'Angers wishes to see you," the man announced. "He sent us to bring you to him."

Rather than reassure the girl, this news seemed to make her more wary. "Why did he not call on me at DeCourcey?"

"He knows your father is ill and had no wish to trouble him with company," the man said blithely. Calum saw the girl's mouth tighten.

"You mean he knows my father is ill and hopes to force me to marry him so that he might take over DeCourcey and merge it with his land once Father is dead," she said shortly. "You may tell him I am not interested."

"I fear you shall have to tell him yourself. I have orders to bring you to him, and bring you to him I will."

"Kidnap me, you mean," she said bitterly.

The man inclined his head. "Call it what you will. I have my orders."

Calum watched the girl, seeing the way her eyes now shot around the clearing from her clothes, to her mount, to the surrounding woods, then along the riverbank. She was seeking an escape route, but there wasn't one to be had. One of the four men had taken her mount by the reins, the other had gathered up her gown and chemise. The men now simply stood, waiting. If she tried to swim up- or downstream, they would follow. Her only choice was to stay in the water until they tired and went in after her, or come out under her own power.

Calum shifted in the silence, telling himself it wasn't any of his business. Despite that, his gaze kept returning to the girl, noting the pretty face, the lovely, honey hair, and the proud, grim expression that belied the fear he could sense coming from her.

She was in a fix, that was certain, and she was alone against four men. One chit against four men hardly seemed a fair fight to him. On the other hand, it wasn't any of his business, Calum reminded himself again. He'd merely stopped to rest for the day before continuing on with his journey at sunset, but . . .

"Ah, hell," Calum muttered under his breath and started to push his way through the bush at the mouth of the cave.

Sarra DeCourcey stared at the men before her with frustration. She was in a fine bind and knew it. D'Angers had hinted at his intentions when her father's health had first begun to fail, suggesting a merger of their lands and titles could be of great benefit to them both. Sarra had stared at him with open horror at the suggestion. The man was her father's age and had buried three wives already: two were lost to childbirth, along with the wee babes they would have brought into this world; the other died most recently from a fall down the stairs that was questionable. All knew d'Angers wasn't pleased that his last wife wasn't bearing fruit despite five years of his dedicated efforts to plant his seed. It was suspected the accident wasn't an accident at all. Being Lady d'Angers was obviously perilous.

While that had been the first time d'Angers had suggested marriage to Sarra herself, she knew he'd talked to her father of it before. He'd tried to talk her father into a merger at least three times since she'd come of age, but Lord DeCourcey wouldn't hear of it. It appeared now that her father's health was failing, d'Angers had decided to force the issue.

Sarra knew without a doubt that if his men took her to d'Angers, she would be forced into the marriage whether she wanted it or not . . . and then forced into bed to consummate it.

The thought wasn't a pleasant one, and her panicky gaze slid from Jocks to the other three men with him. One held her chemise and the pale blue gown she'd worn over it, his grubby hands smoothing over the material again and again as he licked his lips and peered at her.

Sarra shuddered and shifted her gaze to the man next to him; this one had the reins of her mount twisted around his talonlike fingers. Both her clothes and her mare were lost to her, she supposed unhappily, her gaze sliding past the last of the three men with Jocks and along the embankment. Could she swim downstream and get out before they caught her? And then what? A naked run through the woods back to DeCourcey?

She grimaced at the very idea of one of these men tackling her to the ground in such a state, then recalled the secret passage to the castle. The entrance was a long tunnel that started in a hidden cave in this very clearing. If she could lure the men away, and slip back here unmolested . . . Even if they followed, she would soon lose them in the rocky twists and turns of the tunnel.

Even as her gaze slid to the hidden cave, the bushes filling its mouth suddenly parted to allow a man to slip through. He was tall, broad-shouldered, lean, and moved with the sleek grace of a cat. He was also dressed in a kilt, giving away that he was a Scot, and Sarra watched in fascination as he crossed the clearing.

Catching her eye, the man gave what Sarra suspected was supposed to be a reassuring smile, but what really looked to her like a fierce grimace. Still, for some reason, she was less afraid of this stranger than of the four men between them. Sarra supposed it had something to do with the way d'Anger's men were leering at her lasciviously. In contrast, the newcomer wasn't paying any attention at all to her nudity—his focus appeared to be wholly on the men he approached.

Her gaze slid back to the three men. None of them seemed to hear the stranger approach, and for a moment, Sarra felt sure he would take them by surprise. But then one of the men—the one holding her gown—stiffened and started to turn as if he'd heard or sensed something.

Panic coursing through her, Sarra did the only thing she could think of to distract him—she stood up in the water. It was a nervous, jerky action and loosed her hair once again, allowing it to flow down to help cover her naked body before it disappeared in the water that reached her waist.

D'Anger's man promptly stopped his turn, his eyes locking and widening on her naked flesh. He received a cosh on the side of the head with the flat of the stranger's sword for his trouble.

Of course, the sound as he crumpled to the ground caught the attention of the other three men, and Sarra sighed with relief as they tore their eyes from her to note the newcomer to the clearing. There was a moment of complete silence and stillness, then Jocks asked, "Who the devil are you?"

"Calum MacNachton," the man answered easily.

"MacNachton," she breathed. Sarra had heard of the clan. Everyone had heard of them. It was said they were fierce warriors and there were whispers that there were witches and changelings and other boogeymen threaded through their clan. Sarra didn't put much truck with gossip.

"Well, what business do you have here?" Jocks asked with a frown, a wary look having come to his face.

"Naught," Calum acknowledged easily, then added, "But then I'm thinkin'neither ha'e ye."

Jocks' eyes narrowed. "I am here for the lady."

"Aye, well, Goldy doesnae appear to wish to go with ye," he pointed out.

Sarra blinked. Goldy? Her hand went unconsciously to her hair as her mind made the connection to the reason for the nickname.

"This is none of your business, friend," Jocks said grimly. "Leave now and I will not have my men kill you."

Calum raised a vaguely amused eyebrow and countered, "And if *ye* leave now, I'll no ha'e to kill ye and yer men."

Sarrra bit her lip anxiously as his men glanced to Jocks. They all watched the conflict on his face, and then he heaved a sigh and shook his head. Her heart sank as he drew his sword and moved forward, his men following his lead.

She'd hoped he'd consider it too much trouble and just leave, but it had been a foolish hope. Calum MacNachton was just one man against the three. She very much feared he would be quickly and easily dispatched and then she would be taken anyway. Sarra would not see this brave man die in a courageous but doomed attempt to save her. She opened her mouth to say as much, but had left it too long, she saw, as the battle began and the first clang of metal against metal rang out in the clearing. Sarra quickly began to make her way out of the stream.

Water was difficult to move quickly through unless you were swimming. It was a lesson Sarra had learned long ago, but still, the fact annoyed her as she struggled through the shallow water to shore. She was impatient and slightly frantic by the time she rushed up the bank to snatch her clothing back from the hands of the unconscious man who still held them. Unfortunately, the idiot had fallen on both her chemise and gown and she had quite a struggle getting the items free.

Sarra managed to pull the chemise out from beneath the man and don the thin undertunic. Once that was on, she bent to try to free the gown, glancing over her shoulder as she did. Much to her alarm, the MacNachton seemed to be struggling. He was holding his own against the three men, but barely, and all it would take was a misstep or slip for them to be on him.

Momentarily giving up on retrieving her gown, Sarra straightened and glanced around the clearing, searching for something to use as a weapon. The unconscious man had a sword, but he was presently lying on it.

Spotting a long, thick branch lying further along the bank, she rushed to grab it. The branch was heavy with water, but she managed to heft it and lug it back up the bank. Sarra then had some trouble raising it over her shoulder and almost overbalanced when she finally did.

Steadying herself, she stepped a little closer to the nearest of Jocks' men and swung the branch forward with a grunt, satisfaction coursing through her at the solid thud as she hit the man soundly over the head. He went down like a sack of wheat.

Her gaze slid to Calum MacNachton then. Sarra wasn't sure what she'd expected. A thank-you perhaps, or at least a smile of gratitude. Instead, he scowled at her for her trouble and snapped, "Dress, woman."

Sarra blew her breath out with exasperation.

"That's gratitude for you," she muttered, dropping the wood and turning back to the first unconscious man to grab for her gown again.

"'Tis not as if I am naked. See if I bother to help him again," she added in a growl as she began to tug at her gown anew. She was put out, and that irritation went into her pulling so that she did manage to tug her gown free this time. Unfortunately, Sarra wasn't prepared for it to come loose so abruptly, and squawked as she stumbled backward and fell on her behind on the muddy embankment.

She'd barely registered the bone-jarring jolt to her bottom when a rough hand caught her arm and dragged her back to her feet.

"Quit muckin' about and get dressed," Calum MacNachton hissed.

"Mucking about?" Sarra echoed with disbelief, turning in time to see him raise his sword against a blow from Jocks. Releasing her then, the man returned his full attention to the battle, and Sarra snatched up her gown again.

"Stupid, arrogant, bossy . . . *men*," she muttered as she struggled with the gown, but her efforts halted when a startled oath caught her ear.

Lowering the gown, Sarra glanced toward the three men left fighting. Much to her horror, the MacNachton had backed up and tripped over the branch she'd thoughtlessly left lying in the way. Her eyes widened with alarm as he went down and the two men moved in to take advantage of the mishap.

Moving quickly, Sarra dropped the gown again, grabbed up the sword beside the man she'd felled with the branch, and moved between Calum and the other two men. Jocks and his man stopped at once, irritation flashing across their faces.

"Get out of the way, girl," Jocks snapped, and tried to move around her to get to the fallen man.

"Lady DeCourcey to you, Jocks," Sarra snapped, stepping to the side to block him. She immediately realized her mistake as the second man moved forward through the opening she'd left and raised his sword for a blow. Much to her relief, she heard the clang as metal met metal. Calum had recovered and was on his feet, back in the battle.

Sarra would have continued at his side. She had no idea what she was doing, and the sword was extremely heavy, but if nothing else, she could distract Jocks long enough for the MacNachton to finish off the other man. Or so she thought, until she felt a hand clasp the back of her neck and push her away.

"Dress," came the grim growl as she stumbled a couple of feet away under his impetus. It seemed the man didn't want her aid, she realized with irritation. Honestly, he was a grumpy, bossy sod. And really, Sarra wasn't at all used to being bossed about, or grumped at. Her father had always been a kind, good-natured man, not prone to bossiness or orders when it came to his daughter. In truth, he had probably spoiled her.

Irritated enough to listen to the man and leave him to

their tender mercies, Sarra dropped the sword and moved back to her gown. Still muttering under her breath, she snatched up the gown again, noting that it was now stained with grass and mud from its ill treatment.

Noting that her problem in donning it had to do with the fact that it was inside out, she began to turn it right side out. Her gaze drifted back to the battle as she did, and Sarra frowned when she noted that the stranger appeared to be weakening. He was still holding his own against Jocks and the other man, but his moves were definitely growing slower and more labored.

She wasn't at all surprised. He'd been fighting twice and three times as hard as either opponent. It seemed obvious that if he didn't soon finish them off, he would fail and possibly die at the hands of her neighbor's men.

Sarra knew he wouldn't appreciate her interference, but couldn't just leave him to such a fate. Shaking her head, she threw her gown over the horse's back and reached for the sack she'd hung from her saddle pom. She raised the long, narrow bag, retrieved her bow and arrow from inside and was just notching a bow when a grunt drew her attention back to the battle. Her eyes widened with horror when she saw that Calum MacNachton stood, his sword embedded in the chest of the last man standing with Jocks. That didn't upset her so much as the fact that Jocks had obviously taken advantage of his sword being momentarily occupied and embedded his own sword in the MacNachton's side. The three men were frozen in an interlocking tableau, Jocks man staring at the sword in his chest, the stranger staring at the sword in his side, and Jocks unharmed and smiling at Calum with grim triumph. A heartbeat passed, then Calum suddenly raised his head, glared at Jocks, and his free fist shot out, punching d'Angers' man in the face.

Sarra winced at the crunch of bone breaking as Jocks' head flew back. She wasn't surprised when he landed on his back in the dirt, out cold. The blow had been a sound one.

Her gaze slid from the prone Jocks and back to Calum in

time to see him pull his own sword free. The other man fell at once, leaving MacNachton the only one still standing. Though he wouldn't be for long, Sarra feared, as she saw the way he was swaying. Her eyes widened when he suddenly dropped his own sword and reached down to grasp the grip of Jocks' sword, which was still embedded in his own stomach.

Surely he wouldn't . . . ? He couldn't . . . ?

He did. Sarra stared in horror as he pulled the weapon from his side and flung it away with a roar of mingled rage and pain. Dropping her bow and arrow, she rushed forward, reaching him just in time to catch him as he would have fallen.

Sarra grunted as she slipped beneath his shoulder and took his weight. The sound, or perhaps the action, seemed to rouse him some and he straightened slightly. Calum frowned when he opened his eyes to find her there, supporting him. His hand tightened on her shoulder briefly, then he opened his mouth to speak.

"Get," he began breathlessly, then paused to cough.

Sarra frowned with concern as he clasped his wound and bent forward under the cough; then she spotted his sword and realized what he was trying to say.

"Get your sword?" she asked, and reached quickly to grab it from the ground where he'd dropped it. "Here. 'Tis right here."

Sarra slid the sword back into his belt where it belonged, then moved back under his arm.

He touched the grip as if comforted by its presence, but shook his head. "Get—"

Sarra put a hand to his chest to brace him as he coughed again. Her gze slid to his wound as she did. There was surprisingly little blood, considering the nature of the injury, but she began to suspect from his coughing that he may have nicked a lung.

"Get help?" she guessed as his coughing fit ended. "I will.

I shall take you to help. I just need to look at your wound first."

He shook his head with apparent frustration and tried once more, "Get d-dressed."

Sarra froze, all of her concern evaporating as amazement replaced it.

"You . . . I . . . Ohhhhh," she said with exasperation, flinging his arm off her shoulder.

Leaving him to stand, or fall, on his own, she whirled away and stomped to her mare to retrieve her gown. He was the most annoying, exasperating, *foolish* man she'd ever met. He also seemed inordinately obsessed with her state of dress.

Sarra tugged the gown on with angry jerks, took the time to straighten it, then turned to face the bloody-minded man. "Is this better? Can I save your sorry life now and stop the bleeding? Or shall I don my shoes as well and fix my hair . . ."

Sarra's words died slowly as she realized the man was no longer where she'd left him. Nor was he collapsed in a heap on the ground as she would expect.

Turning with amazement, she spotted him halfway across the clearing. While she'd been busy dressing, he'd tried to make his way back to the cave entrance from which he'd come. However, he didn't have the strength for the journey. Even as she glanced his way, Calum fell to his knees a good ten feet from the bush that concealed the cave entrance.

"What on earth do you think you are doing?" Sarra cried, rushing to his side.

Slipping under his arm, she pushed upward with her legs, managing to get them both upright. She then tried to turn him back toward her horse, but he wouldn't be turned.

"We have to get you on my horse and get you to help," she said, trying once more to turn him.

"Nay." Calum shook his head. "Sun. Weakens me. Cave."

"But—"

"The cave," he hissed, and Sarra hesitated. He'd taken a

bad wound to the side and shouldn't be moving around so much. However, he seemed determined to get to the cave and it couldn't be good for him to upset himself like this.

Her gaze slid back to her horse and then to the cave as she considered the best option. Were she to take him to the horse, she would have to get him on her mare, then keep him on it to ride back to the castle before she could tend his wound. Sarra wasn't at all sure he could stay on the mount on his own. She also didn't think she had the strength to keep him on it. If they could even get him mounted.

However, if she took him to the cave, she could quickly tend his injury, then leave him hidden inside the cave while she rode back to the castle. Surely he would be safe in the cave while she went for help.

"The cave," Calum gasped insistently, sounding desperate.

Relenting, Sarra took a moment to adjust her grasp on him, planting herself more firmly under his arm, then struggled forward, half-dragging him to the bush that concealed the cave. They were both breathless and exhausted by the time they struggled through the bush and into the cool, shadowed cave. Sarra paused to catch her breath once inside, her gaze slipping around the dark interior.

It had been years since she'd been inside. Not since her father had shown it to her as a child. A secret passage only worked if it was a secret, and traipsing in and out wouldn't keep it a secret for long. A path would have been trod through the bush, giving away its existence, or at least the existence of something of interest.

Now, she blinked and peered around the dim interior curiously. Fingers of sunlight were creeping through the bush, leaving the first chamber half lit. There wasn't much to see. A dirt floor, stone walls . . . and a horse.

"Yours, I presume?" Sarra murmured as the horse moved forward and nosed them. Calum's answer was a grunt. She took it as a yes.

Her gaze went to him with concern. He'd grown heavier

against her, supporting himself less and less, and she decided it would be best to sit him down before he fell down.

"Here." She urged him to the side of the cave and tried to get him to sit, but he resisted.

"Out o' the light," Calum insisted.

"We *are* out of the light," she assured him. "Just sit."

"Out o' the light," he repeated, gesturing toward the small, stray beams peeking through to land on them. "It weakens me. Die . . . if I stay out here."

Sarra frowned at his words. She could believe the man had a sensitivity to the sun. She'd heard of the malady before, people whose skin reacted badly to exposure to it, but suspected his panic about even this much was a result of his wound. He was pale, and sweating, and breathless, and obviously off his head.

On the other hand, it couldn't be good for him to be so upset, either, so she closed her mouth and helped him to the back of the cave, following when it curved to the right. The moment they turned the corner, all semblance of light disappeared. She now couldn't see a step in front of her.

Before she could complain, Calum paused and his weight was lifted from her. Confused, she felt for him in the darkness, relieved when she found his plaid-covered chest. Obviously, he'd leaned himself against the cave wall.

Unsure how long he could remain on his feet with just the wall to brace him, Sarra peered around the darkness with a frown. She wanted to look at his wound, but needed light to do so.

"Wait here," she instructed, then felt for the wall beyond him and followed it further into the darkness. There had been torches in the cave when her father had brought her here. They would still be there, and she knew he kept them in good condition in case they were needed, checking and changing them every once in a while. Sarra supposed that would soon be her job. Her father's health wasn't good and she didn't expect him to recover. He had a wasting disease and grew weaker each day.

A pang of grief tried to claim her, but her hand brushed a torch just then. Grateful for the distraction, Sarra lifted it out of its holder and then felt along the ledge for the flint she knew would be there. Much to her relief, she found that, too. Now, she just had to light the thing. Easier said than done, Sarra knew. She had never been very good at this sort of thing.

Gritting her teeth, she set to work and managed the task, surprising herself when she did so relatively quickly.

Releasing a small breath of relief as the torchlight chased the worst of the dark back into the cavern, Sarra set the torch back in its holder and returned quickly to Calum. He was still leaning against the cave wall, but his eyes were closed, his face slack with the barest hint of a grimace of pain on it. She wasn't at all sure he was fully conscious, despite his remaining upright.

Leaving that worry for the moment, Sarra urged his hand aside so she could look at his wound. Worry consumed her as she peered at it. The light was poor and she couldn't see it as clearly as she'd hoped, but saw enough to know it was bad.

Muttering under her breath about the stupidity of men and cursing d'Angers and Jocks and the others to hell, Sarra ripped at the hem of her gown to use as a bandage. It was a temporary measure until she could get him help . . . which was her next step.

She'd barely had that thought when Sarrra became aware that the man had leaned forward and down so that his head rested on her shoulder. His face was turned into her neck, his breath hot on her throat.

Sarra was about to pull away when he suddenly thrust her away, as if she'd been the one mauling him.

"Go," he gasped. "Ha'e to go. Can no . . ." He fell silent, gasping as if he'd been running.

Sarra frowned at the state he was in, then said quietly, "I am going for help."

She frowned more deeply when there was no response from him. His eyes were squeezed shut, his face a grimace.

"Do you understand?" she asked, not wanting to leave him thinking she'd abandoned him. "I am going for help. I shall be as quick as I can, I promise. Just lie down here and rest until I return."

Sarra tried to urge him to lie down, but he resisted, and after a brief moment, she gave up. No doubt he would fall down soon enough . . . and probably hit his head or do himself some other further injury when he did, but despite his wound, he was stronger than she and she couldn't force him.

Leaving him where he stood, Sarra hurried back into the first cavern, surprised to see that the horse had returned here. She'd heard him follow them into the back of the cave earlier and hadn't realized he'd left until now. Apparently, he hadn't liked the dark any more than she and had returned to the front of the cave where it was at least dimly lit. She must have been too distracted with the torch to notice, Sarra supposed.

Giving the horse a sympathetic pat, Sarra moved past him to the mouth of the cave, but paused abruptly as she saw that the clearing was now full of activity. Three of the men were awake and on their feet. Only the one that had been run through with the sword was still down. She wasn't going anywhere.

Two

"She cannot have gone far. Her horse is still here."

Jocks' words drifted easily to Sarra inside the cave. She waited anxiously as he peered around the clearing, relieved when his gaze skated over the bush hiding the entrance without stopping.

"She would not get far on foot with an injured man," he added.

"Maybe MacNachton had a horse," the man she'd knocked out said.

"I did not see one." Jocks didn't look pleased at the suggestion. "Spread out. Search for them."

"What about Jasper?" The man Calum had first knocked out gestured to the one who'd been run through. "He needs looking after."

"Leave him for now," Jocks ordered.

"But he could die," the fellow protested with alarm.

"So?" Jocks asked heartlessly. "Do you want to be the one to explain to Lord d'Angers that she got away because *one* man felled us all?"

The fellow's eyes widened in fear, then he turned to move into the woods, apparently resigned to leaving the hapless Jasper to his fate. It only took a glance from Jocks to make the third man move off quickly as well. It left Jocks alone in the clearing. Sarra watched him glance about, then stiffened with worry when he moved toward her mare.

Much to her satisfaction, the moment he neared the animal, her mare reared up, then turned and bolted off into the woods. Probably headed for the castle, Sarra thought, and hoped so. It would raise the alarm and make sure men were sent out. If that happened, Jocks and the others would flee for d'Angers' land. At least she hoped so.

A small sound from the back of the cave made her glance back, and Sarra frowned. Her rescuer didn't have time to wait for the men from the castle to come looking for them. She needed to get him back to the castle quickly.

Her gaze slid back to the clearing, but there was nothing out there for her. Her mare was gone and Jocks was there, waiting. She knew he was hoping to hear that one of his men had spotted her. What he was more likely to hear was that men from the castle were coming, but she couldn't wait that long. Well, *she* could, but the man now bleeding out in the back of the cave couldn't.

Calum's horse shifted, drawing her gaze, and Sarra eyed him thoughtfully as she considered her options. The first that came to mind was getting both herself and Calum on the horse and riding out of there, but Jocks' presence and Calum's weakness could be a problem. If they weren't quick enough to avoid Jocks attacking them . . . And if Calum fell off the horse . . .

Another option was to mount the horse alone and ride back to fetch help. Sarra had no doubt that alone she'd be quick enough to avoid Jocks stopping her, but he'd no doubt see where she came from, discover the cave, and might go in and look around. Both the secret tunnel and an undefended Calum would be discovered then, and she couldn't risk either outcome.

Sarra's gaze slid to the back of the cave again. The chamber Calum waited in went off in two different directions. One tunnel led to various other tunnels and would leave anyone who didn't know their way lost; the other led to the castle. If she could get Calum on his horse and lead it through the tunnels back to the castle, they should arrive there not long after her own mare, perhaps even before her men left DeCourcey. She could tell them who exactly they were looking for and where Jocks and his men were. She could also get Calum some help before he dropped dead on her.

Her gaze went back to the clearing again. Jocks had now settled himself on a boulder and was peering around the clearing. His gaze never once moved to the injured man on the ground. He didn't even bother to try to stop the flow of blood that must be seeping from his wound.

Shaking her head with disgust, Sarra turned away from the scene and moved to Calum's mount. Catching his reins, she ran a soothing hand down the horse's head and whispered, "We have to get your master to help. Will you come with me without trouble?"

Not expecting an answer, Sarra didn't wait for one, but began to lead the animal deeper into the cave, wincing at the loud, harsh, clop-clop of his hooves on the cave floor. The sound seemed loud to her as it echoed off the surrounding stone, but she was hoping it didn't reach the clearing outside the cave. Fear of it being heard kept Sarra glancing back to the cave entrance as she led the animal deeper into the torchlit cavern. She didn't relax until she'd led the mount around the corner into the new cavern. By that point she was hoping that if Jocks should happen to hear the noise and move to the cave entrance to investigate, all he would see was a dim cave and he would not look further.

He might, she knew, and that fact made her work quickly to get to Calum's side.

Much to her relief, he was still upright, leaning against the cave wall. Sarra glanced from him to the horse and frowned.

"Calum," she murmured quietly. "Do you think you can mount? I need to get you to the castle to take care of your wound properly."

Sarra could see the whites of his eyes as he slowly opened them in the darkness and felt sure his gaze moved from her to the horse and back. He remained still for a moment, then straightened slowly and shifted forward to lean against the horse's side.

Releasing the reins, Sarra immediately moved to help him, interlinking her hands to make a step for him to use to mount the horse and then bending her knees to ensure it wasn't too high for him to reach. Calum stared at her briefly, then grasped the pommel and slowly raised one foot to place it in her hands.

The moment he began to put weight on her hands to push upward, Sarra straightened her knees, forcing herself upward; she also lifted her hands themselves at the same time in an effort to give him a little extra impetus to insure he got into the saddle. He went up all right. Unfortunately, he just kept going. Apparently lacking the strength to catch himself and stay in the saddle, Calum sailed right over it, landing on the ground on the other side of the horse with a thud and a grunt.

"Oh!" Sarra gasped and rushed around the horse to peer down at him.

The man was lying flat on his chest. Sarra hurried to kneel beside him and peered at his face. His eyes were closed, his mouth open, and the side of his face pressed to the ground was kind of squished-looking.

"Lord MacNachton?" she said tentatively. "Are you all right?"

When she received no answer, Sarra bent forward to hold a hand an inch from his nose and mouth. Relief coursed through her when she felt his breath soft and warm on her fingers.

"I did not kill you, then," she said with relief.

"Yet," Sarra added when her only response from Calum MacNachton was a groan.

Sighing, she glanced up at the horse and then back to the man prone on the cave's dirt floor. Her gaze then shifted nervously back to where the cave curved toward the entrance. She really wanted to get him away from the entrance as quickly as possible, just in case it was discovered.

Sarra turned her eyes back to her rescuer.

"Excuse me," she whispered nervously. "Do you think you could wake up now and get on your horse?"

When there was no response, she added hopefully, "I promise not to push you off again."

When she still got no answer, Sarra sighed and got to her feet. It seemed she would have to do it herself.

"You can do it," Sarra assured herself. "Maybe."

Rolling her eyes at her own doubt, she shifted to stand over him, one foot on either side of his hips. He wore a tunic with the kilt around his waist, then over his chest and down his back in a narrow band. Sarra bent to grasp a handful of the tunic in each hand, took a deep breath, and straightened.

A small puff of excited surprise escaped her lips when his chest rose a couple of inches off the ground. The rest of her breath left in a dismayed whoosh, however, when the sound of tearing cloth reached her ears and she was left holding the back of his shirt, the front having gone with Calum as he collapsed back to the ground.

"Oh dear," Sarra breathed, realizing that the side seams of his tunic had given way.

"Well, that was not well made at all," she commented, dropping the limp cloth and trying not to feel guilty. She was contemplating the chances of his kilt tearing or unraveling if she tried to lift him by that when she heard a faint whisper from the man.

Hope rising in her, Sarra bent her ear closer to his face. "Did you say something, my lord?"

"No . . . a . . . laird," he gasped. "And what . . . the bloody . . . hell . . . are ye . . . doin'?"

Fortunately, there was no real strength behind the words, else Sarra might have had her feelings hurt. Telling herself that he was a little testy because he was wounded, she patted his back reassuringly.

"I am trying to get you on your horse," she explained, then asked hopefully, "Do you think you could help?"

There was a moment of silence, then Calum slowly moved one hand and then the other closer to his sides and began to push himself upward.

Relief coursing through her, Sarra stood and bent to grab one arm, tugging in an effort to help him upright.

Between the two of them, they managed to get him on his feet, though it was slow, hard work, and even Sarra was breathless and exhausted by the time he was upright and leaning heavily against his horse. The animal was well-trained and stayed put, which was a good thing because Sarra was sure the man was barely conscious by that point and the horse's solid bulk was the only thing keeping him upright.

Sarra was taking a moment to catch her breath when Calum whispered something. Leaning closer, she asked, "What was that, my lord?"

"Tunic," he breathed with confusion, one hand raising weakly. He didn't have the strength, however, and the hand fell away before reaching his chest. No longer connected, both parts of the tunic had fallen away as they struggled to get him upright and he was now bare-chested except for the bandage she'd wrapped around his stomach and the plaid hanging down one side.

"Er . . ." Sarra murmured, then decided to just ignore his questions about his tunic and turned his attention to mounting instead. "We need to get you on your horse, my lord."

"No a . . . laird," he gasped, but Sarra just waved that

away, too, and urged him to turn along the beast until he was facing it, his chest and face pressed to the animal's side.

Once she had him positioned, Sarra knelt and wrapped her arms around his legs, then glanced up the length of him. "I am going to lift you, my lord. Think you, you can help?"

She thought she heard him mutter something, but didn't straighten to have him repeat it. Instead, Sarra took a breath, tightened her hold on his legs, and pushed upward. It took much grunting and straining to get upright with his weight, and Sarra suspected it was only desperation that allowed her to do it.

Her feeling of success was brief, however. Once she was standing straight, it became obvious that she'd chosen a poor position. Calum went up and over the horse so that he was lying across the animal's back. He was on, and when she carefully released his legs, he stayed there, but he wasn't exactly mounted.

Biting her lip, Sarra ran around to the other side of the horse to peer at his head and arms hanging down this side. Grabbing him by a handful of hair, she lifted his head and tilted her own until she could see his face.

"Do you think you can get your leg over and sit up?" she asked, despite the fact that his eyes were closed.

Sarra then waited for a response, but he didn't even blink his eyes. He was unconscious.

"Damn," she breathed and let his head drop down again. Stepping back, she peered at him silently. He was on the horse, but she didn't think it was probably good for him to be lying on his injury. She couldn't see any way to fix that while he was apparently unconscious, however. On the other hand, Sarra had to wonder how long he would remain across the horse's back once it was moving. He was likely to slide right off with the first step or two, and then she'd be back to trying to get him on the mount.

Sarra considered the matter for a moment, then bent to grab the torn hem of her gown and tore off several more long strips. She stepped up to the horse, caught one of Calum's hands, and started to tie it to the stirrup on this side of the horse, only to pause as it occurred to her that if he did slip, he might take the saddle with him.

Muttering under her breath, Sarra removed the first strip of cloth and tied it to the others to make one long length. She then wrapped it around both of his wrists and tied it securely.

Sarra paused then and placed a hand to the horse's side as she announced, "I am going to crawl under you, boy. Pray, do not stomp on me."

There was no reaction from the animal to indicate whether he heard and understood her, but Sarra merely sighed and crawled under the beast, taking the free end of the cloth rope with her. She didn't breathe again until she was safely on the other side of the horse. After taking a moment to pat the animal's flank in gratitude for not kicking or stomping her, Sarra then carefully tied the free end of the cloth rope around Calum's ankles.

Satisfied that she'd done what she could to keep him on the beast until they reached the castle, she brushed off her hands and got to her feet. Sarra moved to the head of the horse then, and ran one hand soothingly down its nose as she whispered, "We have to get your master back to the castle so I can tend his wounds now. I am going to mount you. I hope that is all right."

The horse stared at her for the briefest moment and then turned his nose into her hair and began to eat it.

"I shall take that as a yes," Sarra said on a soft laugh. Pulling her head out of his reach, she gave him one last pat and then mounted.

It was a bit of a struggle. Calum was in the way, and her muscles were a tad weak after wrestling to get the man on the horse, but she eventually got herself settled behind him. She gathered the reins then and sat back with a sigh, only to realize that she didn't have the torch. Sarra glanced at it with a scowl. She'd set it in its holder while she worked and wasn't pleased at the idea of climbing down, collecting the thing, and then trying to mount again, this time with one hand hampered by having to hold the torch. It would be easier if Calum was conscious and could hold it while she mounted.

Sarra paused to cast a scowl down at Calum for being unconscious, only to pause as she found herself staring at the full, round curves of his bottom. She blinked at the sight. The man was bottom-up on the horse, and his kilt had flipped down to cover half his back, leaving no doubt that Scots didn't wear anything under their kilts. She had an unimpeded view of his butt. It was, she noted, a fine bottom, round and firm-looking. Curiosity urging her on, Sarra reached tentatively to poke one finger at one rounded curve to see if it was as hard as it looked.

Her eyebrows rose as she felt that it was firm yet soft. Unable to help herself, she cupped him with her whole hand and gave a good squeeze, nearly leaping out of the saddle when a groan sounded from the vicinity of his head.

Retrieving her hand quickly, Sarra peered toward where his upper body disappeared down the side of the horse, then leaned to the side to try to get a look at his face, but all she could see was his shoulders from her angle. Sarra hesitated, considering asking if he was all right, then changed her mind. She was really hoping he was unconscious and completely unaware that she'd been feeling his bottom. And if he wasn't and was aware of what she was doing, she really had no desire to know it.

Shaking her head, Sarra quickly tugged the kilt back to where it belonged, only to watch as it slid down to hang over his back again. Biting her lip, she tried once more, then gave it up when the same thing happened.

Forcing herself to ignore the naked bounty before her, Sarra peered toward the torch again and scowled. She was not getting off and back on this animal. After a hesitation, she squeezed her thighs around the horse and clucked her tongue, urging it forward. Once beside the torch, she pulled lightly on the reins, relieved when the beast stopped. Shifting the reins to her left hand, she stood in the stirrups and leaned to the side to reach the torch.

Sarra settled back in the saddle a moment later, torch in hand and relieved that she'd managed the task without unseating either herself or Calum.

"There," she breathed as she rearranged both the torch and the reins so that she had a firm grip on both.

"We are off, then," she murmured, and urged Calum's mount to a slow walk.

Sarra held the torch out as far as she could as the stallion moved forward. It lit the way a good five or six feet ahead of them, and she divided her attention between where the horse was going and keeping an eye on Calum, afraid the man would slide off the horse despite her precautions against such an eventuality. Every time she glanced down, however, she found her eyes lingering on his bottom.

Sarra found herself fascinated by the sight of him. She had seen lots of men in various stages of dress and undress over the years. It was difficult not to with so many soldiers and servants in the keep, but a lady did not look at such things. So, while she may have caught glimpses here and there, she'd never had the opportunity to examine one up close . . . until now. Calum was half-naked and right in front of her and completely oblivious. She could look to her heart's content and no one would ever know. She hoped.

Unfortunately, Sarra was so distracted by looking at the man before her that she took the wrong turn in the tunnels at one point. Luckily, she realized her mistake almost the moment Calum's horse started down the tunnel. Also very fortunately, the tunnel they had turned down was a wide one and she was able to turn the animal in the space rather than back him out. Once headed down the right tunnel again, she released a small sigh of relief and reprimanded herself to stop ogling the poor wounded man before her.

Feeling suitably chastised, Sarra endeavored to ignore the man before her and concentrate on negotiating the labyrinth of tunnels that led to the castle. She did such a fine job of ignoring Calum that she didn't notice that his position on the horse was slipping with each jarring step the animal took . . . until he shifted enough that gravity took over and Calum suddenly swung off the horse. Sort of.

Sarra pulled hard on the reins with a cry of alarm as she saw his behind go sliding past her. Fortunately, the cloth rope she'd made held, and he ended up hanging under the horse, his hands and ankles on either side of the saddle and the cloth rope strained over it.

Letting out a little sigh, Sarra leaned to the left to see his head dangling back from his upraised arms, his expression slack. The fall hadn't awakened him. She leaned to the other side, to peer at the horse's legs, wondering if they could continue. She was afraid the horse would unintentionally kick his master with each step. After a hesitation, she urged the horse to take a step, watching the entire time. The horse took one short step forward and Sarra breathed a small sigh. From the looks of it, so long as she kept him to a walk and didn't try a trot or anything, Calum should be safe enough.

Straightening in the saddle, Sarra took a moment to consider where they were in the tunnels. They were nearly at the end, by her measure. Another few moments and they should reach the entrance to the castle dungeons.

Leaning to the side, Sarra lowered the torch slightly and peered at Calum's face again. Even slack-jawed and mouth open, he was a handsome man. He had long, dark hair that her fingers itched to run through. Sighing, Sarra turned her attention to his face, noting the firm jawline and high cheekbones and wishing his eyes were open so she could see the color. She hadn't really noted their color in all the earlier excitement and was now curious.

As if her thoughts were spoken aloud, Calum's eyes suddenly opened and she found herself staring into their deep, dark depths. Noting the confused look to his eyes, she smiled down at him reassuringly and opened her mouth to say something kind, only to pause and frown as the scent of something burning reached her. Wrinkling her nose, she glanced around, but the only flame anywhere was the torch and that—

Gasping, Sarra jerked the torch upward as she realized she'd allowed it to get too close to the man's head and it was melting his hair. Unable to reach his head from where she was, Sarra jerked her foot out of the stirrup with the intention of dismounting and ensuring she hadn't done him any damage, but her actions were uncontrolled in her panic and she ended up kicking the man in the side of the head.

"Oh!" she cried, forcing herself to sit still lest she do the man more damage. Sarra stared down at Calum. His eyes were no longer open. She suspected she'd knocked him out with the kick. But he wasn't on fire, either, though the hair on the side of his head was a mess. Other than that, he seemed fine.

Sarra rolled her eyes at her own thoughts. Oh aye, other than her having melted his hair and knocked him out with a kick to the head, he was just fine. Sighing, she straightened in the saddle and glanced along the tunnel and decided in the end that alighting to examine him might not be a good option. It would be better just to get him back to the castle. Now.

Clicking her tongue, she urged the horse forward again, relieved when the wooden frame of the secret entrance came into view moments later.

Sarra rode the horse right up to the entrance before dismounting. She did so carefully, not wishing to do her rescuer any more damage. She'd done quite enough already.

Grimacing at herself, she paused to examine Calum's face and hair, careful this time to keep the torch safely away from him and the horse.

The hair on the side of his head would have to be cut away, and there was a bruise on his temple where she'd kicked him, but other than that, and the no-doubt-gaping wound in his stomach, he seemed just fine.

Shaking her head, Sarra straightened and carried the torch to the holder beside the secret entrance. There was an unlit torch in the holder already. She removed it and replaced it with the lit torch, set the unlit one on the ground, then moved to the secret entrance. Sarra knew it led into the dungeons of the basement of castle DeCourcey. Now all she had to do was recall how to open it.

It had been years since her father had shown her this secret entrance. Sarra stood at the large rectangle and stared slowly over the wood on either side of the door she knew was there. Her mind raced as she tried to recall how to open it. She was a little surprised when she recognized the stone she had to press to release the rock. Sarra pressed her palm flat against it, shoulders sagging with relief as the stone door slid inward on its hinges. Breathing out slowly, she then leaned through the small opening to peer around the dungeon beyond.

Much to her relief, the cell beyond was unused and the door open. Seeing this, Sarra turned back to grab the horse by the reins and urge him slowly forward.

The entrance was small, just over her height, and she had to urge Calum's horse to lower his head to get him through it. Sarra was so busy concentrating on that, that she wasn't paying attention to Calum until a grunt drew her eyes back to him. While the entrance was just wide enough to let the horse slide through, Calum's arms, shoulders, and head were hanging out on one side of the animal and his legs and behind hung out on the other and would not fit through the door. He was rammed against the frame of the entrance when his horse tried to walk through.

"Whoa," Sarra said quickly, making the horse stop. Moving along the stallion's side, she peered through the small space left over and looked worriedly at Calum's face. He was awake again—and not at all happy, by the looks of the expression on his face.

"You are awake," she said with forced cheer, wondering if he recalled her accidentally kicking him in the head.

"What the hell?" Calum gasped, peering up at the horse's belly and side. "What ha'e ye done to me?"

"Nothing," Sarra said guiltily. If he didn't recall her kicking him, she wasn't offering the news. "Just a moment."

Moving back to the horse's head, she caught the reins and smoothed one hand down his nose, murmuring, "You have to back up, boy. We have to get Calum off you. Both of you will not fit through the door together."

The horse nickered and began to step backward, slowly and carefully. Sarra waited until he was wholly inside the tunnel again before urging him to stop.

"Good boy," she murmured, giving him one more pat before releasing his reins and moving around the side of the horse to Calum.

"How are you feeling? Do you think you can walk out of the tunnel by yourself? Or do I need to get some help?" Sarra asked, wondering how she could do that, even as she asked the question. The tunnel was a family secret. Only she and her father were to know about it. She really couldn't bring anyone down here. At least not until she had him out of the tunnel.

"What the hell did ye do to me?" Calum repeated rather than answer, but Sarra took heart. His voice was much stronger than it had been before she'd got him over the horse's back. She was hoping that meant that with some help from her, he might be able to walk out of the tunnel. Once she had him in the dungeon and the entrance closed, she could fetch help in getting him above stairs—once she got him off the horse.

"Get me down," Calum grunted.

"Yes, of course, right away," Sarra said quickly, moving around to the other side to peer at the rope she'd tied around his ankles. Unfortunately, his weight was being held up by the rope and making it impossible to untie the knots. After a hesitation, she slipped her hand through a small slit in her skirt and found the small pocket hanging under it.

Pulling it out, Sarra opened the drawstring and retrieved the small dirk resting there, then used it to cut the rope around his ankles.

"Get ready," she warned just before the knife finished slicing through the cloth and his legs dropped to the ground.

Rushing back around the horse, she peered down at Calum. He lay on his back under his horse's belly, eyes closed, a grimace of pain on his face.

Sarra knelt beside him and reached out to touch his cheek. "Are you still conscious?"

Calum's eyes slowly opened and he glared at her. "Yer tryin' tae kill me, are ye no? If so, jest do it quick and put an end to all this torture."

Sarra sat back with annoyance. "I am not trying to kill you, my lord. I am trying to save you."

"Yer savin' will be the death o' me," he muttered and rolled onto his side.

Sarra straightened slowly, unsure whether to try to help him rise or not. He seemed a tad annoyed at the moment. Perhaps he recalled her kicking him in the head after all, she thought, and wondered if she should apologize or not. If he didn't recall it, it would be foolish to remind him by apologizing for it.

Sarra's thoughts were scattered by the realization that while she'd cut his ankles loose, his hands were still tied by the cloth rope and he was struggling to get it off his hands.

"Here, let me help," she murmured, moving around in front of him and kneeling to cut the cloth with her dirk.

Calum spotted the dirk and jerked back abruptly.

"I am just going to cut the cloth," she said with exasperation and proceeded to do so.

"See?" Sarra tossed the bits of cloth aside, then sat back to eye him. "Shall I help you up? Can you get up, do you think?"

Calum scowled. "I dinna need help. I can do it meself."

Sarra rolled her eyes and straightened to get out of the

way as he rolled onto his stomach and managed to gain his hands and knees. It was her experience that Englishmen could be bloody stubborn at times, and it seemed Scottish men were no different. She watched anxiously as he crawled out from under the belly of his horse. He moved to the wall thusly, then used various jagged edges in the wall to pull himself upward. Calum was trembling and panting by the time he was upright. He was also swaying on his feet like a lady about to swoon.

Mouth tight, Sarra couldn't resist anymore and moved to his side, wordlessly placing herself under his arm to help take some of his weight. Calum didn't protest her aid this time and Sarra feared it was a bad sign. She suspected it meant he wasn't as strong as his voice had led her to believe and that he'd used up much of his strength getting to his feet.

Gritting her teeth, she urged him around the horse and to the entrance. His breath was a pained gasp in her ear as they stumbled into the dungeons together. Worried by the harsh sound, Sarra glanced up at his face, only to have her worry increased by his expression. The MacNachton was so far gone, he hardly seemed aware he was on his feet again, let alone that she was urging him through the DeCourcey dungeons. Sarra heard the secret panel close behind them, but didn't even glance back, her concentration taken up with keeping both of them on their feet as she and Calum struggled through the dark, silent dungeons.

As far as Sarra knew, no one had been kept in the small, unpleasant cells during her lifetime, though she supposed they may have been used a time or two while she was a child. It wasn't something a parent shared with a child.

They reached the stairs leading to the first level of the castle and Sarra contemplated them with dismay. There was no way she could get him up the stairs on her own.

However, there seemed little choice. Grinding her teeth together, she straightened her shoulders and put her foot on the first step, then paused and glanced up with surprise when the upper door opened and light spilled down the stairs.

Sarra blinked in the sudden, blinding sunlight that poured down on her from the kitchens. The door from the kitchens out into the gardens behind it was obviously open, she realized, just as Calum suddenly groaned and collapsed on the stairs beside her.

Three

"My lady?" A voice called out uncertainly. "Is that you?"

Sarra glanced helplessly from Calum to the figure silhouetted in the door above just as the kitchen door was closed, making the light more bearable.

"Hadley?" she said uncertainly, recognizing her father's head man.

"It *is* you!" The older man immediately started down the stairs toward her. "I was just finishing my nooning meal in the great hall when one of the maids rushed out to tell me she thought she'd heard noises coming from the dungeons," the man explained as he came. "So, I thought I'd best come have a look."

Hadley paused two steps above where she stood beside the slumped Calum and frowned from one to the other with uncertainty. Finally, his gaze settled on her and he asked, "Who is this? And how did the two of you get down here? I thought you had gone down to the clearing. What—"

"I shall explain all later," Sarra promised, interrupting his questions. "Right now, I need you to help me with him, please, Hadley. This man saved my life and was injured in the doing. He needs help."

Her father's man didn't question her further. Moving to Calum's other side on the thankfully widish stairs, he drew that arm over his own shoulder, removing at least half his weight from Sarra as they started up the stairs.

"You say he saved you?" Hadley asked, his voice strained with the burden they carried between them. "Saved you from what?"

"From d'Angers' men," Sarra panted, glancing up the stairs to see how much further they had to go. It seemed a long way to her. She'd barely had the thought when Hadley forced them to a halt by stopping abruptly. She glanced his way with surprise to see that he was peering anxiously back toward the dungeons and she realized he thought she meant he'd saved her from d'Angers' men right here in the dungeons.

"In the clearing," Sarra explained. "As you said, I rode out to the clearing. I was bathing. Jocks and three of d'Angers' other men appeared, demanding I accompany them to d'Angers."

"We have no quarrel with d'Angers," Hadley said with a frown. "Mayhap he just had some news he wished to share with you."

"They were to take me there whether I agreed or not," Sarra said grimly. "I fear now that father is ill, d'Angers' intends to force his suit, marry me—willing or not—and take over DeCourcey. I got away only because of this man, and we came back through the tunnel."

Hadley glanced sharply at her grim expression, but kept his mouth shut. He had known about the secret entrance for years. Not its exact location, perhaps, but that it existed. Whether her father had ever troubled to tell his first where the entrance was, Sarra didn't know, but she suspected not. He'd always said it was a family secret, not to be shared with others.

When Hadley continued to stare at her, a frown on his face, Sarra shifted impatiently and glanced to Calum. "We need to get him above stairs. I needs must tend his wound."

"Oh, aye," the older man muttered and started to move again.

They were silent for the rest of the journey up the stairs, but Hadley began shouting orders the minute they reached the kitchens. Servants began running willy-nilly, one rushing to open the door between the kitchens and the great hall for them as the cook himself moved to replace Sarra in taking Calum's weight.

Sarra stepped aside with relief and followed the men into the hall just as the keep doors flew open and Malcolm, one of the men under Hadley, rushed in, panic on his face.

"My lady's mare just rode through the gates and Lady Sarra was not on her. She—" He paused abruptly as Sarra stepped out from behind the two men carrying Calum.

"My lady, you are safe," he said, and there was no mistaking the confusion in his words or on his face as he tried to sort out how she could be coming from the kitchens when she'd ridden out on her horse and it had just returned without her.

"Aye, she is safe. See her ladyship's mare is tended to, Malcolm. She is fine," Hadley ordered, a tad breathlessly.

Malcolm nodded and started to turn away, but Sarra called him back and said, "Have six men ride down to the clearing to see if d'Angers' men are still there. They have probably given up and returned to d'Angers by now, but if they have not, capture them and bring them back here."

Malcolm's eyes widened, his gaze sliding to Hadley. The older man nodded, and once the younger man had left, glanced to Sarra. "I am sorry, my lady. I understood that this man had taken care of them already, else I would have ordered a search for d'Angers' men at once."

"He knocked out three of them and ran the fourth through," Sarra explained, and then added, "but they were all conscious and beating the bushes for us when we headed back to the castle."

"I see." Hadley nodded, then asked, "Where do you want him, my lady?"

Sarra followed his gaze to Calum, her mind working quickly. She wanted to tend to him herself. It was the least she could do when he'd been injured saving her. However, she tended to spend all her time in her father's room since his illness, leaving only once a day to ride down to the river for fresh air, sun, and a bath. She had no intention of changing that pattern and running between two sickrooms.

"My lady?" Cook prompted, then added apologetically, "Tonight's stew shall burn do I not watch over it."

"My father's room," Sarra announced firmly.

When Hadley frowned at the suggestion, Sarra reminded him, "He was wounded saving me from d'Angers' men. I wish to watch over him to be sure he heals well."

Hadley didn't look pleased, but kept his opinion to himself and turned toward the stairs.

Breathing a little sigh of relief that he wasn't arguing with her, Sarra caught up her skirts and followed as they carried the man across the great hall to the stairs to the second level of the castle. She paused, however, when she spotted the maid hurrying down the stairs toward them.

"Milly, I need boiled water and fresh cloth for bandages," she instructed as the woman reached them.

"Aye, my lady."

When the maid ran off toward the kitchens, Sarra followed the men as they started up the stairs. Once in the upper hallway, she hurried around them to reach her father's door first and open it for them.

"My lady!" Bessy, the maid Sarra had left to sit with her father, stood in surprise as they entered the room.

Sarra nodded at the girl, but her gaze moved to her father as the frail old man forced himself into a sitting position in bed to stare at Calum as Hadley and Cook dragged him into the room. "Sarra, my dear. What is this?"

"Please lie down, Father. You will wear yourself out," she said, frowning at his pallor and the sweat that broke out on his brow at the small effort.

Sarra started toward the bed to see him settled against the pillows, but paused when Hadley asked, "Where shall we put him?"

She turned to survey the room with a frown, unsure where she should have him put. She hadn't thought ahead to the fact that there was only the one bed in the chamber.

"Who is he?" Elman DeCourcey asked as Bessy moved to settle more furs and pillows behind his back so that he could sit upright without having to support his own weight.

"His name is Calum MacNachton, Father. He saved me from Reginald d'Angers' men. Unfortunately, he was injured in the doing."

"Reginald d'Angers' men?" her father echoed with surprise. "Why would you need saving from Reginald's men? We have no quarrel with our neighbor."

Sarra sighed, unhappy to have to explain. "It would seem we do now. They said Reginald wanted me at d'Angers and they were to bring me back whether I wished it or not."

Her father's mouth tightened. "He thought as I was ill he could force you to marry him."

"That is what I suspect," Sarra admitted.

Her father nodded solemnly, then glanced toward Calum.

Sarra followed his gaze, then sighed. "Come, Bessy. Bring some furs. We shall make a bed here by the fire for him."

"On the floor?" her father asked with amazement.

Sarra grimaced, but nodded. "I would tend him while I tend you, and it will be easier if you are both in the same room."

"You cannot put him on the floor like some dog," he said firmly. "The man saved your life."

"Aye, but—" Sarra glanced around the room helplessly. Where else could she put him?

"Here." Her father pulled aside the furs on his bed and thumped the empty bed beside him. "Put him here. There is plenty of room. You can tend his injury more easily, and he will not be on the floor."

Sarra hesitated, surprised at the offer, but Hadley and the cook were already moving toward the bed, eager to be free of their burden.

"Are you sure?" Sarra asked as she rushed to move the furs for the men.

"Positive. He saved your life, child. The least we can do is offer him a warm bed to rest and recover in."

Nodding, she stepped out of the way for the men to set Calum on the bed. He was a large man, seeming larger next to her father's shriveled, illness-wracked body. Elman DeCourcey had always seemed larger than life to her and it pained Sarra to see him so reduced in countenance. Pushing away the sadness this caused, she moved forward as soon as the men were out of the way and bent to Calum's wound.

"I will be below," Hadley announced, following Cook, who was hurrying for the door, eager to return to his stew. "I want to know what the men found as soon as they return."

Sarra nodded absently as she quickly removed the temporary bandage she'd covered Calum's injury with down at the cave. She tossed the stained bit of cloth aside, peered at the wound, then paused and frowned.

"What is it?" her father asked as the door closed behind the men.

"I am sure the wound was larger . . . and there is so little blood," Sarra muttered. "It must be the light in here. I need more light." She said the last more loudly.

Bessy rushed away to the window and had opened the shutters before Sarra recalled Calum's aversion to sunlight. The way he began to thrash the moment the sunlight splashed into the room reminded her, however, and she barked, "Close the shutters!"

Eyes wide, Bessy quickly closed the shutters again. Much to Sarra's relief, Calum settled the moment the sunlight was blocked out. Sighing, she moved to grab a candle and bring it closer to the bed.

"I forgot he has an aversion to sunlight," she explained to her father. "He says it weakens him."

"Hmmm. A MacNachton, you say?" her father asked,

leaning forward to watch as she held the candle close to the wound.

"Aye," Sarra murmured absently, her attention taken up with examining his injury. Truly, to her eye, it did look smaller than it had been, and really, for the sort of wound he'd suffered, the amount of blood that had stained his now-missing tunic had been pitifully small indeed. It didn't appear he'd bled since then, either, despite all her bumping and dumping him about.

"Here you are, my lady." Milly rushed into the room with the water and bandages Sarra had asked her to fetch.

"Thank you," Sarra murmured. Setting aside the matter of the size of the wound, she concentrated on mending him.

Calum slept through her cleaning of the wound. Sarra stitched it closed with small stitches, then bandaged him up while her father, Milly, and Bessy watched. She was relieved to finish the job and found herself rubbing the small of her back as she straightened. It had gone stiff after having bent over him so long.

"You should go have your nooning meal and a drink," her father said quietly, eyeing the way she was stretching her back and rubbing it. "Bessy, Milly, and I shall watch him while you take care of yourself. It will do none of us any good if you make yourself ill," he added when she opened her mouth to protest.

Sarra nodded reluctantly. She *was* hungry and thirsty. Besides, now that she'd finished tending the man, she was recalling his horse, and the fact that she'd left the poor beast in the tunnel.

"I will not be long," she assured her father as she moved toward the door. Then she glanced to the maids to add, "Fetch me if there is any problem."

Hadley was seated at the great hall table. Sarra paused long enough to assure him her father and Calum were fine and to learn that the men had not yet returned from the clearing. Sarra nodded at this news, suspecting it meant that d'Angers' men had given up their hunt and fled the clearing by the time the men reached it. She suspected the DeCourcey men were pursuing them to the edge of their land, but feared they wouldn't catch them up.

Frowning over this, Sarra continued on to the kitchens, where she paused again, this time to request that some bread and cheese and mead be taken out to the trestle table for her to eat when she returned. She then lit a torch from the fire in the kitchens and continued on down into the dungeons. The place was much more spooky on this journey. Sarra could only think it was because she was alone.

Eager to get the task done and get back upstairs, Sarra hurried to the secret entrance. She paused then long enough to glance behind herself to be sure she had not been followed and was alone, then turned the torch holder that opened the entrance from this side. The darkness beyond the opening made her pause. Sarra had left the lit torch in a holder in the tunnel, but it appeared to have gone out. She was now facing a deep dark that made the hair on the back of her neck stand on end. There was no sign of Calum's horse, and she at first feared the animal had wandered off in search of light as he had in the caverns earlier.

"Hello . . . er . . . horse?" she said uncertainly, and moved a reluctant step into the darkness.

"Oh," Sarra gasped with relief when Calum's black beast stepped forward and his nose suddenly appeared in the darkness before her.

"Hello, boy." Reaching out, she patted his nose in greeting, then felt for his reins and urged him to follow her out of the darkness and into the lighter dungeons.

"Good boy." Sarra patted him again once they were out of the tunnel. "I am sorry. I didn't realize the torch was so close to running out, or I never would have left you alone in there," she assured him as she led him into the center of this first room.

Feeling bad for having abandoned him in the dark as she had, she took a moment to pat his side and murmur soothing nothings to him. Then, noting that he was covered with cobwebs and dirt from the tunnels, Sarra brushed him down with one hand, apologizing the whole time.

"There, that's much better," Sarra assured him as she finished brushing the dust and cobwebs away. "You *are* a pretty boy, are you not? Yes, you are. So, that's what we shall call you then. Pretty Boy."

Smiling, she gave him one more pat, then turned back to close the entrance to the tunnel only to find that it had closed on its own as it had the first time. Relieved to be able to leave the dungeons, Sarra caught the stallion's reins and led the way to the stairs, talking the whole way.

"Your master is well and resting now. I tended his wounds, but they were not as bad as I first feared," she announced, then added, "and soon you will be in a nice, warm stall in the stables. I shall have the stable master give you a good brushing-down and get you something to eat. And I shall give you a special treat of carrots for being so patient and waiting in the tunnel in the dark as you did."

Sarra had no idea whether he understood her or not, but Calum's horse moved docilely along at her side until they reached the stairs. He paused there and looked up the narrow stone staircase with what she would have said was equine doubt. Sarra didn't blame him—while wide, they were steep and narrow and could be treacherous to humans. No doubt they would be doubly so for a horse.

Sarra eyed the stairs and blew her breath out on a sigh. They would be tricky, and Cook would hardly be pleased to have a horse traipsing through his kitchens, but there was no other way out of the dungeons.

"Perhaps we can sneak you through the kitchens while Cook's back is turned," she murmured to the horse, but he didn't appear any more convinced than she that this was a likelihood.

Sighing, Sarra released his reins and patted his nose again. "I shall go open the door at the top and have a look about, shall I?" Her gaze slid to the steep stairs again and she added, "I shall definitely give you a carrot when we reach the top."

Leaving him at the foot of the stairs, Sarra made her way up to the top. She eased the door open and peered out to see that Cook was busy at a pot over the fire. They might yet manage to slip past him, she thought, but glanced over her shoulder with alarm as a sudden clatter sounded on the stone steps. Seeing the big, black beast charging up toward her, Sarra thrust the door open and stepped into the kitchen to get out of the way.

"What the devil!" Cook whirled to peer at her with amazement, then frowned. "Oh, my lady. I—what the devil is that racket?"

"Oh, well, you see, I . . ." Sarra's voice died as Calum's horse burst through the open door and trotted to her side to rest his head against her shoulder.

Cook's eyes went wide with amazement. "How the devil did that beast get in the dungeons?"

"He is not a beast, he is Pretty Boy," Sarra said quickly, patting the animal soothingly in case he was offended. When Cook raised one doubtful eyebrow, she sighed and said, "He needs a carrot. I promised him one. If you would send one out with the cheese and bread, we would both greatly appreciate it."

Not waiting for his response, Sarra then grabbed up Pretty Boy's reins and hurried from the kitchen out into the great hall. Calum's mount followed docilely enough. He seemed a fine horse, well-mannered and obedient. She was most impressed.

"There you are, my lady." Hadley stood as she approached, his eyebrows rising at the sight of the horse following her. "MacNachton's horse?"

"Aye. I had to leave him in the tunnels while I brought Calum in," she explained. "I would have ridden right into the dungeon on him, but the opening was not large enough."

"No, I do not imagine it would be," he murmured, rubbing his chin as he eyed the beast.

"I fear the torchlight went out while we were gone and he was left in the dark," Sarra admitted guiltily, turning to run an apologetic hand down the animal's side.

"He seems well enough for all that," Hadley murmured, then asked, "Shall I have him taken down to the stables?"

"Aye, please. But Cook is sending out a carrot for him first."

Hadley nodded and they both glanced to the kitchen doors as a maid rushed out with the requested food. Sarra smiled at the girl as she set it on the table, then reached down for the carrot and held it out to Calum's horse. The stallion accepted the offer graciously and Sarra left him to eat it and sat down to eat the cheese and bread she'd ordered.

Hadley kept her company, speaking on estate matters while she ate, telling her what was happening, but not saying anything that required an answer. Sarra was just finishing when the keep doors opened and Malcolm entered. She waited expectantly as he crossed the great hall to make his accounting.

Sarre wasn't terribly surprised when he announced that the clearing had been empty when they'd arrived. D'Angers' men had apparently taken their fallen comrade and fled. Malcolm and the others had followed their trail to the border between d'Angers and DeCourcey, hoping to catch them up, but hadn't come across them. It was no more than Sarra had expected, but she was still disappointed.

"I suppose I shall have to refrain from riding out alone for now," she said unhappily, once the man had finished speaking. As much as it pained her, Sarra knew it was no longer safe to make her daily journeys down to the clearing. The knowledge was depressing. It was the only time she usually took for herself in a day. Before this meal, Sarra had eaten every meal with her father and sat by his side from the time she rose until the time she retired, except for that brief hour when she rode to the clearing to bathe. It pained her to give that up, but she had little choice so long as d'Angers had determined to force her hand.

"That is a shame, my lady," Hadley murmured. "'Tis the only break you allow yourself from your duties." He frowned over the matter and then said, "Perhaps myself or one of my men could accompany you in future. You would have to forgo bathing, but the fresh air and exercise would still do you good."

"Do you think one man would be enough to deter them?" Sarra asked doubtfully. "I would rather there was no more fighting over me. I would not see anyone else injured for my sake."

After taking a moment to consider the matter, he allowed, "Well, perhaps myself *and* one of the other men would be better."

Sarra smiled faintly and patted his hand. She could see it upset him to admit it might take more than one man to keep her safe and supposed it rankled to admit that while Calum alone had saved her, there were few men under his leadership who could have managed the feat. In fact, Sarra doubted there was a single man at DeCourcey who could have got her out of that situation as Calum had. She didn't say as much to Hadley, however, but finished her mead and stood. "Very well, Hadley. I shall not go out alone in future. Now I had best go up to check on Father and Calum."

Sarra headed for the stairs, recalling Pretty Boy only when the heavy clop-clop of hooves on stone followed her. Pausing, she turned back to find the horse on her heels. Hadley and Malcolm were moving toward them, even as she took the animal's reins and glanced their way.

"Never fear, my lady," Hadley said as they reached her. "Malcolm here can take the beast down to the stables. He shall see him tended to."

"Thank you," Sarra murmured and handed the reins over to the younger man. "See he gets a turnip or something and a good brushing, please, Malcolm."

"I will, my lady," the young man assured her.

Nodding, Sarra turned back to the stairs, pausing after a few steps when she realized the clop-clop was still following her. Glancing over her shoulder, she turned with amazement when she saw that Calum's horse was following her despite the hold Malcolm had on his reins and his efforts to stop him. The horse was ignoring the man's tugging and simply dragging him along behind him.

"No, no," she said to the horse, moving back to rub his nose. "You have to go down to the stables. I shall come visit you there later to see that all is well."

Much to her amazement, the horse blew his breath out and shook his head as if he understood what she said and was protesting. Sarra frowned at the animal.

"You go on, my lady—we'll take care of him," Hadley said, moving to add his strength to the reins. The moment the words left his mouth, the horse reared up on his hind legs, pawing the air in protest before slamming down onto all fours and moving determinedly forward as Sarra slowly backed away. Hadley and Malcolm were fighting him, both men pulling on the reins, but it didn't seem to be holding the animal back much at all.

"Enough," Sarra said, concerned the animal would hurt himself or someone else in his upset. Moving back to the horse, she took his reins and rubbed his side to try to soothe him. "I will take him to the stables myself."

"That may be for the best," Hadley murmured, wiping his brow; then he stiffened and they all glanced upward as a sudden roar sounded from above stairs. Before anyone could react, Calum's horse had pulled his reins free of Sarra's slack hold and charged up the stairs toward the sound of his master's pained shout.

Cursing under her breath, Sarra grabbed up her skirts and gave chase, aware that Hadley and Malcolm were on her heels.

Four

Calum's horse was at the door to her father's room when Sarra reached him. Concerned by the continued roar coming from the room, she pushed past the beast and opened the door, only to be nearly trampled when Calum's mount pushed past her. Catching herself on the door frame, Sarra managed to keep her balance and staggered into the room, hard on the animal's heels. She took in the situation at a glance. Bessy was nowhere to be seen and Milly stood frozen by the open shutters of the room, staring in horror at Calum as he thrashed about in the bed like a fish out of water.

Lord DeCourcey was shouting at the girl to close the shutters, but the maid didn't seem able to follow the order, if she even heard it over Calum's screams.

Hurrying across the room, Sarra pushed the girl out of the way and quickly slammed the shutters closed.

Calum went quiet at once and Sarra sagged with relief as she turned back to the room. Her sigh was echoed by her father.

"Milly opened them before I realized what she was up to," her father said when she glanced his way.

Sarra nodded, but frowned. "Where is Bessy? She knew not to open the shutters."

"She went below to fetch your father a drink," Milly said, biting her lip anxiously.

Sarra frowned at the claim. She hadn't seen the girl pass on her way to the kitchens and had no doubt the maid was off canoodling with Petey somewhere and would return much later with the drink she was supposed to be fetching. *Young love*, she thought with disgust. The maid had been undependable since Petey had arrived at DeCourcey. The two had set eyes on each other and appeared to have forgotten anyone or anything else existed.

"I am sorry, my lady," Milly said anxiously. "I just thought as it was such a nice day your father would enjoy some sunshine."

Sarra nodded and waved away her apology. "Bessy should have told you before she left. Sunlight makes Calum anxious. It is miasma to him. Never open the shutters."

"Aye, my lady," Milly said.

Satisfied that the woman wouldn't forget again, Sarra now turned her attention back to the bed. Calum's horse was standing at the bedside, head lowered over the man, chewing at his hair as if hoping to wake him thusly.

Sighing, she straightened her shoulders and moved to the bedside to check that Calum hadn't reopened his wound with his thrashing. Sarra pushed the horse determinedly aside and started to bend over the man in his place, only to find herself bumped back as the horse pushed *her* out of the way.

Scowling, she glared at the beast. "I have to check his wound."

Pretty Boy stared back for a minute, then sidestepped away to make room for her as if he really understood. Which was ridiculous, Sarra told herself as she bent to pull the furs aside and peered at the bandages.

There was no sign of blood showing through to suggest he'd ripped his stitches and was bleeding again. Sarra was debating whether to remove them, just to be sure none of the stitches had given way, when she became aware of a hot breath on her neck. Calum's horse was hovering over her as she worked.

Sarra scowled and turned her head to glare at the animal. "I can not do this with you breathing down my neck. Go over there, Pretty Boy."

She pointed to the corner, but the horse didn't move. Straightening slowly, she propped her hands on her hips. "Very well, then I will not tend him."

"Er . . . Sarra," Elman DeCourcey said, and she glanced at her father to see that his expression was torn between concern and amusement. Her gaze slid to the others in the room. Milly, Hadley, and Malcolm were all staring at her, wide-eyed.

She was talking to a horse, Sarra realized. On the other hand, she was quite sure he understood her.

"He's a very intelligent animal," she muttered by way of explanation.

Hadley cleared his throat and nodded uncomfortably, then gestured to Malcolm to join him in trying to get Pretty Boy out of the room.

Ignoring them, Sarra turned her attention to tending to Calum. As far as she could tell, everything was fine. At least, he didn't appear any worse off than he had been when last she'd looked at him.

"He will be fine," Sarra murmured to the room at large as she straightened.

"He has a very bad reaction to light," her father commented as she pulled the furs back into place and straightened.

For some reason, the comment made her glance nervously to where Hadley and Malcolm were wrestling with Pretty Boy, trying to drag the unwilling horse from the room. Hadley was pulling on the reins, while Malcolm pushed on his flanks from behind. The horse wasn't moving; however, they were suitably distracted and didn't seem to have heard. Keeping her voice low, she murmured, "Aye. He said he reacts badly to it. It weakens him. I suspect he is merely sensitive to it, but injured and insensate as he is, his mind is making him overreact to it."

"Hmm," Lord DeCourcey murmured thoughtfully. "And he took on four men on his own?"

"Three, really, I suppose," Sarra said slowly. "He knocked one out before they even realized he was there, then had the other three to deal with. He was very strong . . . and fast," she said with admiration, her gaze on the man as she recalled his maneuvers in the clearing.

"A MacNachton who is strong and fast and with an aversion to the light," her father murmured thoughtfully, and Sarra glanced at him curiously. There was something about her father's expression that troubled her. He was eyeing Calum like there was something odd about him, and she supposed he *was* a little unusual. Most men wouldn't dare even attempt to take on four men on their own, and certainly few would succeed at it. The rumors about his clan came to mind again, but she pushed them away.

"I knocked one out for him," Sarra announced quickly and it was true, though he had battled the three men for several minutes before she'd done so . . . and held his own. Shaking these thoughts away, she tried to turn her father's thoughts from their guest. "How are you feeling today?"

"Fine, fine," he said absently, then smiled at her and added, "Today is a good day."

Sarra smiled slightly. Her father's days were made up of good and bad days. Much to her alarm, however, there were more bad days than good of late. He seemed to grow smaller and weaker all the time and his body pained him more and more with each passing day. And each of those days forced Sarra to face the fact that he was dying. What he had was one of the wasting diseases, something she couldn't fix with all her medicinals. Sarra feared she was losing him and the very idea filled her with fear and pain. She would be alone then.

"Sarra. We should talk."

She forced her thoughts away and managed a smile as she noted her father's sad expression.

"We need to figure out what to do about d'Angers before—"

"Do not fret, Father," Sarra said quickly, interrupting him. She wasn't ready to talk about his dying. He was all she had. "We will talk. But first I need to see to Calum's horse."

She turned away before he could protest and approached Pretty Boy. Patting his head, she leaned up to his ear and whispered, "Follow me and I shall find you another carrot."

Sarra then turned and left the room. Pretty Boy immediately trotted after her, leaving a panting Hadley and Malcolm gaping after them.

The room Calum opened his eyes to was dark, barely lit by the glowing embers of a dying fire. He could smell the wood smoke in the air and it was so unexpected, when he'd gone to sleep in a cave, that he started to try to sit up. That was when he discovered he was wounded. The pain in his side was a sharp contrast to the constant gnawing of his stomach. Calum lay back and closed his eyes, sorting the matter. He was warm, wounded, lying on something soft and comfortable, and he was hungry and thirsty.

"If you are thirsty, there is mead in the jug on the chest beside the bed."

Calum's eyes flew open, his entire body jolting at the sight of the wrinkled old face leaning over him. A man's face . . . belonging to the man under the furs with him in his bed.

In the next moment, Calum had propelled himself out of the bed. It wasn't something planned out. His mind and body reacted of their own accord, jerking and scooting sideways away from the fellow until he was suddenly tumbling from the bed. He landed on the floor with a grunt, his body tangled in linens and furs, and really, it did him little good. The man just followed, his head poking out over the side of the bed to eye him with amazement.

"Are you all right?" the old man asked with concern. "Did you do yourself an injury in any way? Sarra will be annoyed if you did."

"Sarra?" Calum asked warily, his alarm fading as he started to wake up.

"My daughter," the old man explained. "She put a lot of effort into sewing you up and shall surely be annoyed if you rip your stitches so she has to do it again."

Calum frowned, his mind seeking answers. He recalled that he'd been traveling to London to take care of some business for his uncle. Again. He had been taking on such chores more and more often of late now that his brother, Bothan, had found his mate and married her. It left Calum alone at Cambrun. Bothan had invited him to live at Bantulach, but Calum felt like a third wheel around the newly married couple and missed the old camaraderie he and his twin had shared. The two of them used to be quite close, talking about and sharing everything, but that had changed with the arrival of Kenna Brodie of Bantulach in his life. His twin had found his mate and a new home, and Calum had found himself alone at Cambrun. Not wholly alone, of course—there were many others there, but not Bothan and he felt his absence like a missing limb. Calum had been leaving MacNachton more and more often since, volunteering for every chore that came up to get away from the home that reminded him of his loss.

He was on one such chore now and had stopped to rest in one of the many caves he used on his journeys, only to be awoken by the most god-awful singing he'd ever heard.

Ah yes, Calum recalled. The golden-haired creature in the water, the four men who had accosted her, his decision to intervene on behalf of Goldy, as he'd come to think of her.

"Goldy."

Calum blinked in surprise as the man echoed the name. He hadn't realized he'd been speaking aloud, but he must have been.

The old man was smiling as he added, "A thoroughly appropriate name, but we call her Sarra. She brought you back to the castle through the tunnels and tended your wounds. She wished to keep you in here with me where she could tend both of us more easily, which is how you ended up in this bed. It was either in bed with me or on the floor, and the floor seemed too mean a resting place for the man who saved my daughter."

Calum grunted at this news and glanced around for the daughter in question, but the room—what he could see of it from his position on the floor—appeared empty.

"She has gone to her own chamber to sleep now. Bessy is watching over us tonight."

Calum raised an eyebrow at this news. "And where be this Bessy?"

"Off giggling in the hall with one of the men. Petey. They are in love." He rolled his eyes, then assured him, "She will not be gone long, though. And one little call and she would be right here. Do you need help getting back in bed? Shall I call her?"

"Nay," Calum said quickly and proved the point by getting to his feet, though he was shaky and sweating by the time he managed the feat.

"Well . . . you *are* a strapping fellow, are you not?"

Calum frowned. The old fellow was gaping wide-eyed at his nudity. Calum shifted uncomfortably on his feet. "Where are me clothes?"

"Clothes?" The old man looked surprised at the question, then frowned in thought as he apparently tried to recall.

Calum was hoping to dress and slip from the castle while its inhabitants slept. His hopes were dashed, however, when the man shook his head and admitted, "I have no idea. I do not recall anyone taking them away. They must have done it while I was asleep."

Calum frowned. "And me horse?"

"I would guess he is in Sarra's room," the old man said with a laugh. "She spent a good hour trying to put him in the stables, but he wouldn't remain there no matter what they tried. I gather he kicked a hole in the wall of the stables at one point when she managed to get him into a stall, and then tried to leave. She finally gave up on it and allowed him out. He has been following her around like a great, faithful dog ever since."

Goldy's father shook his head. "I have never seen the like."

Calum's frown deepened at the man's words. He wasn't at all sure he even believed it. His horse, Black, was a loyal beast, never letting anyone but Calum near him, including his own twin brother, Bothan. He simply couldn't fathom the idea that the horse had shifted his loyalty to the little slip of a blonde he'd rescued that afternoon.

Scowling, he tossed the furs and linens on the bed for the old man and turned to head to the door.

"Oh, say! You cannot go about like that," the old man protested, scrambling off the bed to chase after him in his nightshirt. "Besides, your side is not healed."

Calum turned back to snap at the man, but frowned and took his arm to brace him when he saw the way the man was swaying. Of the two of them, the old man was the one in the worse shape. Calum sniffed the air in the room, recognizing the sweet stench of death. The man was rotting away of one of the wasting diseases, and wasn't far from the end, and yet troubled himself to worry about him. Feeling himself soften a bit, Calum scooped up the old man and carried him back to the bed.

"Rest," he growled not unkindly as he set him down.

"You should rest, too," the old man argued, sitting up

the moment he set him down. "Sarra will be upset if she catches you up and about."

"I thought ye said she was sleepin'," Calum pointed out. He'd hoped to slip into her room, retrieve his horse and some clothes, find something to eat, and slip from the castle without disturbing anyone, but it would be impossible to do so if the lass was awake.

"She may be. Or mayhap not. Sarra has not slept well of late," the old man murmured. "She worries about me, you see. She knows I am dying and often wakes up in the night and checks on me. I suspect she fears each time that she will find me dead. And, no doubt, one night she will."

Calum felt a pang at the words and that pang just managed to redouble his desire to get out of the room. He had enough troubles of his own without taking on the burdens of others. He pushed the man back on the bed, grunted "Rest," and quickly left the room before the man could protest further.

The hall was dark and appeared empty at first; then Calum heard a soft, breathless giggle followed by a moan and peered more carefully into the shadows of the hall. On second glance, he could make out a couple locked in an embrace at the end of the hall. Bessy and her Petey, he supposed. Fortunately, they were too wrapped up in each other to notice him. Calum eyed them briefly, considering stopping for a quick bite. He didn't have to feed often, but had lost a lot of blood to his injury and had been weakened, which put him at about mortal strength, by his guess. A bit of blood would help his wound heal more quickly and return his strength to him.

Another giggle drifted down the hall and Calum sighed. He hadn't bothered to feed off the old man—his illness made his blood weak. This pair was both robust and healthy and their blood was hot with their passions, but . . .

He glanced along the hall with a frown. Calum preferred not to feed on people he knew. He didn't know this couple, but they belonged to Goldy—Sarra, he corrected in his mind. He may have started out trying to save the girl, but she in turn had saved him. Calum would never have made it into the safety of the cave without her. He would have lain where he'd fallen and died under the hot midday sun. Sarra had saved him by helping him into the cave, tending his wound, and bringing him back here to the castle through the secret tunnel. He wouldn't repay her by feeding on one of her servants. The best thank-you he could offer would be to find her room, slip in and retrieve his clothes and horse without waking her, and then leave the castle.

Sighing, he turned away from the amorous couple and moved silently along the hall, sticking to the shadows. The hunter in him had taken over. He was silent and stealthy and unseen until the door he was approaching suddenly opened and a woman stepped out.

Calum froze, noting at once that it wasn't Sarra. The woman was older and larger and in the rough clothes of a servant. She was humming under her breath as she walked out of the room and pulled the door closed. The woman then turned to walk up the hall, pausing sharply when she spotted him.

Calum saw her mouth open to cry out in surprise and moved instinctively, catching her around the waist with one hand, the other slipping over her mouth to silence her as he backed her into the door she'd just come out of. He opened it and quickly backed her through it.

The maid went with little fuss, her eyes wide and fastened on his groin. Noting this, Calum rolled his eyes. The English were rather prudish about such things, in his experience. Pushing the door silently closed, he glanced around the empty room, then forced her head upward until she peered at his face.

"Where be yer mistress?" he asked.

The maid stared back at him, wide-eyed.

Sighing, he tried an easier question. "Be this her room?"

Much to his relief, she nodded.

"Where is me horse?"

A silent shake of the head was his answer. Calum took that to mean the maid had no idea where the animal was, and sighed. He had no intention of wandering through the castle in search of his clothes and horse while he was as naked as the day he'd been born, but his clothing wasn't likely to be here. If the woman had taken it away, she'd probably done so to wash and repair the items. No doubt there was a large hole in his tunic from the sword, and blood on both it and his plaid. It seemed reasonable his clothes had been taken away for a good wash and repair. And if so, no doubt they would still be hanging somewhere drying, else they would have been brought back to the room.

As for his horse, from what the girl's father had said, Black would be trailing Sarra around, and who knew where *she* was. She may be below, or she may already be back at the room he'd just left, wondering where he'd got to. His best bet seemed to be to go back to the room he'd left. It wasn't really a bad idea—he was still weak and even a bit weary, and another day's rest wouldn't go amiss.

The maid shifted slightly in his arms, drawing Calum's attention once more. She was a robust creature, reeking of good health and blood so sweet it made his teeth ache just to inhale it. Unfortunately, it reminded him of his hunger and made the gnawing in his stomach increase and his better intentions slip.

A small bite wouldn't hurt the woman, and it would go a long way toward healing him and making him more comfortable.

Calum felt his good intentions evaporating by the moment and tried to fight it, reminding himself that Sarra had saved his life and he owed her. Repaying her by feeding on her servants hardly seemed fair.

His lecture wasn't working, however. Calum just kept thinking that his feeding wouldn't harm the girl.

A small gasp against his hand made Calum glance at the woman to see that her eyes had gone even wider and were fixed on his mouth. It was only then he realized that just the thought of feeding had brought on his teeth.

There was no help for it now, he told himself. It was always easier to wipe the mind of a donor than of someone he hadn't fed off of. He really had little choice but to feed on her and wipe her memory.

Eyes narrowing, Calum slipped into her thoughts as he lowered his head to her neck. A small sigh of satisfaction slipped through him as he pierced her neck and her blood flowed into his body. The gnawing died almost immediately, and Calum would have sworn the ache of his wound eased, too. Robust as she was, the maid had swooned by the time he finished, and Calum set her carefully in a chair by the fire before slipping from the room.

"There you are!" Lord DeCourcey cried as Calum opened the door to the room he'd awakened in. The man was out of bed and almost at the door. Apparently, he'd decided to come in search of him. "I was starting to worry about you."

"There's no need to be worryin'. I'm fine," Calum assured him, catching his arm and turning him toward the bed. "Ye should no be up."

He frowned as he saw the way the man tottered. Shaking his head, Calum once again scooped up the old man in his arms and carried him the few steps to the bed. Sarra's father was pale and breathless by the time he had him bundled back under the covers, obviously exhausted by the small effort. Still, he found the energy to gasp, "You should get back in bed before Sarra catches you up and about."

Calum smiled faintly at his worry. The man made Sarra sound like an ogre with his worries of upsetting her, but he suspected the truth of the matter was the man felt bad for dying on her and didn't wish to see his daughter upset any more than necessary in other matters.

"You look a bit better."

The comment drew Calum's sharp glance. He had no doubt he probably did look better. He was flush with the fresh blood he'd consumed and that his body was putting to good use.

"I'm feelin' better," he grunted, then frowned. He did feel better, but he was also now suffering the lethargy a man enjoyed after consuming a large feast and would enjoy a sleep. He could feel the telltale itching in his side that spoke of his body using the blood to finish healing him. Waiting another day seemed a very good idea at this point to his weary mind and body, and he may as well rest in the comfort of a bed as the cold, damp cave. Besides, he couldn't go anywhere without his clothes and his horse.

Decision made, Calum started to move around the bed, intending to get in and sleep, when the sound of the door opening made him pause and turn back.

"Oh, very well." Sarra sighed with resignation. She'd spent the last hour trying to convince Calum's horse to stay in the barn. Again. She'd tried to convince him earlier in the day as well, but he'd refused to be left in the stables, and she'd given in then, allowing him to follow her around like a dog all day. However, it was night now, and she wished to go to bed, but it had been the living end when the animal had tried to follow her into her room. She'd decided it was time to attend to the matter and had led the animal out to the stables with determination.

Unfortunately, the horse was having none of it. The past hour had made no difference. Sarra could lead him into a stall and even managed to walk out, but the moment she left the stables, he began kicking at the walls of his stall, determined to follow her. He'd kicked out two slats in two different stalls before she'd finally given in to the inevitable. It seemed she had a roommate for the near future.

"Come along, then," Sarra said with a sigh as she led Pretty Boy out of the stables and back toward the castle.

The horse followed docilely . . . now that he was getting his own way.

Grimacing to herself, Sarra led the way into the keep and straight to the stairs to the upper level. It had been a long, eventful day and she was tired. All she desired was to sleep. Normally, Sarra would check on her father before retiring, but couldn't tonight with Pretty Boy following her. She feared he'd wake the men with the sharp clop of his steps.

Bypassing her father's room, she continued on to her own, reassuring herself that Bessy would call her if there was a problem.

Sarra found Milly sound asleep in a chair by the fire and smiled faintly to herself. It seemed she wasn't the only one who'd had a long day. Her smile faded, however, as she noted the pallor to the woman's skin.

Fearing she was coming down with something, Sarra moved to the maid's side and shook her arm gently.

"Milly?" she said softly when the touch on her arm alone didn't wake her. "Milly?"

Sarra almost had to be rough before the woman roused, and her concern had deepened by the time she managed to wake her.

"Oh, my lady," Milly murmured sleepily as she sat up. "I'm ever so sorry. I never meant to sleep. I only sat down for a minute."

"'Tis all right, Milly," Sarra said quietly. "Are you feeling all right? You are terribly pale."

"Fine," Milly assured her as she sat up. "A little weary is all."

Sarra stepped back out of the way as the woman got to her feet, but the maid seemed steady enough, with just the wobble of weariness to her.

"Well, you should take yourself off to your pallet," Sarra said quietly. "I would not have you ailing, too. Two sick and ailing are enough for now."

"Oh, nay, my lady. I am fine, really," Milly assured her. "I have not been sleeping well of late is all. I shall help you undress, then retire."

"That is all right, Milly. I can manage on my own tonight. You—"

"Nay, I am fine," Milly insisted. "Here let me help you off with your gown."

Sarra hesitated, but then gave in. She was unwilling to argue the point when she suspected it would be faster just to let her help her disrobe and send her on her way.

"I see you were not able to convince Pretty Boy to remain in the stables."

Sarra grimaced at the woman's comment and glanced toward the horse now standing by the door.

"He would not be left in the stables," she said on a sigh. "He seems determined to stick with me, which I do not understand at all. I would more easily understand his insisting on remaining close to his master than his following me about as he is doing."

"Mayhap he feels safe with you," Milly suggested as she removed Sarra's gown. "After all, his lord is not awake to tend him."

"Aye, mayhap he does," Sarra agreed reluctantly and wondered if it meant the horse would switch his allegiance back to his master once the man woke up. Her thoughts continued to ponder the matter as Milly helped her remove her chemise and don a fresh one to sleep in, but then she pushed the thoughts away and frowned at the maid.

"This is good enough, Milly. 'Tis time for you to find your own bed," she insisted as the maid moved to fetch the ewer of water for her to wash with before she retired. "I can manage the rest on my own."

Milly set the ewer down on the chest by the fire and nodded wearily. "Very well, my lady."

For some reason her acquiescence worried rather than relieved Sarra and she followed her to the door, fretting over the possibility that the maid was falling ill. The last thing she needed was another person to add to the sickroom.

"Will you be all right?" Sarra asked as the woman slipped out into the hall.

"Of course, my lady. A little sleep and I shall be right as rain," Milly assured her.

Sarra nodded and even managed a smile and quiet "good night," but still watched as the woman walked up the hall. She waited until Milly headed down the stairs to the lower level and had started to back into her room when a soft sigh caught her ear.

Pausing, Sarra peered up the hall, her eyes narrowing in an effort to pierce the dark shadows at the far end. When that didn't help much, she stepped out of her room and started along the hallway, pausing when she was able to make out the dark shape of a couple embracing.

"Bessy," she hissed, able to guess who it was without seeing more than the shadow of a couple in an embrace. Bessy and Petey were forever being caught in passionate embraces of late.

A gasp of alarm reached her ears as the couple separated.

"Sorry, my lady." Bessy moved quickly up the hall toward her. "Petey just came to ask me a question."

Sarra managed not to snort aloud at the excuse. Just. Mouth tightening, she said, "Aye, well he can ask you tomorrow. Get back in there and sit with Father."

"Aye, my lady. I am sorry, my lady," Bessy said quickly and changed direction to scurry into the room even as Petey hurried toward the stairs and the escape they offered.

Sarra shook her head and started to withdraw back into her room, pausing abruptly when a screech sounded from her father's room. Whirling back toward the hall, she ran for the still-open door of her father's room, aware that Calum's horse was hard on her heels.

Five

Sarra reached the door to her father's room at the same moment as Petey. The two tried to scramble through the door together, collided, clogged the entrance, and were helped along by Calum's horse. The animal pushed them through with a nudge of his massive head, apparently eager to get inside as well.

Muttering an apology, Petey caught Sarra's arm to steady her as they turned to survey the room in search of the source of the trouble that had caused the scream. Their eyes went wide, jaws dropping at the sight before them. Sarra wasn't sure what she'd expected, but it wasn't what she found. An obviously shaken Bessy stood just ahead of them, eyes wide and round, one hand over her mouth, goggling at their guest.

Frowning, Sarra turned her attention to the man at the foot of the bed and nearly screeched herself. Calum's expression was as startled as theirs. He'd obviously been caught by surprise, she realized. He stood at the foot of the bed, frozen in place and as naked as the day he'd been born.

Unable to help herself, Sarra found her gaze sliding over him, taking in all that pale, muscular male flesh. His skin was almost as white as the bandages around his stomach, she noted, but he was nowhere near frail. He was big, strapping, and well-formed, she thought as her eyes drifted down over his wide chest, his bandaged stomach, his well-formed hips, and finally to . . .

My, she thought faintly, *he* is *well-formed.* Sarra found herself waving a hand in front of her face as she became aware of the stifling heat in the room.

Bessy made a little cheeping sound, distracting her, and Sarra glanced to the girl to see that her gaze was also settled on points south on their patient. The maid was now also fanning herself. It seemed she wasn't the only one suddenly aware of the stifling temperatures in the room.

Petey appeared less impressed as he moved to the maid's side, and he showed no sign of being affected by the temperature in the room, either. He did, however, puff up like a rooster preparing for a cockfight.

An unfortunate description for her mind to settle on, Sarra thought, as her gaze slid back to Calum. Realizing where her eyes had gone, she forced them away and gave herself a mental shake. Taking a deep breath, she focused her eyes on his face and started forward.

"What are you doing out of bed?" she asked in stern tones as she rounded the bed.

"He was helping me to bed," her father said quickly, and Sarra glanced his way with concern. Elman DeCourcey looked pale and shrunken in the bed, and there were beads of sweat on his forehead, proof that he had been exerting himself.

"I was up and about, but came over weak of a sudden," he explained. "Calum carried me back to bed and was just about to get back in himself when Bessy opened the door."

Sarra's eyes narrowed on her father. She'd known him long enough to be able to tell when he was lying and he was doing so now . . . or, at least, not telling the whole truth.

"And why were *you* out of bed, Father?" she asked archly as she reached Calum's side. Sarra instinctively slid under his arm as she'd done so many times earlier that day, determined to help the man back to his bed. Not that he seemed all that weak. He didn't lean on her for strength as he had earlier in the day, but didn't remove his arm from over her shoulder, either, leaving it there in what felt almost like an amorous fashion rather than the supportive manner she'd meant it to be.

Sarra glanced up at him with surprise, blinking when she saw his expression. The look in his eyes was that of a sleepy predator and made the oddest sensations rise up in her. She forgot all about her father's purpose in being out of bed as she became aware of the odd responses of her body to this man. Her breathing was suddenly fast and shallow, and she could feel the flush rising up to warm her cheeks as a sort of excitement coursed through her.

Uncomfortable with her own reactions, Sarra was relieved when they reached his side of the bed. She ducked out from under his arm, pulled the linens and furs back for him to get in. Once he'd lain down, she bent to begin unraveling his bandages, but Calum suddenly closed his hand over hers, stopping her.

"What are ye doin'?" he growled.

Sarra glanced to his face with surprise. "I need to check your wound and be sure you have not ripped the stitches or done yourself injury."

"'Tis fine."

"But—"

"'Tis fine," he repeated firmly, then took his hand away, lifting hers with it to reveal the still-clean bandages. "See? There's nay blood. Had I torn the stitches, there'd be blood. 'Tis fine."

Sarra hesitated, but then gave in and stopped trying to look at the wound, drawing up the linens and furs to cover him instead, automatically tucking them around him until his eyes caught hers. Sarra paused then, staring into the dark depths of his beautiful eyes, touched by the soul-deep loneliness and yearning there. Then his eyes dropped to her mouth and it was almost as if he caressed her there. Her lips began to tingle as if they'd been kissed. She was trying to sort out that response when he suddenly reached up to brush his fingers lightly over her cheek.

Sarra found herself turning her cheek into the caress, like a cat in search of petting. She was sorely disappointed when his hand then slipped away. When she felt a tug at the front of her gown, she glanced down to see him tugging lightly at the cloth of her chemise. It was only then that Sarra realized she wore only her chemise. Alarm and embarrassment were just claiming her when a snort from Pretty Boy and the clop-clop of his hooves on the wooden floor drew her attention to the animal. He had crossed the floor to the foot of the bed and was now nipping at the furs, attempting to pull them off the bed.

Sarra straightened abruptly and scowled at the beast. "Let him sleep, Pretty Boy. He needs rest to heal from his wounds."

"Pretty Boy?" Callum growled, his voice husky.

"Aye. He *is* a pretty boy and I did not know his name," Sarra explained. "So I have been calling him Pretty Boy."

Calum scowled. "His name is Black."

Sarra's eyebrows rose, but she simply said, "Thank you for rescuing me. I am sorry you were wounded in the doing."

Looking suddenly uncomfortable, Calum grunted, and then his eyes returned to her lips. They immediately began to warm as if the sun was shining on them, and Sarra almost raised her fingers to touch them before catching herself. Turning away, she moved around the bed to her father's side and fussed over him briefly, seeing that he, too, was tucked in and that he hadn't done himself any harm with his little jaunt. She was aware of Calum watching her the entire time, could feel his gaze like a physical touch as she fretted over her father's wearing himself out.

Finally, satisfied that neither of them had done themselves too much harm, Sarra straightened with a sigh, wished them "good sleep," and turned toward the door. She had crossed half the room when Calum's voice drew her to a halt.

"Where are ye takin' me horse?"

Sarra paused and turned back, her gaze sliding over the big, black animal, and then to the bed where the horse's master rested beside her father. She was so used to the animal following her, she hadn't even taken note of his trailing her to the door.

"I am not taking him anywhere. It seems to me that Pretty Boy, like his owner, does exactly what he wants. He has been following me around ever since I fetched him after seeing you tended to."

While her words were put out, her irritation was belied by the way she reached up to pat the horse's head affectionately.

"Black," Calum corrected irritably.

Sarra smiled faintly, finding his disgruntled expression amusing, but merely said, "If you need anything, Bessy will fetch it for you. Sleep well."

Sarra gave the maid a meaningful look then, full of warning that she wasn't to leave the room again, before turning toward the door. She caught Petey's arm as she passed him, urging him out of the room with her. Once in the hall, Sarra waited for Pretty Boy to follow her out, then closed the door before turning to Petey.

Propping her hands on her hips, she arched her eyebrows and pursed her lips briefly before saying, "I do not want you on this floor again, Petey. You have no business here and you distract Bessy from her work. Calum and my father are not well and should not be up and about . . . and they would not have been had Bessy been in the room watching them as she was supposed to be doing instead of out here in the hall, gallivanting about with you."

"I am sorry, my lady," Petey said quickly. "It will not happen again."

"No, it shan't," Sarra said solemnly. "Else I shall have to speak to Sir Hadley. Do we understand each other?"

"Aye, my lady. It will not happen again," he assured her once more.

Satisfied, Sarra nodded. "I shall wish you good night, then."

"Good sleep, my lady," he murmured and turned to head for the stairs.

Sarra watched him go, reaching up to absently pat Pretty Boy as she waited for the soldier to disappear down the stairs. Once he was out of sight, she turned and made her way to her own room, hardly aware of the clop-clop as Pretty Boy followed. She was so used to the animal following her that she led the way into her room and automatically waited for him to follow before closing the door.

Ignoring the horse after that, Sarra pulled the furs back and climbed into her bed. She settled herself under the furs, breathed out a little sigh, and peered around the room, finding her weariness had disappeared with the bit of excitement in her father's room.

Her gaze slid to Pretty Boy. The horse had positioned himself by the dying fire in the fireplace and Sarra frowned, aware that once the fire was completely out, the room would quickly cool. It was late summer and while the days were warm and mostly sunny, the evenings were growing cool. She had her furs to keep her warm, but the horse did not. Perhaps she should cover him, Sarra thought.

Sarra had no idea how the horses were kept warm in the stables of a night. Perhaps the stable master kept the fire going, or perhaps he left the animals to suffer. She had no idea, but couldn't go to sleep knowing Pretty Boy would suffer in the cool night air.

Pushing the furs aside, she got out of bed, took one of the larger furs from her bed, padded across the floor, and laid it over the animal's back, cooing nonsensical nothings as she did. Pretty Boy stood still for the coddling, nudging her shoulder with his nose in gratitude. When she'd finished, Sarra smiled and patted the animal.

"You *are* a very handsome animal," she informed him with a smile, gave him one last pat, and scurried back across to her bed. Once settled again, Sarra smiled at the covered beast and closed her eyes to sleep.

It hardly seemed like any time had passed at all when she was opening her eyes again. Sarra knew she'd slept, but to her mind it seemed as if she couldn't have slept long before she opened her eyes to stare blankly at the figures leaning over her. On one side was Pretty Boy, his reins trailing down across the furs covering her. On the other was Calum, a curious expression on his face as he took in her rumpled state on awaking in the circle of light spilling from the candle he held.

Sarra glanced from one to the other with incomprehension, wondering how Calum had followed her out of her dream. It was the hot drip of wax splashing down on her hand on top of the furs that woke her to the situation. Gasping, she drew the furs up to her neck.

"What are you doing here?" As soon as the words left her mouth, concern replaced her shock and she sat up, forcing both horse and man to straighten away from the bed. "'Tis my father, is it not? He—"

"Yer father is fine," Calum said, and Sarra relaxed, her attention turning to him with fascination. The man had a voice that made shivers run up and down her spine. She'd never reacted like that to a mere voice before. Actually, she'd never reacted to anyone as she did to Calum. For some reason she seemed to have trouble breathing in his presence. As she was now, Sarra thought, aware that her breathing had become fast and shallow as if she had been running.

Frowning, she tried to force it to slow down and drew the furs closer about her again, her expression becoming a touch wary. "Then what is it? Why are you here?"

"Ye normally bathe down at the clearing during the noonin' hour."

Sarra blinked at the comment, completely flummoxed by what that could possibly have to do with his presence in her room in the middle of the night. Or what she suspected must be the middle of the night. It was pitch-black in the room where his candle light did not reach.

"I was told yer excursion to the clearin' was a daily trip, taken at noon to allow ye to bathe and get fresh air and a short break from yer father's sickroom. Is that no' so?" Calum asked, sounding impatient.

Sarra turned her gaze back to his and nodded. "Aye, but I shall have to cancel them now, of course. 'Tis no longer safe."

"No' cancel," he said. "Reschedule."

Sarra stared at him with bewilderment, finding it unimaginable that he had crept into her room in the dark of night to discuss her bathing habits. "I do not understand—"

"Yer pattern has always been to bathe at the noonin' hour. Apparently 'tis well known among yer people, and the information somehow made its way to d'Angers' ear. Hence, he sent his men to the clearin' at the noonin' hour to bring ye to him. However, after yesterday, he'll no' expect ye to return. Especially no' in the predawn hours."

"No," she agreed, with confusion.

Nodding, as if she'd agreed to something, Calum stood, taking the glare of the candle with him. "Aye, so get ye dressed. Black and I'll wait in the great hall."

"Get dressed?" Sarra sat up and stared after him as he led his horse to the door. "Why? 'Tis the middle of the night. I—"

"'Tis nearly dawn," he corrected. "If we're quick, we can ride to the clearin', ye can have yer bath, and we can be back ere dawn. Now hurry. I'll go ha'e the servants pack somethin' to break our fast with while there."

"But my father," Sarra protested as he opened the door. "I need to check on him and—"

"Yer father is fine. He's sleepin'."

Sarra shook her head. "He wakes early and will worry if I—"

"He'll no' wake early this morn," Calum assured her.

"He was up most of the evenin' talkin' with me. And he'll no' worry. 'Twas his suggestion."

"It was?" she asked with amazement.

"Aye. He appreciates yer dedication, but does no' wish ye to lose what little time ye take fer yersel' in a day. He suggested the mornin' trip and asked that I escort ye so he needn't worry o'er yer runnin' into trouble on yer own. Now, get dressed."

"Get dressed." Sarra sighed as the door closed behind him and Black. It did seem he was constantly chivvying her to dress. Shaking her head, she pushed the linens and furs aside and slipped her feet to the floor, but remained seated as she considered what he'd said.

Her father had been up half the night talking to him? And *he'd* suggested this early-morning excursion? Aside from the fact that she was shocked that her father had found the energy to stay up all night, it seemed obvious that he'd taken a shine to Calum to make such a suggestion. He'd also given the man his own clothes to wear. They were tight on Calum, but she'd recognized the blue tunic and braies he wore as being the outfit Sarra herself had made for her father for his last birthday.

Her thoughts were interrupted when the door opened again and Calum stuck his head into the room. He didn't appear surprised to see her still seated on the bed, nowhere near ready.

"I ha'e to be back by dawn. Dress," he growled.

The door closed and Sarra stood and quickly began her ablutions, her mind returning to his panic at being in sunlight the day before. Calum did seem to have an aversion to it. Her thoughts on that subject scattered and Sarra grimaced as she splashed cold water on her face. Milly brought her fresh, warmed water every morning to attend her ablutions. However, never this early. She had to make do with the cold water left over from the night before. It wasn't so bad, Sarra decided as she washed. The water was cold, but not unpleasant. It was rather invigorating, and she found herself humming as she went through her ablutions and dressed.

Sarra was as quick as she could be and was rather proud of herself when she hurried out into the hall little more than a couple of moments later. However, her shoulders sagged with confusion when she found the hall empty.

Frowning, she made her way up the hall to her father's room and eased the door open to peer inside. Her father was sound asleep in bed, a smile on his face that made her pause. It had been a while since Elman DeCourcey had smiled in his sleep. Most often he had a restless night. From the occasional murmur she'd heard him utter in his sleep, she knew his dreams were disturbed by nightmares brought on by his worries over how she would get along once he was dead and no longer there to protect her. She knew he'd feel better if she were married with a husband to protect her once he was gone. It seemed his talk with Calum had distracted him sufficiently from this worry that he was sleeping peacefully for the first time in weeks. Sarra was grateful for the small blessing.

A sound drew her gaze to the fireplace where Bessy sat slouched in a chair by the dying embers, softly snoring. Smiling faintly, Sarra eased the door closed and glanced toward the stairs. It seemed obvious Calum had taken Black below. It was only then she recalled his saying he would have some food prepared for them to break their fast.

No doubt she would find him in the kitchens, Sarra realized, and hurried for the stairs, aware of the passing time.

As it happened, Calum and Black weren't in the kitchens. He was much faster than she'd expected. Calum was seated at the table, feeding a carrot to his horse, a small sack she suspected held bread and cheese on the trestle table beside him. He finished feeding the carrot to Black as she stepped off the last step and promptly stood to lead the way to the keep doors, leaving her to follow.

Sarra smiled wryly as she trailed after him. Manners obviously had not been a large priority in this man's training, but then she knew from his name and accent that he was Scottish. That explained a lot. Smiling to herself at the mild insult she'd dared to think, Sarra followed him out the keep doors and down the stairs, her steps faltering when he stopped and mounted Black at the foot of the stairs and then held his hand out to her. Surely, he didn't expect her to ride with him? It was hardly proper.

"Come. 'Twill be faster and safer on Black."

Sarra hesitated, then raised her chin. "I would rather ride my mare. 'Twill only take a moment to saddle her and—" Her words died on a gasp of surprise as she reached the bottom step and he suddenly leaned down and caught her about the waist. In the next moment, she'd been lifted up onto his mount in front of him.

"Very well, I shall ride with you," Sarra conceded dryly as he took up the reins and sent Black toward the castle gates.

The gates at DeCourcey were closed each night and opened at the first crack of dawn, but it wasn't yet dawn and the gates were open. Sarra supposed that meant that Calum had gone to talk to the men either before coming to wake her, or while she was dressing. She supposed she shouldn't be surprised. He appeared an efficient man, one likely to get his way in most things.

They rode out to the clearing in silence. There was no choice. Calum urged Black into a run the moment they were through the castle gates. Talking would have been difficult, if not impossible, so Sarra tried to relax in the saddle and peered around as they rode.

She'd never ridden at night before. In fact, Sarra had rarely been outside the castle at night and then only in her father's company. She found the play of shadows and moonlight on the leaves and trees around them surprisingly beautiful and endlessly fascinating. It was almost like another world, she noted with surprise, and was almost sorry when they reached the clearing and Black slowed to a halt.

Calum slid to the ground, then lifted her off without a

word before moving Black to the water's edge to drink. The bag she'd seen lying on the table beside him in the great hall was hooked to the pommel of Black's saddle and he unhooked it, then carried it toward her.

Sarra waited uncertainly, surprised when he moved past her. Turning, she watched him walk to a large boulder on the edge of the clearing and settle himself there. He glanced at her then, raised an eyebrow, then patted the large portion of boulder beside him. "Sit."

Sarra smiled faintly at the order. Get dressed. Sit. He was obviously a man of few words. Had he not spoken to her in whole sentences in her room, she would have wondered if he were capable of proper speech. Shaking her head, Sarra joined him on the boulder as he began to pull items from the bag—bread, cheese, a skin of mead. It appeared they would be breaking their fast before she swam.

"Thank you," Sarra murmured as she took the food he offered.

"I didna think to bring anythin' to pour the mead into," he said with a frown, then offered an apologetic glance. "We'll have to drink from the skin."

Sarra nodded, not minding at all. Her interest was more in finding out more about him. She peered at him curiously as she ate the bread and cheese. "So, you and Father talked?"

Calum glanced at her briefly, then away as he nodded.

"He must like you," she commented softly.

"He's a nice mon," Calum said quietly. "'Tis a shame he's dying."

Sarra caught her breath with the shock of the words. She knew it was true and had slowly been coming to accept it over the last weeks, but to hear the words said aloud . . .

"He worries about ye," Calum murmured with a frown.

"He should not," Sarra said quietly. "A man should not spend his last days worrying about those he leaves behind."

"Aye. He should," Calum countered. "Yer neighbor appears determined. Had I no' been here yesterday, he'd ha'e ye already. He'll try again, and the closer yer father gets to death, the harder he'll try."

Sarra frowned at the reminder of just how little time had passed since the incident here in the clearing. It hadn't even been twenty-four hours since d'Angers' men had attacked and since Calum had been run through with a sword. She opened her mouth to suggest that she should look at his wound, but before she could speak, he said, "Bathe."

Sarra blinked uncertainly. "Bathe?"

"Aye. Ye're done yer cheese and bread and dawn is approachin'. We'll ha'e to return soon. Ye should bathe while ye've the opportunity. I'll stand watch."

Sarra hesitated, but then stood and moved to the water's edge. She wanted to argue and insist on seeing his side, but the truth was that she liked to bathe every day and didn't wish to risk missing out on a bath to argue with him. She could always pester him about his side afterward, and he certainly didn't seem troubled about it.

Sarra undid the lacings of her gown, her gaze slipping back to the man on the rock. He sat as still as a stone statue, his head turned away, eyes slipping over the trees surrounding them. He didn't seem interested in looking her way at all, and yet she didn't strip down completely. Instead, she kept her chemise on today. It would be wet when she came out and uncomfortable until she could return to the keep and change, but she just didn't feel comfortable bathing nude with him only feet away.

Letting her gown drop to the ground, Sarra stepped out of it and moved into the water, sighing as the cool liquid enveloped her. Sarra loved water. It never failed to relax her and make her feel that all would be well. She didn't know why, it just always had, ever since childhood.

She'd never swum at night before, and Sarra soon wondered why. The water felt ever so much warmer in comparison to the cool evening air. It was like warm velvet as it slid around her body and she reveled in it as she lay back in the water and peered up at the stars overhead. Though she noticed there seemed few of them left in the sky and suspected this meant that daylight was creeping closer.

A rumble from Calum disturbed her, but was distorted by the water in her ears and Sarra straightened quickly and turned in the water to see him still with his back to her.

"Did you say something?" she asked uncertainly.

"Aye. I said, talk. 'Twas so quiet I feared ye'd drowned and I was guardin' a corpse."

"Oh," Sarra said with surprise. "Of course."

She searched her mind briefly for something to say, then blurted, "You are Scottish."

"What ga'e me away?"

She could hear the amusement in his voice and knew it had been a silly thing to say. Ignoring that, she asked, "From where?"

He hesitated, then admitted, "Cambrun."

Sarra nodded silently. Cambrun was the seat of the MacNachtons, but there were MacNachtons in other parts of Scotland. At Bantulach, for instance. The new lord there was a MacNachton. She'd heard much of that particular MacNachton just lately. Though she couldn't recall his first name, she'd recently heard much of the man's courage and skill in battle. It appeared this courage and skill was not restricted to the one MacNachton. Calum had shown both in the battle with d'Angers' men.

"Are you related to the MacNachton at Bantulach?" she asked curiously.

The question appeared to startle Calum and he actually started to turn before catching himself.

"Bothan," he said after a moment and Sarra recognized the name she'd briefly forgotten. She forgot it again when he added, "He's me twin."

"Really?" she asked with surprise. It had never occurred to her that he might be a twin and she found the idea fascinating. Two such handsome, strong men. "He is married to Kenna of Bantulach, is he not?"

"Ye ken a lot about me brother," Calum growled and didn't sound pleased to say so.

"A traveling minstrel came through several weeks ago. He had spent time at Bantulach and came away with many tales in song," Sarra explained. "Some were funny, some sweet, some . . ."

"Some?" he prompted when she hesitated.

"Unbelievable," she admitted after a hesitation.

Calum was silent, but Sarra sensed that he wasn't pleased, though she wasn't sure which part he wasn't pleased with.

"Where is this minstrel now?" he asked finally.

Sarra's eyebrows rose at the question. She inferred from it that he *wasn't* pleased there was a minstrel traveling about the countryside singing the praises of the courageous Bothan MacNachton of Bantulach. Most would have been flattered and proud of the fact. She wondered if he might be jealous, but didn't think that was the case. The man had proven himself equally courageous and skilled and he didn't seem the sort for petty reactions like jealousy.

"I am not sure," she said at last. "He went on to d'Angers from here, but I heard he headed further south several days ago."

Calum grunted at this news and they sank into a brief silence, but then Sarra recalled that she was to talk and commented, "You are far from home."

"Aye. I'm on a chore fer me uncle, the laird of Cambrun," he admitted.

"Oh." Sarra frowned. "Where were you headed?"

"London."

His voice sounded somewhat disgruntled and she supposed he was irritated at having his journey interrupted. Sarra contemplated his silhouette in the moonlight, noting how stiff and still he sat. He was like a statue, his skin glistening like a fine pearl on black velvet. He seemed to suit the night.

"Was it a very urgent chore?" she asked finally, distracting herself from his looks. A prolonged silence was his response and Sarra took that to mean yes. Guilt plaguing her, she offered, "I am sorry your trip was delayed by your saving me."

"I'll be leavin' tonight to finish it. 'Tis soon enough," he said with a shrug.

"Tonight," she murmured. Sarra knew he didn't mean this night. It was almost over, and with his aversion to sunlight, he would hardly travel during the day. She supposed Calum meant he would be leaving when the sun set that evening. The idea saddened her. She didn't really want him to leave, but could hardly say as much, especially since she had no idea why the idea distressed her. She hardly knew the man.

"What about your wound?" Sarra said finally. "You really should not be traveling so soon after such a serious injury. In fact, I wish you would let me check your wound. Just to be sure 'tis not festering, or—"

"I ha'e checked it, 'tis fine," he assured her firmly. Then he added, "The sun'll be up soon. We should return."

Sarra glanced skyward to see that he was right—the sky was definitely lightening. Sighing with regret, she waded out of the water and immediately shivered as the cool air touched her damp chemise and skin. It encouraged her to dress quickly, more quickly than she probably should have. The next thing she knew, Sarra was quite tangled up in her gown. Her arms were up over her head, caught up in the material, and she couldn't lower either them or the material.

"What is it?" Calum asked suddenly, and Sarra bent forward so that she could look out at him through the hole at the top of the gown. He still had his head turned away, but had gone terribly still, as if sensing she was in difficulty, but obviously uncertain what it was.

Sarra hesitated and then sighed and admitted, "Somehow I have got my gown all tangled up."

"Diya need help?"

She paused and straightened to try to rectify the matter herself, but it was impossible.

"Yes, please," Sarra said meekly.

Calum was at her side in an instant and she was untangled shortly after that.

"There," he said as he smoothed the gown over her body and she was able to lower her arms.

"Thank you," Sarra murmured, lifting her face to glance at him.

Calum nodded, but his eyes had dropped to her lips and Sarra found herself suddenly holding her breath. Her mouth was tingling under his glance, her whole body suddenly warm, and if she'd had the capacity, she would have wondered at this effect he had on her. However, she didn't have the capacity. Her mind seemed to have turned to mush as she waited to see if he would kiss her.

"We should go back," Calum growled, and Sarra nodded, but neither of them moved, they simply continued to stare at each other, then he finally lowered his head. His hands were nowhere near her and his head made a slow and careful descent, leaving all the time in the world for her to say no or to move away. Sarra did neither. She didn't even breathe until his mouth touched hers, then a sigh slid from her lips and into his partly open mouth.

Sarra's little sigh seemed to act like a signal for Calum. One moment he was kissing her as carefully and gently as a brother, and the next all that caution and care dropped away to reveal the passion beneath. Sarra suddenly found herself enveloped in his embrace, overwhelmed by his scent, his touch, and his passion as his mouth opened fully over hers and his tongue slid between her lips to urge her mouth further open as well.

Sarra gasped, her body arching instinctively against his as she was overwhelmed with feelings she'd never encountered before. Passion, desire, heat, want—they all rose up inside her like an uncontrollable inferno, consuming everything in its path, including any sense of propriety or pretense at ladylike reticence.

A growl rose up in Calum's throat, vibrating through his lips to hers and adding to the sensation. Sarra groaned in response, her body thrumming as she became aware of his hands sliding up her back, pressing her closer. Her gown no longer seemed chill and damp—it was warm and wet, heated by her excited flesh.

One of his hands slid around to cup her breast through the damp material and Sarra gasped, her body jerking against his. She groaned her pleasure as he kissed her, then moaned her distress as his mouth left hers and traveled to her throat. Sarra felt him nibbling softly there, shuddered against him, and was wholly unprepared when he suddenly stiffened and jerked his head away.

"What—?" she began with confusion, but he immediately covered her mouth with one hand. It took her a moment to realize that he was listening, but even then she wasn't sure what he was listening for. She didn't hear anything.

In the next moment, Sarra realized that this was odd in itself. There should have been the sound of night birds and the stirring of the small woodland creatures, but there was none of that.

Sarra had barely grasped the fact when Calum suddenly released her mouth, caught her hand, and hurried her to his horse. At first, she thought he meant to mount, but instead he grabbed Black's reins and dragged both of them across the clearing to the cave.

"What is it?" she asked in an uncertain whisper once they were safely inside.

Calum waved her to silence, his attention on the clearing.

Biting her lip, Sarra moved to his side. She peered out into the clearing just as Jocks and several riders broke from the woods. It seemed this hadn't been a safe time to come here after all.

Six

"They are not here."

Calum's mouth tightened as Jocks cursed and yanked on his reins, forcing his horse to an abrupt halt in the clearing. The move would no doubt tear at the animal's mouth, causing damage. Calum hated to see animals abused. Seeing this made him doubly glad he'd interfered on Sarra's behalf the day before. A man who treated his horse thusly could be expected to show little care for children and women as well, and Calum wouldn't have had a man like that working for him. The fact that this d'Angers did, suggested Sarra's neighbor had little care for those under his rule. He wouldn't like to see Sarra married to a man like that.

"Are you sure he said they came down here?" Jocks asked, turning threateningly on one of the men.

"Aye. He said MacNachton was bringing the girl down to bathe," the man answered quickly, then added, "but they could have been here by the time he reached d'Angers with the news. By the time I got the news to you, you gathered men, and we left and rode here . . ." He shrugged. "Perhaps they have been and gone already."

"They must have," Jocks muttered, scowling around the clearing. He heaved a heavy sigh. "D'Angers won't be happy."

"Nay," one of the men agreed.

"Very well," Jocks decided, turning his horse toward the woods. "We shall scour the woods between here and DeCourcey. They are not aware we know they are out, or that we are here, so they may be taking their time on the ride back to the keep. If we are lucky, we might yet find them."

"And if we don't?" one of the men asked.

"Then I shall be leaving you and three other men behind to watch the castle in case she leaves again," he announced. "And if she does, you are to capture her and bring her back to d'Angers."

Calum heard the small, unhappy sigh that slipped from Sarra as she realized that Jocks had just consigned her to being virtually a prisoner in her own castle. He scowled over the matter as the men turned and rode out of the clearing, but couldn't think of anything he could do about the matter himself. Nothing short of her marrying someone else was likely to turn her neighbor's attention elsewhere. DeCourcey was too attractive a holding, as was the lady herself.

Calum could kill d'Angers for her, but the truth was that once her father was dead, there would be many more men like d'Angers sniffing around. The lass needed to marry.

"Shall we take the tunnels?"

Calum stiffened as she whispered the question in his ear. He was so distracted by the feel of her warm breath on the skin of his ear and neck that it took his mind a moment to understand what she was saying.

"What?" he asked with shock when it finally sank in. Calum couldn't believe she'd made the suggestion. While it was true she'd taken him to the castle through the secret tunnels before, it was while he'd been injured. He didn't recall much about the trip and wouldn't have been able to travel the tunnels again on his own without getting lost.

Right now, however, Calum was in perfect health—well, nearly perfect health, he acknowledged. His injury had almost healed, which was why he wouldn't allow her to look at it. Explaining how he had healed so quickly would be impossible without revealing what he was, and he'd never do that. The point was, however, that he was relatively healthy, lucid, and would definitely recall every aspect of the journey through the tunnels this day. He couldn't believe Sarra was willing to reveal such a family secret to him and said as much.

"How could ye even be suggestin' sech a thing? 'Twould reveal the route o' yer tunnel to me and could jeopardize yer verra safety should I gi'e or sell the information to anyone."

"I trust you," Sarra said simply.

Calum stared at her blankly. Dear God, she trusted him. The woman was as naïve as a babe.

He only realized he'd spoken the words aloud when she stiffened with outrage. "I am not naïve."

"Yer set to trust a complete stranger, lass," he pointed out gently. "That's naïve."

"You are not a stranger," she argued. "And you have already proven yourself trustworthy."

Calum's eyes went wide with amazement at the claim. "How?"

Sarra blew her breath out with exasperation, then said, "Let us see. I gather you were resting in here quietly until night fell and you could continue your journey?"

"Aye," he said warily.

"But then you heard us out here in the clearing and looked out to see what was happening?"

"Actually, 'twas ye I heard. That god-awful screechin' that ye seem to think is singin'," he said dryly. "Ye woke me from a good sleep, too."

Sarra flushed, but continued, "And then, despite not knowing me from Adam, and my waking you from a sound sleep with my 'screeching,'" she added dryly. "And despite your sensitivity to sunlight, you risked yourself by taking on not one, but *four* men to save me. I would say that says a lot about your character, my lord. And it does not suggest that you would betray the confidence of where the tunnel is."

Calum found himself squirming. She made him sound better than he was, or better than he was comfortable seeing himself, anyway.

"Besides," Sarra reasoned when he remained silent. "There is very little else we can do. We cannot go back through the woods with Jocks and his men there . . . and the sun is almost up. The tunnel seems the safest route."

Calum turned to peer out toward the sky, grimacing when he saw how much it had lightened. Even without Jocks and his men out there, they would not be riding back to the castle the normal route—that was certain. At least, he wouldn't.

He considered the matter briefly. Calum *had* to continue on with his journey tonight; it was important he get the message he carried to London, but he was sorely tempted to say to hell with the message and stay here with Sarra. She was beautiful and sweet and had tasted like honey when he'd kissed her, and he'd like many more of those kisses . . . and more. Which was why it seemed wiser to send her on her way, stay here, and avoid temptation.

"Ye take the tunnel back to the castle," he instructed finally. "I'll be restin' here till the sun sets, then am headin' out to continue me task."

Calum saw the way her eyes widened and knew she would argue even before she opened her mouth. Sighing inwardly, he prepared himself for a barrage of protest as only a woman can give it.

"I am not leaving you here to sleep on the stones like a dog. You saved my life, my lord. You shall return with me and rest in a comfortable bed. Besides, I am sure my father would be terribly disappointed did you leave without speaking to him again, and I will not see my father disappointed."

Calum stared at her for a moment, several comments coming to mind. The only one he finally said was, "I be no one's laird."

Sarra blinked at the words, then simply rolled her eyes and moved to catch Black's reins. "I suggest you ride back to the castle with me. Else you will simply have to walk there to fetch your horse. I have no intention of walking through these tunnels by myself."

Calum's lips twitched as he watched her lead his mount into the shadows at the back of the cave. There was a haughty, stubborn stiffness to her back and Black followed her as docilely as a pup. For some reason, both amused him. He would never have thought his horse would willingly follow the hand of another, and Sarra wore haughtiness and determination like a hair shirt. She wasn't at all comfortable with the attitude.

Allowing a full smile to claim his lips, Calum took one last glance out at the now-empty clearing, then gave up his position by the entrance and followed her. He turned the corner at the back of the cave and nearly ran into Black. The horse's coloring allowed it to disappear into the shadows.

Calum patted the beast's flank as he waited for his eyes to adjust to the darkness. It didn't take long. His vision was perfect for night sight. Within seconds he could make out shadows and shapes. He quickly made out Sarra's shape ahead of him. The woman was feeling her way along the cave wall, in search of something. Not having his vision, she was, of course, blind in here.

Giving Black one last pat, Calum moved along the cave to her side.

"Stay here—I shall get the torch," he said, guessing what she was seeking.

Calum moved past her, walking confidently as his eyes continued to adjust. He bypassed the first torch holder—it was empty. No doubt it was the torch she'd used on the last journey, he thought. The second torch holder did have one in it. He lifted it out and then grabbed the flint and quickly lit it before carrying it back to where Sarra stood blinking in the sudden light.

"Ye'll ha'e to replace both torches we've used," Calum pointed out quietly, placing the torch in her hand. "Yer father will no be able to do it. 'Tis up to ye now."

Sarra nodded grimly as she accepted the torch from him.

"Wait here. I'll bring Black." Moving past her, Calum caught Black by the reins and led the animal back to her side. He then lifted her quickly up into the saddle, hesitated, and then followed her up and hesitated again. His mind was still telling him that the sensible thing would be to refuse her the horse and send her on her way through the tunnels on foot. He should rest here until the sun set, then head out, but he didn't want to do the sensible thing. He wanted to spend that day with Sarra . . . and refused to ask himself why. He just did.

"Shall I hold the torch out in front as far as I can?" Sarra asked suddenly, leaning her upper body forward to show him what she meant. The problem was, the moment she leaned her upper body forward, her behind seemed to press back more snugly against him. Calum stiffened as her bottom rubbed against him in a most improper fashion.

"Er . . . nay," he said gruffly, then cleared his throat and reached for the torch. "In fact, I shall take—oh hell," Calum cursed as he managed to bump Sarra's hand and knock the torch from her grasp.

They both watched in horror as the light fell to the ground and promptly went out.

For one moment, they both sat silent and still in the darkness that descended. Calum spent that time suffering an increasing awareness of her body before him in the saddle. Sarra was no longer leaning forward and he could feel the entirety of her back pressed against his chest and smell the sweet scent of her soap. She felt perfect in his arms, her body fitting itself to his like the missing half of a broken plate, and God, she smelled good. He found himself leaning forward to press his nose lightly against her hair, wishing it wasn't up in its habitual bun but was flowing around them both, cloaking their naked bodies.

Calum closed his eyes on the images his mind was flashing him.

"I shall get it," Sarra said, and started to try to dismount to go after the torch.

"Nay," Calum said quickly, snatching back the hand that had been moving toward her hair to loose it. Taking a deep breath, he forced himself to forget such fantasies and pay attention to the matter at hand. "'Tis fine. I can see well enough to get us where we're headin'."

"You can not possibly see," Sarra protested. "Besides, I cannot and I am the one who needs to tell you where to go."

Before he realized what she was about, she'd swung her leg over the horse and dropped to the ground to feel around for the torch.

Scowling, Calum followed her down and nearly fell over her. The woman stood, bent at the waist, feeling blindly around with her hands. It left her bottom in the air, and this is what Calum stumbled into.

"Oh!"

"Sorry," Calum muttered, instinctively catching her hips to keep her from overbalancing forward. Then, realizing the position they were now in, he released her abruptly and stepped back.

Unfortunately, in his eagerness to escape the suggestive pose, Calum unintentionally pushed her forward as he released her and Sarra immediately fell on her face. He heard the grunt as she hit the ground and rushed to help her up.

"Are ye a'right? I'm sorry, I did no . . ." Calum's words trailed away as he got her upright, only to have her hair tumble out of its bun and fall around her shoulders like a cloak. He could see it, not well, but he *could* see it. More importantly, he could feel it as it brushed across his hands like living silk. And his sense of smell, always heightened when his vision was impaired, no matter how slightly, was overwhelmed by her sweet scent. It drifted around him, enveloping him in a pleasant cloud.

"Calum?" Sarra whispered, and he saw her hand reaching out toward him uncertainly. "Are you there?"

Calum caught her hand, reminded that while he could see, she couldn't.

"Oh," Sarra sighed with relief. "You *are* there. Did you find the torch?"

Calum hesitated, then slid past her and bent to pick up the torch. "I have it. We'll need a flint to light it."

"There should be one under the next torch or the one after. Father put one out at every other holder for just such an occasion."

"Hmm." Calum glanced along the tunnel. The next torch was a distance away. The one behind them was closer, but he could see well enough that there was no need to backtrack.

"Come," he murmured, taking her arm to urge her back to Black. "We'll stop at the next torch holder to see if there's a flint there."

"Can you really see in this darkness?" Sarra asked, sounding confused.

"Aye. A bit," he admitted. "So long as there is a drop o' light, I can see, and though there is verra little, some light is still creepin' around the corner from the main cavern and makin' its way here."

"Oh." Sarra sounded rather doubtful. Calum ignored that and lifted her onto the horse, handed her the dead torch, and then mounted behind her.

Riding with her seemed different in the dark, more intimate somehow. Calum had no idea why until he realized that she was sitting closer now that they were in the dark, almost nestling into him. He knew without considering that it was because of the darkness itself that she felt a need to be closer to him and was almost burrowing into him to get away from it like a child almost cowering into its mother's warmth to battle against the cold. He doubted she was even aware she was doing it.

"'Tis spooky in here, is it not?" Sarra whispered, and Calum found himself taking one hand from the reins to slip it around her waist, allowing it to rest against her stomach in a reassuring manner.

"'Twill be fine," he growled to reassure her and sensed rather than saw her tilt her head to peer up at him.

"I am glad you came with me. I should not like to have to travel the tunnels alone."

Calum didn't know what to say to that, so simply gave her a reassuring squeeze.

"Besides, you should not sleep in the cave when there is a perfectly nice, warm, comfortable bed waiting for you in the keep."

"Aye. Yer father's," Calum said wryly and could hardly credit that he'd slept in the same bed as another man. Actually, he hadn't in the end. Well, he had the first day while unconscious, but last night he'd been unable to sleep and had sat up in a chair by the fire, ignoring Bessy's protests and pleading that he return to the bed . . . Just as Elman DeCourcey had when he'd decided to join him.

Calum had almost added his own protests to Bessy's when the old man had toddled over to join him, but then had merely gone to fetch one of the furs off the bed to tuck around the man. Elman DeCourcey was a grown man, something those caring for him seemed to forget. He would leave him his dignity.

The two men had spoken through most of the night, on countless subjects, but somehow their talk had seemed to keep returning to Sarra and the old man's worries for her. Calum learned a good deal about the woman presently in his arms from her father. Most of what he'd learned was that he liked the man, and that Elman DeCourcey loved and was proud of his daughter.

"Do you miss your brother?"

Calum blinked in surprise at the question from Sarra. "Why would ye ask a thing like that?"

He felt her shrug in his arms, her body moving against his.

"It just seems to me that twins are closer than normal siblings and that you would miss that closeness now."

Calum grunted, a sound that could have been taken as agreement or not, but the truth was, he missed his brother terribly. The two had been inseparable from birth, spending almost every moment of every day together until the arrival of Kenna. Bothan was his best friend as well as his brother, but he had a life at Bantulach now, one Calum didn't really fit into, and he felt like he was wandering through life missing a limb since Bothan's marriage.

"Ye had a twin," Calum said quietly. Elman had told him about his second daughter. The child had died while still young, along with her mother. Both of them taken by fever. Sarra, he'd said, had been devastated. Calum understood that. To lose a mother or sister was bad enough, but a twin . . . There was a special bond there, especially when young.

Sarra stiffened in Calum's arms as his words pierced her. Even now, after more than ten years since her twin's death, she ached at the thought of her twin, Joan. They had been as close as two peas in a pod. When the fever had made the rounds of the inhabitants of the castle, it had bypassed Sarra, but hit her sister and her mother. They, along with many others, had died of the ailment. Sarra had been crushed at the loss of them both, but Joan's death had been the hardest for her to deal with. Along with a sense of loss and sorrow, she'd suffered intense guilt over not getting ill. She and Joan had always done everything together, including getting the same colds and so on, until that time when Sarra had stayed well and Joan had died.

"Sarra?" Calum murmured, sounding worried, and Sarra sighed, thinking that she liked the way her name sounded when he spoke it, rolling the r's in his soft burr. She thought it might actually be the first time he'd addressed her by name.

"Aye," she said at last. "I had a twin sister. Joan."

"It must ha'e pained ye to lose her," he murmured.

"Aye," she agreed. "So, I understand the loss you must be feeling over Bothan."

Sarra sensed his gaze on her as he said, "'Tis hardly the same thing. My brother is alive and at Bantulach. I will see him again."

"And, according to the church, my sister is happily in heaven, looking over me, and we, too, shall meet again," Sarra said softly. "But they are both far away, are they not?"

She felt Calum's arms tighten around her and smiled faintly, knowing he was trying to comfort her the only way he could. Sarra found her hand moving lightly to cover his hand, trying to comfort him back as she narrowed her gaze on the tunnel ahead. She thought she could just make out a difference in the wall and that they might be nearing the entrance.

"I think we are nearly there," she said quietly.

"Aye," Calum murmured.

They were both silent for the last little distance. Once there, Calum drew Black to a halt and quickly dismounted. He then turned back and held up his arms to her. Sarra hesitated, worried about the torch she still held, but then slid her leg over the horse's back and allowed herself to slide down into his waiting arms, trusting him to catch her.

"Oh damn," she breathed as her elbow bumped against his shoulder and the torch tumbled from her fingers.

They both froze then, Calum holding her aloft by his grip on her waist as they watched the torch drop to the cave floor.

Calum's curse joined hers as the torch rolled on the ground and went out.

Sarra sighed as the darkness enveloped them, again wondering if she would be able to find the stone she had to push to open the entrance in the dark.

As if her sigh had reminded him he still held her aloft, Calum finally began to lower her, and Sarra caught her breath as her body slid along his. She was a bit breathless by the time her feet touched the ground and she had to grab at his hands to steady herself.

"Be ye a'right?" Calum asked. His voice was husky, his breath warm on her cheek. He seemed to be looking down at her through the dark, and she wondered if he could see her in this stygian light, but found it difficult to believe that he could.

"Aye," Sarra said finally. Embarrassed at how breathy her voice sounded, she made herself step away, feeling for Pretty Boy as she did. She sensed Calum's moving away and supposed he was retrieving the torch. Sarra strained her ears, listening to the soft rustle as he moved. When the rustling stopped and there was no further sound, she frowned and stared nervously into the surrounding darkness, wishing she could see him.

"Calum?" she whispered uncertainly after a moment.

He made a shushing sound. It was followed by another moment's silence—then he asked, "What is that sound?"

Sarra tilted her head in the dark and listened. At first she didn't know what he was talking about, but then she became aware of a soft tapping sound. Frowning, she took a step toward the direction the sound seemed to be coming from, then another before she brushed against him. His hand covered hers in the dark. Comforted by the warmth and strength it offered, she moved a little closer as she tried to sort out where the tapping was originating.

The hair on the back of her neck began to creep as the tapping continued, seeming to move closer. Someone was in the dark with them.

Seven

"'Tis coming from the other side of the wall."

Sarra let her breath out on a sigh at Calum's words. The fear that had gripped her that someone was standing in the dark with them slowly slid away.

Of course it was coming from the other side of the wall, she realized. It was too faint a sound to be coming from inside the tunnel itself, where every sound seemed magnified and the smallest rustle sounded loud.

"Yer father said only ye and he ken where the tunnel is," Calum commented after a pause.

"Aye," Sarra agreed, then added, "I think others know it exists, but not where 'tis."

"What others?" Calum asked.

"Hadley," she said, then frowned and admitted, "I am not sure who else."

"How did ye get me out o' the tunnels?" he asked. "Surely ye did no manage it on yer own."

"You were semiconscious, and between the two of us, we got to the stairs. Hadley helped me from there."

"Hadley?" he asked.

"Aye," she said and explained, "One of the maids heard us in the dungeons and he came to check on it. He helped me get you up the stairs. Cook then took over, helping to get you to my father's room."

"So Cook and Hadley ken ye came from the dungeons?"

"Aye." Sarra nodded, then added, "And a handful of servants."

"A handful o' servants?" Calum asked on a sigh.

"Aye." Sarra bit her lip, then added, "And more servants saw me bring Pretty Boy back up later."

"Black," Calum muttered.

Sarra smiled faintly at the annoyance in his voice, then asked, "Why are you asking who saw me bring you out, my lord?"

Calum didn't answer right away and silence fell around them except for the tap-tap-tapping. Sarra blinked as understanding dawned. "You think someone is looking for the secret entrance."

"Aye," Calum murmured.

Sarra frowned, her eyes searching the darkness, trying to place where the entrance was. "I suppose 'tis not safe to leave until they go away, then."

"Nay," he agreed.

"Can we at least light the torch?" Sarra asked hopefully.

She could hear the frown in Calum's voice when he said, "I'm no sure. If the entrance has the smallest crack around the edges, the light may be seen from the other side and lead them to the entrance."

Sarra sighed, but recognized the wisdom of his words. It seemed they would have to wait a bit . . . in the dark. At least until the tapping stopped. They both fell silent and the moment they did, she became extremely aware of the fact that Calum was still holding her hand in his warm, firm grip. More than that, his thumb was moving gently back and forth across the back of her hand in what she suspected was a subconscious action. Sarra stood completely still, concentrating on the touch, feeling the rough pad of his thumb sliding along her soft flesh as she recalled his kiss in the clearing. It had been the most incredible experience of her life, and one she wished she could experience again.

"Sarra?"

She blinked, aware that his voice sounded closer than it had when last he'd spoken. At first, she thought he'd moved closer to her, but then Sarra realized that she'd leaned toward him, like a flower in search of the sun. He was obviously aware of her action. At least she thought he must be and was calling her attention to it.

Flushing with embarrassment, she started to straighten, "I—"

The apology she'd been about to offer died in her throat when his mouth suddenly covered hers. Unable to see it coming, Sarra nearly swallowed her own tongue in surprise when his lips descended on hers and for one moment she was too stunned to even respond as they brushed softly across her own. It wasn't until Sarra felt his arms slide around her waist and draw her against his chest that her body relaxed its tensed stance and she melted against him, a small sigh slipping from her lips.

Had Sarra been able to speak, she would have said, *Oh, yes, please*. But it was difficult to talk with a tongue in your mouth. For several moments, Sarra simply enjoyed the way his tongue explored her—then it occurred to her that perhaps her tongue was supposed to join in and she slid it forward tentatively. Finding the moan this elicited from Calum encouraging, Sarra became more enthusiastic.

Her hands crept up around his neck and she pressed closer, eager to feel all of his body pressed against hers. Calum immediately complied, tightening his embrace until there wasn't a breath between them as his kisses became deeper and more aggressive.

It wasn't until she felt the cool air on her breast replaced by a warm hand that Sarra realized he had somehow worked her gown and chemise off one shoulder, baring the breast to his attention. She moaned as he squeezed the delicate orb, her body shuddering against his, though not in protest. Dear God, she'd touched her breasts countless times in her life while washing and dressing, but never once had a mere brush of fingers across them brought on a response like this. Her flesh actually ached in his hand so that she could barely stand it, and a strange heat she didn't understand was pooling between her legs.

"Calum," she pleaded against his lips, though Sarra couldn't have said what she was asking for. He seemed to understand, however. She felt his leg slide between both of hers—then he shifted his other hand to her bottom, urging her lower body closer and higher so that she was almost riding his thigh as if it were a horse, but riding a horse had never felt like this.

Her attention divided between the sensations his caresses were causing in both her breasts and between her legs, Sarra lost all ability to concentrate on kissing and hardly noticed when his mouth left hers. Hands caught tight in his hair, she simply turned her head to the side and groaned at the sensations overwhelming her as his mouth trailed to her ear, then down her throat.

Calum's lips nibbled down her neck, seeming to trace a straight line; then she felt something sharp brush her skin, but had hardly noticed it when he suddenly went still.

Confused, Sarra waited, becoming aware that she was panting and clutching him as if her life depended on it, her body screaming for him to continue, as if knowing some great event waited not far ahead, but he didn't. Calum remained completely and utterly still.

"My lord?" Sarra whispered uncertainly.

"Hush, lass." His voice was harsh and breathless. "Gi'e me a minute to get control."

Sarra bit her lip, her hold on him easing, her body slowly pulling away as the excitement began to slip out of her. Even before it had completely left her, Calum eased her away. She felt a tug on her gown and it took a moment for her to realize that he was straightening her clothes for her.

Suddenly self-conscious and embarrassed, Sarra brushed his hands away and completed the task herself, aware that her cheeks were on fire with a blush.

Calum cleared his throat, then murmured gruffly, "The tappin's stopped. I think 'tis safe to go now."

Sarra let her breath out slowly and reached for the cave wall to balance herself in a world suddenly unsteady. She heard Calum moving around, but had no idea what he was doing and didn't pay it much attention. Instead, she concentrated on pulling herself together, both her clothes and her thoughts. Sarra was suddenly suffering an overwhelming sense of embarrassment. She tried to tell herself it was good that he had stopped them—certainly she wouldn't have been able to. She'd lost total control of herself.

Light suddenly exploded in the tunnel. Calum had lit the torch and it was blinding after being in the darkness for so long. Sarra squeezed her eyes shut and covered them with her hands for a moment, then felt Calum's fingers brush lightly down hers.

"'Tis sorry I be, lass. I should ha'e warned ye I was lightin' it."

Sarra hesitated, then slowly lowered her fingers and opened her eyes. Blinking rapidly, she glanced toward Calum. His eyes were mere slits, but other than that he showed no sign that the light bothered him. It seemed light bothered him no more than dark did.

"Come." He offered a crooked smile. "Let's find our way out o' here, hmm?"

Managing a weak smile of her own, Sarra turned to the wall and found the stone that would open the door.

"Wait here, jest a minute," Calum instructed quietly as the panel slid open.

Sarra watched him step cautiously out into the cell and peer about, then walk to the door and look out along the row of cells. It took her a moment to realize he was checking to be sure the tapper had gone. She'd quite forgotten all about him during Calum's kisses. He apparently hadn't, and for some reason the knowledge depressed her.

Sighing, Sarra turned to Pretty Boy and ran a hand down his jaw. "Your master is handsome, smart, and a very, very good kisser, and I think it may be a good thing he is leaving at sunset. He could break my heart did he stay much longer."

Pretty Boy nickered softly and began to chew her hair in response. As comforting went, it was better than nothing, Sarra supposed, a smile breaking out on her face as she pushed his head away.

"'Tis clear."

Sarra glanced over her shoulder to see that Calum had returned. Nodding, she ran her hand down the horse's nose, then caught his reins and turned to lead the way out of the cell. The horse followed docilely.

"Yer ruinin' me beast," Calum muttered as she led the horse past him.

"He is not a beast, he is a pretty boy," Sarra said firmly and was sure she heard the man growl. For some reason the sound made her smile. Shaking her head at herself, she led the animal out of the cell and along the row of them to the stairs leading to the second level. Releasing Pretty Boy's reins then, she left him at the bottom of the steps and quickly ascended to the door. She listened briefly at the wooden panel, then eased the door open to peer inside. It was busy with servants rushing this way and that. The castle was awake and everyone would be sitting down to break their fast. There was no hope that they would slip by unnoticed.

Sighing, Sarra pushed the door the rest of the way open, smiled wryly at Cook as he turned to glance at her in surprise, then peered back down the stairs as Pretty Boy charged up with his master behind him.

"My lady," Cook began in protest, then fell silent, eyes going wide as Calum followed his horse into the room.

"I am sorry, Cook," Sarra murmured, catching Pretty Boy's reins and leading him quickly to the door. "I do not think it shall happen again."

Cook's shoulders sagged with defeat and he merely shook his head and turned back to what he'd been doing as they slid out of the kitchen.

The great hall was bustling with people coming and going from the trestle tables. Sarra managed a smile when she caught Hadley's surprised eye, but merely headed for the stairs to the second floor, intending to check on her father. She wasn't at all surprised when Pretty Boy and Calum followed her.

"Do you keep Pretty Boy in your keep in Scotland?" Sarra asked curiously as they made their way along the upper hall.

Calum grimaced at the question and shook his head. "Nay. He stays in the stables there. I shall take him to yer stables for the day if ye like," he added.

Sarra hesitated, knowing she really should let him wrestle the horse to the stables, but she feared even with Calum performing the task it might be a hard, long, drawn-out battle to get the beast to stay in the stables, and she was reluctant to be parted from Calum.

"Nay," she said finally. "The way he follows me about seems to amuse my father and he has had little enough to smile at of late."

When Calum remained silent at this, Sarra added, "You appear to make him smile as well. I fear he has only had myself and the maids for company of late and he is enjoying your short stay with us."

"I enjoy his company as weel," Calum murmured as she opened the door to her father's room.

"Sarra! There you two are. I was starting to fret. 'Tis well past dawn. I expected you back ages ago."

Sarra forced a smile for her father as she moved to the bed. "I am sorry we worried you, Father. We would have been back a while ago, but were held up."

Elman DeCourcey frowned as he took in her expression. "You are a bit flushed. Was there trouble at the clearing after all? We had hoped that by going so early you could bathe in peace."

"D'Angers' men showed up," Calum announced without preamble. "We heard them coming and managed to get into the . . . out of the clearing ere they entered it," Calum changed his choice of words midsentence as his gaze slid over Milly sewing by the fire. Sarra supposed he was reluctant to give away any more information than necessary about the hidden cave and secret entrance.

"Oh dear," her father murmured, then glanced toward Milly and said, "I would like a nice glass of mead, please, Milly. Will you fetch me one, please, girl?"

"Right away, my lord." The maid set aside her sewing and slipped from the room.

"We came back through the tunnel," Calum announced as soon as the door was closed and they were alone. "But there was a tappin' comin' from the other side o' the entrance when we reached it and we thought it best to wait 'til whoever it was went away."

"A tapping?" her father asked, eyes narrowing.

"Aye." Calum hesitated. "I think someone's lookin' fer the secret entrance. And that is no all. We overheard Jocks talkin'. Someone sent news to d'Angers that Sarra was goin' to the clearin' first thing to bathe."

Sarra bit her lip as her father's face tightened. "We have a traitor, then."

"Aye. That would be me guess," Calum murmured.

"Well, forewarned is forearmed, is it not?" her father commented. "I shall have to find some way to use this to our advantage."

"We shall think on it later," Sarra murmured. "For now, you should enjoy our guest's company. Calum plans to leave us at sunset."

"What?" If anything, her father looked almost as alarmed at this news as she had been. "But why? You are welcome to stay here as long as you wish, Calum. I am enjoying your company and know Sarra is as well."

"He was on his way to London to carry out a chore for his laird," Sarra said quietly. "He only stopped to rest the day in the cave, and his chore has been delayed. He wishes to complete it."

"Oh, aye. Of course." Elman DeCourcey frowned, then eyed Calum solemnly and said, "I hope you know you are welcome to stop here on your return journey, and that you are welcome to stay as long as you wish."

Sarra frowned, sensing that a message was being passed between the two men, but unsure what it was. She didn't get the chance to wonder about it for long. Calum changed the subject and moved to grab two of the chairs from in front of the fireplace. He pulled them over for her and him to sit in by the bed while they visited with her father.

It was quite the nicest day Sarra had enjoyed for a long time and she knew her father enjoyed it, too. She also knew he was as disappointed as she when the day came to an end and Calum stood to move to the window. As if some inner clock told him the sun had set, he pulled the shutters open and peered out on the darkening night.

"'Tis time for me to go," he murmured, his back to the room.

Sarra bit her lip, then glanced to her father when she felt him squeeze her hand. She forced a smile for his benefit, then turned back to Calum and murmured, "It occurs to me that you might do better to leave through the tunnel."

Calum glanced back with surprise at her words. "Why?"

"Jocks said if they did not find us this morn, he would leave several men to watch the keep. I fear they may cause you trouble if they see you pass."

Calum shrugged that away with unconcern. "I can handle any trouble they care to send me way."

"Honor an old man's request and leave by the tunnels," her father said quietly. "I will rest easier knowing that you got away unharmed and untroubled."

Calum hesitated, then shrugged again. "As ye like. It makes no ne'er mind to me."

"Good," Lord DeCourcey said, then glanced to Sarra. "Daughter, go have Cook pack Calum some food to take with him. I would have a word alone with him ere he goes."

"Aye, Father," Sarra murmured and turned to leave them alone. It wasn't until she was pulling the door closed behind her that she realized that Pretty Boy hadn't followed her this time. The fact saddened her terribly. It was almost as if the two were already gone.

Shaking her head about such foolishness over a man she'd known for so short a time, Sarra hurried below to find Cook in the kitchens. She was just overseeing the last of the food being placed in a sack for Calum when he entered the kitchens with Pretty Boy on his heel.

Calum eyed the bulging bag and shook his head as he approached. "What did ye ha'e put in there, lass? A cow?"

Sarra managed a smile as she handed the bag to him. "Dried beef, cheese, bread, some fruit, a skin of ale and another of mead . . ."

"Ah," he murmured wryly as he hooked the bag to Pretty Boy's pommel. "Jest the necessities, then."

Sarra smiled at his teasing, but it was all too much for Cook.

"I do not mean to be difficult, my lady. But, pray, kindly remove that beast from my kitchen," he begged in desperate tones.

"Oh . . . er . . . yes," Sarra murmured and moved toward the door to the dungeons. She opened it and started to move out of the way for Pretty Boy to go down, but paused as she noted the faint light coming from one of the cells.

"What is it?" Calum murmured, obviously sensing something was wrong. He didn't wait for her answer. Spotting the light himself as he peered down, he murmured, "Wait here," and hurried silently down the stairs.

Sarra watched him until he disappeared into the cell below, but when a startled cry sounded, she gave up her stance at the door and hurried down the stairs. She'd barely reached the bottom when the clatter from above warned that Pretty Boy was following.

Worried about his managing the steep stairs, Sarra hesitated. The horse had managed ascending the stairs twice, but descending them was another matter. They were terribly steep. She watched with her heart in her throat as the animal charged down them with as much speed and clatter as he used going up.

Sarra shook her head when he reached the bottom and paused before her, but didn't waste time patting him, or congratulating him. Instead, she hurried to the cell Calum had slipped into to find him holding Hadley up on the wall with a hand at his throat.

"What were ye doin'?" Calum growled, shaking the man as if he were weightless.

Sarra's eyes widened in horror as Hadley's face began to turn blue.

"Calum!" she cried, rushing to his side. "You are killing him. He can not speak with you choking him!"

Calum glared at Hadley, but slowly lowered him until his feet rested again on the ground, then scowled as he released him altogether.

"Speak." It was a cold growl and Sarra could only be grateful it wasn't directed at her.

"I—I was repairing—I—a door," Hadley stumbled over his own words in his fear, and Sarra felt her heart sink as she recognized he was lying. Seeming to realize he wasn't being very convincing, Hadley took a breath and tried again. "When I was down here helping Lady Sarra carry you above, I noticed one of the doors was hanging crooked, so came below to repair it."

"I see," Calum said dryly and then asked, "And tappin' on the walls with the hilt o' yer knife is supposed to repair this door?"

Sarra's eyes sharpened on Hadley at Calum's words as she realized it must have been Hadley tapping when they'd returned earlier.

"I was—" Hadley began, his voice now as panicky as his face.

"Ye were jest tryin' tae find the secret entrance to please yer friend d'Angers," Calum said dryly.

"Oh, Hadley," Sarra sighed with disappointment. He had been her father's first for twenty years now, having worked his way quickly up through the ranks. It hurt her heart to know he'd betrayed them like this.

Her disappointment seemed to knock something loose in Hadley and his fear suddenly turned to rage as he spat, "Do not 'Oh, Hadley' me, you stupid, stupid girl! If you had just married him none of this would be necessary. Why you bother to fight him, I do not know. DeCourcey needs a strong lord and d'Angers could be that lord now that your father is failing."

"Strong?" Sarra said with amazement. "D'Angers is cruel, not strong. How could you side yourself with such a heartless devil?"

Hadley shook his head with disgust. "Better the Devil's first than his lackey. D'Angers is smart and ruthless. He always gets what he wants. Those who fight him are crushed. 'Tis better to work with him and reap the rewards."

Sarra's mouth tightened. "You are forgetting he already has a first. I doubt he would put Jocks aside for you."

"Jocks," he spat the name with disgust. "Jocks is a cockup, constantly failing at the ends he is supposed to achieve. Twice now I have practically delivered you right into his hands and yet twice now he has lost you. Nay." He smiled grimly. "I foresee little difficulty at all in taking his place as d'Angers' first."

"That may be hard to do from these dungeons," Calum said coldly, and before Sarra realized quite what he was doing, he'd clapped one of Hadley's wrists in the nearest manacle attached to the wall. By the time the second manacle was snapped shut, Hadley's eyes had widened with the realization of the fix he was in.

Apparently realizing he would have little luck with Calum,

Hadley turned his pleading face her way. "My lady, please. I was just trying to make the transition easier. D'Angers will siege the castle if necessary to get you to wife and we will have to give in anyway. Is it not better to just get it over with and—"

Sarra stopped listening and turned on her heel to leave the cell, aware that Calum followed her.

Pretty Boy had waited in the hall, watching everything but not bothering to enter the tiny cell. Sarra caught the horse's reins as she left the room and silently led the horse to the end cell in the row.

Calum followed without speaking until she opened the tunnel entrance and stepped aside—then he lifted a hand to her face and peered at her with concern. "Are ye all right?"

Sarra nodded silently. In truth, she wasn't all right at all. He was leaving, which made her heart sore, and she had just learned that Hadley, a faithful retainer to her father for twenty years, had betrayed them all. She was afraid to speak for fear a sob would come out instead.

"At least ye've found yer traitor," Calum murmured after a pause. " 'Tis sorry I am that 'twas Hadley. Yer father speaks o' him with affection, but better ye ken and can stop the damage, than that you dinna ken and he delivers ye into d'Angers' hands."

"Aye," Sarra whispered tightly, keeping a tight rein on her emotions.

Calum frowned at her expression and ran his thumb gently over her lips, "I wish . . ."

Sarra lifted her eyes to his, startled to see the combined yearning and sadness in his eyes. It echoed the feeling in her own heart at his leavetaking and she felt a moment's hope, but then he shook his head and turned to step into the tunnel, leading Pretty Boy. "I shall replace the torches and flints for ye on the way out."

"Thank you," Sarra whispered, watching him mount.

Once settled in the saddle, he turned and peered back at her and his mouth tightened.

"Take care o' yersel', Sarra DeCourcey. Yer father will no live much longer. Yer best to find yersel' a strong husband to keep d'Angers and others like him from yer door," he said grimly, then urged Pretty Boy into a walk.

Sarra remained silent until the stone door slid closed between them, then whispered, "I was hoping I had found him in you, but I guess not."

Eight

Calum blinked his eyes open and stared around the dark woods surrounding him. He'd fallen asleep in the saddle again, something he'd done several times over the last week since leaving DeCourcey. He had known he should sleep the last day ere leaving DeCourcey, but had been enjoying himself too much in their company to force himself to it, so had ridden out that night without any sleep. It was a pattern that had continued the last week as Calum had first completed his task in delivering his uncle's message to London, then had hunted down the minstrel Sarra had mentioned.

Having a minstrel riding about the countryside singing ballads of Bothan's bravery and skill in battle was one thing, but from Sarra's comments about some of his tales being unbelievable, Calum had known the man was touching on subjects that were better left unspoken. The vampirism in his people was the result of an ancestor's breeding with a druid goddess. His uncle was hoping to breed it out of their clan. It was dangerous to be different, breeding fear in humans and what humans feared, they did their best to eradicate. His people had no desire to be hunted. They lived a quiet life, trying to draw as little attention as possible while they worked to weaken the strain and breed it out of the clan. Having a minstrel riding around England singing about them did not aid in that.

Calum had finally tracked the minstrel to a small village near York the night before. Fortunately, the man hadn't spread his tales since leaving d'Angers, and hadn't had a chance to perform much there. Somehow, he'd managed to annoy d'Angers his first night at the castle and d'Angers had personally beaten him within an inch of his life. According to the minstrel, he'd left there half dead, passed out on the road not far from d'Angers, and been found by a traveling merchant who'd felt enough pity to pile him in his cart and take him to his family in the village by York where he'd been recovering ever since.

The beating had been so bad, the man would probably be crippled for life, and Calum had felt enough pity himself for the poor bastard that—rather than threaten him—he'd dropped a bag of coins at his feet as payment to keep him from singing about any of the MacNachtons, leaving him with only the mild threat that he would return and be less kind should he hear the man had not stopped these ballads. He'd then found a spot to settle for the day, but instead of sleep, Calum had lain awake thinking of Sarra and his time at DeCourcey. Both had haunted him since leaving the castle.

He could not get her father's words out of his head. Elman DeCourcey had made several comments through the day that had suggested that he would be happy to have Calum marry Sarra. Comments such as "*You would make a fine son-in-law, Calum,*" and "*I would not need worry about dying and leaving Sarra alone if she had a husband like you.*"

Each comment had made his heart lurch with happiness, then drop into depression. Calum was sure the man meant what he said, but knew he wouldn't feel that way did he know what Calum was. He was positive the same was true of Sarra. He knew she was attracted to him, enjoyed his kisses and his company, and the sadness in her beautiful eyes as he'd left had made his heart ache, but he was sure all of that would disappear like smoke if he revealed what he was. Unfortunately, there was no way he could marry her without doing so.

This is why when Lord DeCourcey sent Sarra to pack him some food and flat-out told him that he wished Calum would think about marrying Sarra, pointing out that he would be the lord of DeCourcey with his own keep and land and so on, it had been hard on Calum. He'd listened to the man list all he would gain did he marry Sarra with a heavy heart. None of that mattered to him. He found Sarra beautiful, funny, and fascinating. The idea of spending the rest of his life with her was like a beautiful dream, and he would have taken her in a heartbeat without DeCourcey, the lands, and all her wealth, but he did not think she would have him.

Sighing, Calum glanced around, realizing that Pretty Boy still was not moving.

"Black," he corrected himself with a shake of the head and tightened his thighs to get the horse moving, only to scowl when the horse did not react except to twitch his ears.

"What is it, boy?" Calum asked in a soft murmur, his gaze shifting around the dark woods they were stopped in, embarrassed to acknowledge even to himself that he hadn't any idea how long he had slept or where he was.

"Where have you brought me?" he muttered with irritation, glancing to Black to see the horse twitch his ears again. Frowning, Calum listened to the soft rustle of the leaves in the trees and then blinked as he realized it wasn't the sound of leaves at all. It sounded like the rustle of hempen cloth flapping in a breeze.

"Tents?" he muttered.

After a pause, he slid off Black's back, patted his side, and murmured, "Stay here."

Calum then moved carefully into the trees, eyes sharp and ears straining as he tried to sort where the sound was coming from. He didn't have to walk far before nearly tripping over the first man. Fortunately, the fellow was asleep, rolled up in a blanket on the ground, blissfully unaware of how close Calum had come to stepping on his head.

Pausing, he glanced around, noting that he wasn't alone—there were others sleeping nearby. Calum stopped counting them after he reached twenty, but knew there were many more than that . . . and they weren't the source of the sound. Weaving carefully around and between them, he made his way through the trees until they ended. Calum found himself standing at the treeline of the woods that surrounded DeCourcey.

He stood in the shadow of the trees, his gaze sliding over a small sleeping army of men. They were huddled close to and in amongst the shelter of the trees, away from the castle and the possibility of missiles being launched on them. When he glanced to the left, he saw a small trio of tents set up.

Calum hesitated, his gaze slipping to the sky overhead. The sky had lightened enough that the stars were twinkling out. Dawn was approaching. His mouth tightened, but he slipped along the edge of the trees toward the largest tent, pausing abruptly as the flap suddenly slapped aside and a tall, blond man stepped out, snapping, "'Tis taking too long. I want this over with ere the king hears about it."

Calum's eyes narrowed as Jocks followed the man out. "Aye, my lord."

"Do not 'Aye, my lord' *me*, Jocks. *Do* something," the man Calum could only think was Lord d'Angers snarled. When Jocks did not respond at once, the man snapped, "What of the tunnel Hadley mentioned? If we went in through the tunnel it would be over by day's end and Sarra and DeCourcey would be mine."

"I have men looking for the entrance, my lord, but DeCourcey covers a lot of land. It could be anywhere."

"Not *anywhere*," d'Angers countered, his expression grim, his eyes calculating. "It must be somewhere near the clearing. Sarra did not take her horse after the first attack and you claim he did not have one . . ." He turned suddenly on Jocks. "Where did this MacNachton fellow come from?"

Jocks shrugged helplessly. "He just appeared behind us in the clearing."

"He had to come from somewhere. What was at your back?"

Jocks hesitated, obviously trying to recall, then said slowly, "The woods behind us on our left, the cliff face on the right."

"The cliff face," d'Angers repeated, grabbing onto the words sharply. "Take a dozen men and examine every inch of the cliff face. I will have Sarra by nightfall or heads will roll . . . yours, for one."

Jocks nodded abruptly and began to walk toward where the rest of the men still slept to rouse the ones he would take with him. Calum didn't stay to watch more—turning away, he made his way quickly back through the woods full of sleeping men to Black.

"Good boy," Calum murmured as he mounted the horse. Were it not for Black bringing him here while he slept, Sarra would have been in great trouble. As it was, if he didn't get to the clearing before Jocks got there, he would have no way to warn her to block off the secret entrance.

Black seemed to sense Calum's tension and urgency; the horse moved, swift and silent, through the woods and within moments they were at the clearing.

Sarra stood on the rampart, staring silently down at the army sleeping outside the bailey walls. They had been there for five days and nights, arriving two days after Calum had left, and two days after Hadley had been locked up in one of the cells. She suspected d'Angers had decided to set siege to DeCourcey when he realized that Hadley had been found out, though she wasn't sure how he'd found out the man had been caught. It was possible that Hadley had made a habit of reporting to him each day and when his reports had stopped, d'Angers had realized he must have been caught . . . Or there was a second traitor who had reported the fact to him. Sarra was hoping it was the first possibility. The thought that someone else in her keep was working for the man was not a happy one.

But then, between Calum's leaving, the steady decline of her father's health, the betrayal by the previously most trusted Hadley, and the fact that they were under siege, there seemed little to be happy about of late.

Sensing she was getting dangerously close to a case of the 'poor me's,' Sarra shook her head and forced herself to straighten her shoulders. All would be well. DeCourcey was well set for food and the other necessities, so they could hold out quite a while. And if worse came to worst, she could ride out through the tunnels and flee to London to speak to the king. The only reason Sarra hadn't already done so was that she feared her father's dying while she was away.

"Lady Sarra!"

Blinking, she focused her gaze on the tents and men beyond the wall to see that Reginald d'Angers was apparently up and ready to throw more insults and threats her way. He had been barraging her with both since setting siege to the castle. And each time he did, she was more and more grateful that Calum had saved her from Jocks and the men that first day. The idea of being married to the cruel, insufferable ass now pacing in front of his tent and eyeing the castle was enough to make her quite nauseous.

"I want Lady Sarra!" d'Angers roared, apparently short-tempered in the mornings.

"You want DeCourcey, too, and shall have neither!" Sarra yelled back, mouth tightening as he spotted her on the wall.

"Ah, there you are," he said more pleasantly, temper apparently appeased at the sight of her.

"What do you want now, Reginald?" she asked wearily,

not bothering to give him the address he supposedly deserved.

"I thought to offer you one last chance to end this amicably before you have no choice. Walk out here willingly to me now and it will go more pleasantly for you than if you make me come in there after you."

"I would more willingly marry a mule than tie myself to you," Sarra responded harshly.

"You shall pay for that, Sarra," he announced, his voice cold and hard.

Her mouth tightened. "Mayhap I shall, but I shall never willingly speak vows in front of a priest."

"Brave words. I shall remind you of them when you are on your knees begging me to marry you."

"Nothing you did to me could bring that miracle about," she assured him.

"Nay?" He laughed coldly. "Well, I shall test that theory when we get inside, and if it turns out to be true, then I shall turn my efforts to your father."

Hands clenching, Sarra turned away and left the wall, unwilling to listen to any more threats. In truth, the last threat was a very effective one. She could suffer much herself, but could not stand the suffering of others.

"There you are, my lady."

Sarra paused at the top of the steps leading down from the wall to the bailey as Seth, the stable master, hurried up to her. "What is it, Seth?"

"Dung," he answered solemnly.

Sarra stared at him blankly. "Dung?"

"Aye. What am I to do with it, my lady?"

Sarra blinked in confusion. Hadley generally handled such problems. "What do you normally do with it?"

"Well now, I usually send it out to be spread over the fields, but we've been trapped in the castle this last week since d'Angers and his men arrived and 'tis piling up and let me tell you, the smell is powerful."

"Powerful?" Sarra murmured, a slow smile spreading her lips.

Seth's eyes narrowed on her smile. "Aye."

"Well, perhaps our uninvited guests can find some use for it. Give it to them."

Seth shifted uncertainly. "Give it to them, my lady? To d'Angers and his men?"

"Aye," Sarra said serenely. "Collect as many men as you think you shall need together, gather it up in baskets, bring it up to the wall and give it to them."

His eyes went wide as plates and Seth was suddenly sporting a grin. "Aye, my lady. It shall be as you wish."

Whirling on the stairs, he hurried back down, eager to do her bidding.

For the first time in the week since Sarra had found herself in charge of a castle under siege, she felt as if she could breathe. She could do this, she realized with relief. The appetite that had been lagging since Calum had left, and disappeared altogether after the siege started, suddenly made a reappearance and Sarra headed to the kitchens intending to break her fast.

Rather than sit about pretending the men outside the gate weren't there, she thought it was time she started to make it known she knew they were there. She wasn't sure how yet, but having the stable master dump the dung on them seemed like a good start. There must be other things they could offer them as well. She just had to think on it. It was going to be a busy day.

The appetite that had returned disappeared the moment Sarra entered the kitchens. The smell that hit her as she came through the door was enough to make her nauseous. Her gaze slid around the kitchen with bewilderment, wondering where it could be coming from. Sarra could almost believe the stable master had been storing some of the excess dung in here.

"What is that smell?" she finally asked with horror as the cook glanced over and noticed her.

"Oh," Cook sighed unhappily, his shoulders hunching as if she'd reminded him of something he'd managed to forget. Though how he could forget that smell, she couldn't imagine, unless his nose just gave up working and stopped smelling anything after a bit, she thought as he shook his head and said, "'Tis the awful, my lady. 'Tis in the courtyard outside the kitchen doors and every time the door is opened the smell fills the kitchens."

"Awful?" Sarra asked with bewilderment.

"Aye." He nodded. "The bits left over and spoilt foods. I have the girls put it in a barrel outside the door and every other day 'tis taken away to be put on the fields."

"Is it?" Sarra asked with interest.

"Aye. But with the castle under siege . . ." He shrugged unhappily.

"Hmm." Sarra paused a moment, then patted his shoulder. "Never fear, I shall have the stable master send some men to collect the awful for you. He may offer it to our guests as well," she announced.

Cook blinked and asked uncertainly, "Offer it to our guests?"

"Aye. We are gathering some things together that are no longer of use to ourselves and that d'Angers and his men may find use for; your awful, the dung from the stables. Things like that."

A startled smile tilted the corner of his mouth and Sarra winked at him, then turned to leave the kitchens, her appetite quite spoiled.

"My lady," Cook called as she started to push through the door.

"Aye?" Sarra asked, pausing and glancing back.

He hesitated, then offered, "I am sure there are other things I could find to . . . umm . . . offer them. Things we have no use for that they might . . . umm . . . enjoy."

Sarra eyed the man. His shoulders were no longer hunched and he was smiling widely. Just the idea of getting back at the men outside the gate had lifted his spirits. This could be very good for morale, something that had suffered during the days since they'd found themselves locking d'Angers' army outside the gate, but by necessity, locking themselves inside.

"Anything you do not need," she said with a nod, then pushed out into the great hall and eyed the table filling with people preparing to break their fast. Sarra watched them, noting the sluggish footsteps and downhearted expressions, then walked to the head table, stepped up on the dais, and asked Malcolm to get everyone's attention. The young man nodded, stood, and hollered for silence. The moment that silence rang, Sarra spoke.

"The stable master and Cook are gathering some things together to gift d'Angers and his men with."

She heard the gasp this caused around the table and smiled widely. "The stable master is giving up the dung from his horses. Cook is offering his awful from the kitchens. Does anyone here have anything they think should be added to this gift?"

There was dead silence for a moment as people slowly understood that she wasn't speaking of your usual gift.

"Well now, I'm thinking I could find a rotten egg or two dozen they might like," Gertrude said, and Sarra smiled at the woman. She had a home outside the castle where she raised laying hens, supplying eggs for the castle. But word of d'Angers' approach had come early enough that the woman had packed all her chickens on a cart and hurried to get them all within the safety of the castle walls rather than risk d'Angers' men raiding her and taking them for meat.

"Aye," the old woman nodded. "The hens always lay off eggs when upset, and they're all unsettled, having been rushed from their homes and dragged within the walls. I might even find I have two dozen questionable eggs to give them."

Sarra opened her mouth to speak, but paused; no one would have heard her anyway, as everyone was suddenly talking, offering various disgusting and unpleasant things they thought d'Angers' men might like.

She let them jabber for a moment, grinning as she heard offer after offer, then raised a hand for silence. Much to her surprise, it fell at once without the necessity of Malcolm's shouting out for her.

Clearing her throat, Sarra said, "Gather together whatever you wish to send to them and take it to the stable master—he is overseeing the matter."

"I am?"

Sarra turned quickly to see Seth standing at her side, a vaguely amused look on his face.

"I was just coming to ask you how you wanted me to give them the dung," he explained. "The men have it all gathered."

Sarra hesitated, then glanced at the people hurrying for the keep doors to gather together what they could. Their steps were noticeably lighter than they had been on entering and they were all smiling and even laughing.

"I think you shall have more to add to the offering," she announced wryly.

"So it would seem," he agreed dryly, then pointed out, "but it isn't going to do much more than land in the moat if we dump it off the walls. A shame to waste such fine . . . gifts."

Sarra frowned. It would be a terrible waste, and the high spirits everyone was enjoying would plummet again if they did that.

"The catapult," Malcolm said suddenly, reminding her he was still at her side.

"Catapult?" Sarra asked with interest.

"Aye. We could stack it on the catapult and shoot it over the wall so that it hits them," he suggested.

"We have a catapult?" Sarra asked with disbelief.

"Aye. Well, really 'tis a trebuchet," Seth explained. "'Tis old, though, and small. Your father had it made when we were under siege some twenty years ago. Hartford had laid siege to the castle and started firing dead animals into the bailey to spread sickness in the hopes of getting us to give up. Your father had a small trebuchet made to fire the horses back." He smiled with admiration at the memory, then nodded and said, "Aye, it might work."

"Well, let us try it, then," Sarra suggested. "Malcolm, pray help him with it."

"Aye, my lady."

Sarra watched the men go, her gaze considering on Malcolm. He was young, but intelligent, and, she thought, trustworthy. He might make a good replacement for Hadley.

She would have to consider it, Sarra decided.

"My lady."

Sarra glanced toward the kitchens at the call from Cook. Seeing the expression on his face, she frowned and moved to meet him as he rushed forward.

"Aye, Cook?" she asked as they met.

The man hesitated, his gaze shifting around to be sure no one was near enough to hear, then asked quietly, "Are you expecting company?"

"Company?" Sarra asked with bewilderment.

"Aye." He raised his eyebrows up and down, his eyes rolling around and around in a suggestive manner that she simply didn't understand.

"Are you having a fit, Cook?" she asked uncertainly.

Blowing out a sigh, the man caught her arm and began to hurry her back toward the kitchens. "There are sounds coming from the dungeons. Again."

"Sounds?" Sarra asked. Then her eyes widened as she recalled the day she'd brought Calum back through the tunnels and Hadley had appeared to help her get him upstairs. He'd said one of the maids had heard noises coming from the dungeons and fetched him to check it out. Just as Cook was now saying there were sounds coming from the dungeons.

"Calum," she breathed, her heart almost stopping dead in her chest. In the next moment, Sarra had pulled her arm free and was hurrying to the kitchens ahead of Cook.

She reached the door to the dungeons and had thrown it open before recalling that Hadley was in the dungeons and may be the source of the noise. Fortunately, it wasn't Hadley she saw standing at the foot of the stairs with Black.

"Calum," Sarra cried happily—then her eyes widened and she stepped quickly to the side as Pretty Boy came charging up the stairs.

It was almost frightening to Calum the way his heart leapt at the first sight of Sarra. Just seeing her face and her welcoming smile as she called his name had made him feel like he'd come home. Then Black charged up the stairs and she disappeared from view as she got out of the way.

Taking a deep breath to steady himself, he followed the horse up the stairs, arriving in the kitchens to find Cook watching Pretty Boy trying to eat Sarra's hair as she patted and cooed to the beast. The usual annoyed expression the man had worn when last Calum had brought the horse through the kitchens was noticeably absent, a beaming smile in its place.

"Welcome back, my lord," the man said, adding to Calum's sense of homecoming.

He nodded at the man, but merely said, "I am no a lord."

Sarra beamed at him as if he'd said something clever, then her eyes widened. "Oh! We must tell Father you are back."

Catching Black's reins, she led the way out of the kitchen, babbling about how happy her father would be to see him, and Calum followed, shaking his head. It was as if she was completely unaware that her castle was under siege and for one moment, he wondered if she was. He knew she spent most of her time in her father's room. If the man had replaced Hadley already, Calum wouldn't have put it past the lord of DeCourcey to keep the siege a secret from her so she wouldn't worry.

He realized how crazy an idea that was when one of the soldiers—Malcolm, he thought the man's name was—came rushing into the great hall as they headed for the stairs.

"We are ready with the first . . . er . . . gift," the man said, nodding at Calum in greeting.

"Oh." Sarra hesitated, then handed Black's reins to Calum. "You go on up and say hello. I shall be up shortly."

Calum watched her go with a frown and considered following her, but it was daylight outside, and he could not go out without weakening himself. Now was not the time to risk making himself ill.

Mouth tight, Calum turned and led Black above stairs and to Lord DeCourcey's room. He found the room empty except for Sarra's father. Frowning over this, he made his way to the bedside to peer down at the sleeping man. His first sight of Elman DeCourcey had the opposite effect of seeing Sarra. Calum's heart sank as he saw how much the man had declined in the short time he'd been gone.

"You returned." The old man smiled weakly when he opened his eyes to find Calum standing at his bedside. "I knew you would. You love her. I could tell."

Calum suspected he might indeed love the woman, but he knew it was hopeless. Unable to say so to the man, he asked instead, "Where are Bessy and Milly?"

"They wished to add some things to the gift Sarra is sending d'Angers. They will be back shortly."

"The gift Sarra is sending d'Angers?" Calum asked with a frown, then paused and glanced toward the door as it opened and Bessy rushed in.

"They are going to send the first volley!"

The girl was so excited, she didn't even seem to notice Calum there as she rushed across the room to the window. She was about to open the shutters to peer out when Elman said, "No, Bessy!"

Pausing, the girl turned back in surprise. When she finally noticed Calum at the bedside, her shoulders sagged with disappointment.

"Go watch from the room next door," Lord DeCourcey suggested kindly.

"But, you—"

"I will be fine," Sarra's father insisted. "Calum is with me."

Brightening, the girl curtsied, then rushed from the room.

"What is she so excited about?" Calum asked as the door closed behind the girl. "And what is this gift?"

The old man smiled. "Sarra has decided to catapult some gifts over the wall to d'Angers to show her opinion of his suit."

Calum's eyes narrowed. "What kind o' gifts?"

"Horse dung, rotten eggs, awful from the kitchens, and so on," the man said with a grin, but rather than smile, Calum felt alarm claim him.

"That'll just make the man furious, no drive him away," he pointed out with worry.

"Aye," Elman agreed with a shrug. "But truly, the man is unpleasant whether annoyed or not. Besides, it will raise the spirits of those of us trapped within the walls."

A roar suddenly rose from the bailey and Calum glanced toward the shuttered windows, wishing he could look out and see what was happening.

"You see, this has boosted everyone's morale," Elman said as the noise in the bailey became recognizable as cheering. "Mind you, your marrying Sarra and sending d'Angers on his way will make them even happier."

"I wish that I *could* marry her," Calum admitted, then changed the subject and announced, "D'Anger kens about the tunnel and is searchin' the clearin' fer it. He shall find it."

Elman frowned, but said, "They will not find their way through the tunnels—they will get lost."

"What if they follow the torch holders?" Calum pointed

out. "I removed the torches on my way in and blocked the entrance in the dungeon after I came through, but—"

"There are torch holders in the other tunnels as well to prevent anyone using the torches as a map," Elman informed him, then frowned and added, "but if you have removed the torches in the tunnels leading to the entrance, that in itself could act as a map for them."

Calum's eyes widened in horror as he realized that he himself may have accidentally made certain they would be able to find their way to the keep entrance.

"Did you block the door well?" Elman asked with worry.

"Aye," Calum assured him, but thought he would go down and make damned sure it was well blocked.

"Are you going to marry my daughter or not? If you did, d'Angers would pack up at once and leave."

Calum glanced away, tempted beyond his wildest imaginings. To be able to claim Sarra as his own, to have the right to kiss and touch and . . . A shudder of desire went through him at the very idea, but he shook his head hopelessly. "She'd no ha'e me."

Elman snorted. "Sarra is as besotted with you as you are with her. She would be happy to marry you."

"If she kenned what I am—" Calum clamped his mouth shut as he realized what he was saying.

"I know what you are," Elman said quietly into the silence that followed his words, and Calum glanced at him with a start.

"Ye ken?" he asked with doubt.

"Years ago I was at court at the same time as a fellow named Janklyn MacNachton." He paused and raised an eyebrow. "A relative of yours, I believe."

Calum kept his mouth shut and waited.

"I liked him," Elman finally went on. "There were a lot of rumors about your clan at the time, and I had occasion to see Janklyn in battle, defending the honor of a young woman in the gardens. A woman he later married. He was feral, and incredibly strong, and his teeth . . ." Elman shook his head. "I suspect if he'd realized I'd witnessed that day, I might have had a problem, but he didn't."

Sarra's father looked him straight in the eye and said, "I know what you are. And it doesn't matter. What matters is your character, and whether you care about and would care for my daughter. I would welcome you as son-in-law."

Nine

It was nearly the nooning hour by the time Sarra made her way off the wall and into the keep. She had been kept busy the whole morning through, overseeing the work with the trebuchet and d'Angers' "gifts," as well as lobbing insults back at him. She'd left once to go check on her father and had hoped to find Calum with him, but her father had said he was overseeing blocking off the secret entrance in the dungeon and had explained that d'Angers had men searching for it.

Sorry she wouldn't get the chance to see him, Sarra had considered going to the dungeons, but her father had seemed to read her mind and had said her presence would just be a distraction while he was busy—besides, she had matters to attend to on the wall. So, Sarra had returned as another sling full of gunk had been loaded and sent over the wall.

Now they were finally out of "gifts" to send d'Angers and were ready for a celebratory meal. Sarra only hoped Cook was ready for them, as they were a tad early for the nooning hour. Her concerns on this matter died as Sarra led the way into the keep and spotted the servants rushing every which way, carrying platters of food for a hastily prepared feast. But it was the sight of her father at the table that made her steps first falter, then pick up as she rushed to his side.

"Father, you should not be up!" Sarra cried with worry as she reached his side. "How did you get down here?"

"Calum carried me," he answered, then added, "and of course I should be here. 'Tis a special day. Celebrations are in order and I will not miss it."

Sarra's smile returned at his words and she clasped his frail hand in both of hers as she settled at the table beside him. "I wish you could have seen it, Father. D'Angers is spitting mad and his men were all cowering in the woods. We would wait until they ventured out, then send another volley. It was brilliant!"

He grinned at her excitement, but said, "That was not what I meant about it being a special day."

Sarra blinked. "It is not? Well, then what—?" The question died in her throat as Calum appeared at her side. His expression was so solemn it was worrisome, and she was sure she must have misheard when her father said, "Today you marry Calum."

The blood roaring in her ears, Sarra turned her head slowly back to her father.

"What?" she asked faintly.

"Calum has agreed to marry you," her father said gently.

Sarra turned back to Calum, noting that Father Hammond stood behind him. Her gaze slid from the prelate to Calum, and then she asked uncertainly, "Are you sure you want to?"

"Aye," he said solemnly with a certainty that lightened her heart, but then clouds crossed his eyes and he said, "If you do not wish it . . ."

Sarra could read the sudden uncertainty in his face and saw the way he stiffened up, as if in preparation of rejection, and felt herself relax. He would not care if she said no, if he did not care. A soft smile coming to her lips, she stood and placed her hand gently at his cheek. "Aye, my lord, I wish it."

"Very good," her father said happily, then picked up the empty goblet before him and banged it on the table to bring silence to the room.

Sarra was aware of the silence that filled the great hall, and knew her father was announcing that she and Calum were to be wed, but she didn't really hear what he said—her attention was on Calum. She could tell by his expression that he was worrying over something, but wasn't sure what it was and that worried her.

"Sarra?"

"Aye?" She turned to her father in question.

"Answer Father Hammond," he encouraged.

Confused, she glanced to the prelate in question.

The man smiled with gentle amusement at her confusion, then said, "Do you, Sarra DeCourcey—"

"Now?" Sara squealed with shock, realizing that while she'd been woolgathering, the actual ceremony had started. "We are marrying *now*? But I—my dress and—"

She touched her hair self-consciously. She was hardly dressed for a wedding. This was not how she'd imagined it happening. Sarra had thought she'd wear a pretty gown and have her hair all done up and look her best at her wedding. Not be wearing a ratty old gown and her hair tumbled about her face in a windblown mess.

"You look beautiful," Calum assured her quietly, taking her hand.

Sarra met his gaze for a moment, then felt her shoulders relax. Her gaze then slid to her father's expectant face and she sighed. "Very well. I do."

"We have not got to that yet, my dear," Father Hammond admonished her. "You must listen to all you are vowing to do. 'Tis most important."

"Aye, Father," Sarra murmured, suitably chastised. She listened quietly and most patiently as he started again.

The ceremony seemed incredibly short to her. Paradoxically, it also seemed to last forever. In truth, Sarra was feeling very odd indeed. Like in a dream where you are running through a tunnel that keeps growing larger, then shorter, so did the ceremony seem to her, and it was a great surprise when it was over and Calum was pulling her gently toward him for the bridal kiss.

She inhaled the scent of him as he bent to her, her eyes drifting closed expectantly, but he merely brushed his lips softly over hers before lifting his head away. Sarra was so scattered at that point that it took a moment for her to realize that the roaring in her ears was the cheering of her people. *Their* people now. And then she found herself suddenly seated at the table between her father and Calum . . . her husband, she realized, a touch faintly. She was married. Moments ago she hadn't been, and now she was. It all seemed quite odd to her and she was having trouble wrapping her mind around it.

"Are ye a'right?"

Sarra blinked and managed a smile for her husband when he leaned close to ask the question.

"Aye," she murmured, and then accepted the wine he offered her and took a sip. She even began to eat, though she couldn't have said what she was eating. Everything kept going out of focus as her thoughts kept returning to the fact that she was married now. How strange.

The celebrations were happy, almost euphoric, and Sarra knew it was because their people realized that it would mean an end to the siege. She smiled and drank whatever was given to her and ate whatever was placed in her trencher, but her mind was quite scattered.

"Sarra?"

Blinking, she tried to gather her thoughts and turned to peer at her father. "Aye, Father?"

"Calum has been riding all night and working at blocking off the dungeons and seeing to the arrangements for the wedding all day," he pointed out gently, then added, "I imagine he would like to rest now."

Sarra stared at him blankly, her mind silently translating what her father was telling her. *Take your husband to bed*, seemed to be what he was saying, and she suddenly realized that she would be expected to share a bed with him. The thought was a startling one. It shouldn't have been, but her mind hadn't managed to move that far ahead of the amazing fact that she was now Calum's wife.

"Sarra," her father prompted when she remained still and silent.

Blinking, Sarra nodded and turned to her husband. "Are you tired, Cal—husband? Would you like to rest?"

Calum hesitated, then simply took her arm and stood.

Whether anyone besides her father noticed their leaving, Sarra couldn't say. She didn't notice—she didn't even notice that Pretty Boy followed them upstairs until Calum paused at her bedroom door and turned to the horse.

"Nay," he said firmly. "Yer sleepin' out here."

Pretty Boy whickered and flicked his head, but moved two steps past the door so that his back was to them, and proceeded to ignore them.

"I'll start to work on movin' him to the stables on the morrow," Calum murmured as he ushered Sarra into her room and closed the door. "I didna get the chance today."

"It was light when you arrived here," she murmured nervously, knowing he couldn't have tried in the sunlight.

"Aye," Calum said, then frowned and glanced around the room, unsure how to proceed. He had allowed Elman DeCourcey to convince him to marry Sarra, but immediately he'd agreed, he'd begun to wonder if it was the right thing to do. Elman may know what he was, but Sarra did not. How would she feel once she did? Should he not tell her first?

In the end, he'd decided to go through with the wedding to save her from d'Angers and then tell her and offer her an annulment if she wished. Unfortunately, now that they were married, part of his mind was urging him to quickly bed her and consummate the marriage so it couldn't be annulled. However, his conscience was urging him to tell her everything before they went further. It was the honorable thing to do. Honor could be a damned inconvenient thing at times, he acknowledged unhappily.

"My lord?"

Calum glanced to her in question. "Aye?"

Sarra hesitated, then said, "Mayhap we should go tell d'Angers we are married and he might as well leave."

Calum smiled faintly at the suggestion, but shook his head. "I fancy lettin' him waste another night out there ere we tell him. 'Tis safe enough—the entrance is well blocked, even do they find it," he added in case she feared otherwise.

"I am sure 'tis," Sarra murmured.

Calum sighed, deciding it was time to get it over with. "Sarra."

"Aye?" she asked.

He hesitated, then sighed again and said, "Before we go further, I need to be tellin' ye something about me people . . . about me."

"I know."

Calum blinked, then asked uncertainly, "Ye know?"

Sarra nodded.

He stared at her blankly for a moment, then asked, "What is it ye think ye ken?"

"You are a vampire, my lord."

Calum's mind whirled at the plain words and he found himself suddenly seated on the side of the bed, just staring at her. Finally, he said with amazement, "Ye ken."

Sarra frowned slightly at his stunned expression. "Of course I know, my lord. What with the rumors about the MacNachtons, combined with your incredible strength and skill while fighting Jocks and his men, how could I not?" she asked dryly, then added, "And then there is your aversion to sunlight and the fact that your gaping wound was closed and half-healed in the short time it took to get you back to the keep . . ." She shrugged as if it had been obvious, and indeed said, "It seemed obvious, my lord."

"I am not a lord," Calum murmured out of habit as he

struggled to realize that she knew what he'd worried and fretted over telling her.

"You are now," Sarra countered. "You are my husband, and soon lord of DeCourcey."

Calum's mouth tightened at the sadness that floated through her eyes, wishing he could change that and somehow ensure her father lived, but he could not. Bracing himself, he put the matter of her father's health aside and made the offer he really had no desire to make. "We can annul the marriage if you do not wish to be married to me."

Sarra stiffened and then managed what looked to be a forced smile as she said, "Surely you did not think to get out of it that easily, did you, my lord?"

Calum was trying to sort out how to answer that comment when her smile faded and she asked uncertainly, "Do you wish to annul it, husband?"

"Nay," he blurted quickly and was glad he had when she relaxed and managed a real smile.

"Well, neither do I, my lord," she assured him. "I am content to let the marriage stand."

Calum hesitated, then asked slowly, "Ye're willin' to stay married to me? Despite knowin' what I am?"

As if this helped her to understand why he'd brought the possibility up, Sarra relaxed, her expression melting to one full of love. "Aye, my lord. I wish to stay married to you, just as you are. I would not care if you had a tail, or . . ." She paused, a worried look entering her eyes. "You do not have a tail, do you?"

Calum laughed at her worry. "Nay, wife. I ha'e no tail."

"Oh, well," she breathed a sigh of relief, then quickly added, "I would love you, anyway, my lord, but may have needed some time adjusting to your having a tail."

Calum chuckled softly and stood to catch her hand and draw her nearer. "I'm thinkin' since we're married and since we both agree to stay married, mayhap we should consummate this marriage so ye can be sure I doona ha'e a tail or any other oddities for ye to concern yerself about."

Sarra nodded, her head ducking, then raised her face to ask, "Will you bite me, my lord?"

Calum went still, struggling with the question. Finally he admitted, "To be truly mated amongst me people, I'd ha'e to bite ye. However," he added quickly in case this news alarmed her, "however, I'll forgo that if ye wish it, Sarra."

Even as he made the offer, Calum wondered if it were possible for him to forgo it. He might start out with the best intentions, but could not be sure he could refrain once his passions were stirred. Sarra had such an incredible effect on him, stirring such deep, hunger and wild desire, he wasn't at all sure it would be possible for him to keep to that promise. He had already found it difficult to refrain from biting her when they had just been kissing and so on earlier.

Much to his relief, he would never be tested in the matter, for Sarra swallowed and said, "If 'tis the way your people mate, then surely we must do it."

Calum breathed a sigh of relief, then frowned as he saw her expression. She obviously had something else to say. He braced himself for whatever was coming, but all she asked was, "Will it hurt?"

Heart softening at the anxiety on her face, Calum hugged her close. "If done correctly and at the right moment, no, it'll no hurt. And I'll endeavor to do it correctly and at the right time."

Sarra nodded against his chest, then lifted her head and eyed him solemnly as she said, "I trust you, my lord."

Calum stared at her, thinking she had just given him the most incredible gift, but then he realized she had trusted him from the start, revealing the path through the secret tunnel to him, placing her own life and the lives of her people in his hands with that knowledge. He recalled that at the time he'd thought her terribly naïve to trust him, but supposed the fact that he'd not betrayed her with that knowledge, and that he wouldn't have, rather bore out her wisdom in trusting him.

"Sarra?" he said quietly.

"Aye?" she asked, lifting her head once more.

"I will endeavor ne'er to betray yer trust."

"I know," Sarra said, a soft smile curving her lips as she raised a hand to brush her fingers lightly across his cheek. "You will be a good husband, my lord. And a good father to our children. If I did not believe that, I would not have married you today."

"Ye did no exactly ha'e a choice with d'Angers at your door," Calum pointed out unhappily, and she chuckled softly.

"Of course I did, my lord. There was always the secret tunnel. If it were not for Father, I would have ridden out dressed as a lad and headed for London."

"London?" he asked doubtfully.

"Aye, my cousin lives there. He would have handled the matter," she assured him.

"Yer cousin?" he asked, doubting that a cousin could have stood in the way of d'Angers' determination.

"Aye. The king."

Calum stiffened. "What?"

"My cousin is the king," Sarra explained patiently. "'Tis why d'Angers was so eager to marry me. He thought 'twould gain him influence and power and—husband, are you all right?"

Calum felt her hands grab at him as his legs gave out on him again and he found himself suddenly seated on the bed.

"Husband, pray speak to me. You have gone quite pale," Sarra begged, fanning his face worriedly.

Calum shook his head, hardly able to take it in.

"Husband?"

"The king is yer cousin?" he asked, his voice cracking, hardly able to take it in. Dear God, he'd married the cousin of the English king. He'd lost his mind. He'd probably lose his head.

"Do not be silly, my lord. You will not lose your head," Sarra said with amusement, letting him know he'd spoken the thought aloud. She patted his hand reassuringly. "Father has no doubt already written a note to be dispatched to London stating that he approves the marriage. All will be well."

Calum didn't comment for a moment, then frowned and turned to ask her, "Why did ye no do it?"

When she looked confused by the question, he explained, "Ye said about donnin' a lad's garb and headin' out through the tunnels fer London. Why did ye no do it?"

"Because of my father," she said simply. "I would not leave him here alone. I feared he might . . ."

Sarra's voice faltered and he squeezed her hand, knowing what she'd been about to say and that she couldn't bring herself to actually voice it. She feared he might die here, alone, with her miles away and unable to see him off. No doubt she'd intended to wait until her father passed and then would have ridden out through the tunnels for London.

"Anyway," she said with forced cheer, "as it happens, I did not need to leave at all, and I owe that to you. Thank you, husband."

Calum gave a disbelieving laugh. She was thanking him for marrying her when while it might have got d'Angers off her door without the necessity of a ride into town, he had gained a lot more than she in the bargain. She was incredible. Beautiful, sweet, intelligent, and yet she made him feel like she was lucky to have him, when the truth was, he was lucky to have her.

"I love ye, Sarra," he said solemnly, drawing her closer so that she stood between his knees. "And I ken 'tis lucky I am to ha'e ye."

"And I love you, Calum MacNachton," she whispered just before he pulled her head down to kiss her.

Sarra sighed as his mouth finally covered hers. Until that moment, she had been nervous, even scared, about the bedding, but the moment his lips covered hers she knew that all would be well. When his tongue slid out to nudge her lips apart, she opened to him without reservation, her arms slipping around his neck as he drew her closer still, until her knees bumped the bed he sat on.

She was vaguely aware of his hands working at her gown as he kissed her, but paid it little attention until he began to draw both her gown and chemise down her arms. Removing her arms from around his neck, Sarra lowered them so that he could remove the cloth barrier between them, shivering as the material drifted down over her waist and fell to the floor.

Calum immediately took advantage of the change in status, his hands smoothing up her stomach to cup and knead her breasts and Sarra moaned into his mouth, her kiss becoming more frantic as her excitement grew. She was terribly distressed when he broke the kiss . . . until he replaced his hand at one breast with his mouth and began to draw on the aching nub. The excitement that had been slowly building until then, shot up in intensity at once and Sarra moaned and arched into the caress, her hands catching in his hair and urging him on.

When the now-free hand then slid down over her hip and then around to make its way up her thigh, she gasped and let one hand drop down to tangle it in the material of his tunic. It was only then that Sarra realized she was completely naked while he was still fully dressed.

Shaking her head to try to clear away some of the desire fogging it, Sarra tugged at the tunic, then at his plaid fretfully, wishing it wasn't there, but she gave that up and was grateful to have the cloth to clutch when his hand reached the apex of her thighs. Every nerve in her body seemed to jump then, and each one seemed to lead somehow to the spot he was caressing.

"Calum," Sarra cried out with alarm as her legs began to go weak, the sound muffled by his mouth.

Seemingly aware of her problem, Calum turned with her suddenly, sprawling her sideways across the bed and coming down on top of her. His tongue thrust into her mouth, filling her, and Sarra sucked at it frantically as his fingers worked a magic she didn't understand. She had the conflicting urges to squeeze her thighs around his hand to make him stop, and to spread her legs wider to give him better access at the same time, and hardly knew which one to follow.

Calum made up her mind for her, urging her legs apart himself and throwing one of his own legs across them to keep them spread as he inserted a finger into her.

Crying out, Sarra arched on the bed, her mind a fuzzy, thoughtless thing overloaded with the sensations he was causing. He lifted his mouth from hers and Sarra immediately began to twist her head back and forth, vaguely aware of the long, drawn-out moan coming from her own mouth. She was aware of the thundering of her heart and the shallow, breathless quality of her gasps, but mostly she was aware of the pleasure he was giving her. She had never imagined the marriage bed could be so wonderful.

Aware that her hands had somehow tangled themselves in his plaid again, Sarra tugged at it fretfully, blinking in surprise when the cloth suddenly pulled free under her hold. Taking advantage of it, she pulled it up, drawing it inch after inch until it was completely free of her husband. She then threw it over her head, so that it slid onto the floor on the other side of the bed, before beginning to work on his tunic.

Calum immediately stopped what he was doing and rose up to tear the tunic off over his own head. It flew through the air and landed somewhere on the floor as well as he came down on top of her, nestling himself between her legs. Now it was his body caressing her, she realized vaguely as he kissed her again, his hardness pressed against the very center of her and rubbing back and forth.

Sarra groaned into his mouth, her heels digging into the bed as she shifted and raised herself into each caress. When he suddenly slid into her, Sarra froze from sheer surprise, her eyes widening incredulously at how easy it was. One minute he was rubbing against her and the next he was in her, filling her. And while there was a small pinch of pain, it was nothing like she'd been led to expect from her first time.

Calum paused and raised up to eye her worriedly. "Are you a'r—"

It was as far as he got before Sarra shifted against him, drawing him further into her. She saw his eyes close and his face tighten and she shifted again, pulling away and then raising herself back up, watching his face with fascination as she did.

When she tried it a third time, Calum suddenly caught her hips and slid backward off the bed to stand at the side of it, drawing her with him so that she rested at the edge of the high bed. Her arms caught around his neck, Sarra went with him, sitting up as he kissed her again and drove himself into her. She moaned into his mouth with each thrust until he broke the kiss, then she turned her face into his shoulder, unconsciously biting at the meaty flesh there as the pressure inside her built to an explosive level. She was aware they were straining toward something, but had no idea what; then his hand slid between them and he began to caress her again even as he continued to love her. That was all it took.

Sarra felt her body clench up and screamed as pleasure exploded through her, hardly feeling the pinch at her neck as he sank his teeth into her. She felt the drawing at her throat and knew what was happening, but her body was convulsing, her mind filled with a rush of pleasure as she'd never experienced and all she could do was hold on as everything exploded around her.

Sarra woke up to find herself sprawled on her husband's chest, his hands moving soothingly over her back as he whispered words she didn't understand to her. She lay still for several moments, listening to the alien words, slowly realizing he was speaking in Gaelic. She had no idea what the words were, but they sounded beautiful and loving and she was feeling warm and limp and happy right where she was, so she remained still and silent until the words faded away and he was silent for a moment.

"Are ye awake, lass?" he asked after a moment and she supposed he'd noted a difference in her breathing.

"Ye've stopped yer snoring, so I ken yer awake."

"I do not snore," Sarra protested at once, lifting her head to glare at him with outrage.

Chuckling, Calum kissed her nose lightly, then shifted her onto the bed and covered her with linens and furs before standing and walking naked to the door. As Sarra watched curiously, he opened it and bellowed out into the hall. He then closed the door, returned to the bed, and scooped her up, furs and all, and carried her to the chair by the fire, where he sat down with her in his lap.

Before Sarra could ask what was going on, the bedchamber door flew open and Bessy and Milly rushed in and hurried to the bed to begin stripping away the blood-stained bottom linen and replace it with a fresh one. While they did that, a dozen more servants marched into the room carrying a tub and pails of water. They were followed by two more servants, one carrying a platter of food, the other carrying wine.

Sarra simply sat gaping as the bed was changed and a tub filled for her in moments. This had obviously been arranged ahead of time by her husband.

"I thought ye might like to wash the blood from our matin' away," he explained once it was done and the door closed behind the last departing servant.

Sarra raised a hand to her throat and he rolled his eyes.

"No there. There is no blood on yer neck," he said dryly, then his hand slid along her leg, and his voice was husky as he said, "There."

"Oh." She flushed.

Smiling faintly, he stood and carried her to the tub.

"I also thought ye may be hungry after . . ." He let his

words trail away as he set her on the floor and unwrapped the furs from around her, letting them drop to the floor. Pausing once he was finished, he asked gently, "Are ye feelin' a'right?"

Sarra nodded shyly. "I am a little hungry, though."

Nodding, he caught her by the waist and set her in the tub, then picked up the soap and a strip of linen. "Then we'd best wash ye quick so ye doona perish o' hunger."

Sarra tried to relax as he lathered the soap and began to run it over her body, but this was all terribly new to her.

"I noticed Hadley is still in the dungeons. I meant to ask yer father what he planned to do with the man, but forgot," Calum murmured as he ran his soapy hands over her back.

"I—we thought to banish him after the siege is over," Sarra murmured, shivering as his hands slid along her sides, brushing the curves of her breasts.

"Aye. Let him go to d'Angers since he wished him to be his lord so badly," Calum said quietly, then allowed his soapy hands to move around to actually cup her breasts. "Malcolm would make a good first."

Sarra gasped as he kneaded her flesh, her hands moving to cover his. It took a great deal to concentrate enough to admit, "I was thinking that myself today."

Calum kissed her ear and she could hear the smile in his voice as he said, "We think alike, then. 'Tis good."

"Aye," Sarra breathed as one hand moved away from her breasts and began sliding down her belly. She gave up any attempt to keep up her end of the conversation when his hand slid between her legs to wash the blood away, instead doing her best not to make a sound, biting back the gasps and moans that wanted to escape as his clever fingers ran over her skin. Finally, she could stand it no more and grabbed his arm. "Oh, Calum."

In the next moment, he'd caught her by the waist and was lifting her out of the tub.

"Yer clean enough," Calum announced in a growl. "Have something to eat while I bathe."

Calum set her on the floor and wrapped her in a linen, then turned her toward the food and gave her a gentle push.

Sarra took a moment to dry herself with the linen, then wrapped it around herself and turned back to the tub. "Shall I help you wash as well?"

"Eat," Calum growled, splashing water every which way as he ran the soapy cloth over his body willy-nilly in the fastest bath ever.

Grinning, Sarra moved to the chairs by the fireplace and the chest the food had been set on. She picked out some cheese and grapes and ate them, then commented, "I suppose Bessy and Milly took the linen to hang it from the banister?"

She grimaced at the idea of everyone below viewing the sheet with her blood on it.

"Nay."

"Nay?" Sarra echoed with surprise. She started to turn to glance back at him, but just then his arms slid around her from behind.

"Nay," Calum repeated, nibbling lightly at her ear before saying, "While that wid be the usual manner to prove yer innocence, I decided on another fer it. I arranged fer Malcolm to hang it from the wall."

"The wall?" Sarra asked incredulously.

"Aye. Off the wall at the front of the bailey with torches around to show the stain." He grinned when she glanced back at him. "And once 'tis hung, he shall inform d'Angers that yer wedded and truly bedded and he is out o' luck."

Sarra gave a disbelieving laugh. "You are cruel at heart, my lord."

"Aye," he agreed, then paused and frowned and asked, "Do you still love me?"

"Aye." Sarra laughed. "Reginald deserves it."

"Reginald?" he asked, arching one eyebrow.

"'Tis his first name," she said, then added with a smile, "He hates it. And so I use it at every opportunity."

Calum grinned. "We suit well."

"Aye," she agreed softly. "I am very lucky."

"Nay," he said solemnly. "'Tis I who am lucky. Here I feared ye'd turn away and be horrified by what I was, and instead you, and even yer father, already kenned it and accepted it easily . . ."

Having heard the frown in his voice and the way his speech had slowed, Sarra glanced over her shoulder at him with concern to find him looking perplexed.

"Why is it ye and yer father accepted what I was so easily?" he asked suddenly.

Sarra relaxed once she realized what concerned him.

"I am not sure why my father did, though I think it has something to do with meeting someone from your clan at court and liking him despite what he was," she admitted.

"Aye, he said as much," Calum murmured, and then asked, "but why did you?"

"For me, I guess, 'twas because . . ." Sarra paused, unsure how to voice it. Turning in his arms, she peered at him solemnly and said, "My lord, I think the fear is out of ignorance. The whispers about your kind are full of descriptions such as soulless, and heartless and other unpleasant things, but I knew this was not the case from the start. A soulless, heartless man would hardly risk his own life to save a lass from an unwanted marriage, would he?"

She didn't wait for him to respond, but continued, "And so I knew that was not so. Besides, my lord. The Bible says that God created all creatures, great and small. This means he created you as well, and if he made you and your clan a little different from everyone else, then he must have had his reasons. And who am I to question his judgment when the very difference in you placed you in that cave to save me that day and brought you into my life?"

Sarra fell silent, concern rising in her as she saw the sheen of what she suspected was tears in her husband's eyes.

"Calum?" she whispered uncertainly, raising a hand to press it against his cheek.

He turned his face into the caress and pressed a gentle

kiss to her palm, then explained, "Our people ha'e been forced to lie low and try to avoid attention like monsters fer so long that I think some of us . . . I . . . began to believe we *are* monsters."

"Oh no," she protested softly.

He pressed his hand over hers on his face and smiled.

"Nay," he agreed gently. "With a few words ye've made me hope it isna so. That we are part of God's plan, too."

"You are," Sarra said softly. "He placed you here for me, husband . . . and for my father, and for every man, woman, and child at DeCourcey. You are a blessing, not a monster."

Calum smiled and hugged her close. "I love ye, lass, and I'm thinkin' we'll suit each other verra weell."

"I love you, too," Sarra murmured. "And I agree, we will suit 'verra weel."

His eyes narrowed. "Ye widna be makin' fun o' me accent, wid ye, lass?"

"Never," Sarra assured him solemnly. "I love your accent. It makes me shiver all over."

"Shiver all over, eh?" Calum asked in a growl, tugging at the linen around her until it slid to the floor. "I have other ways to make ye shiver."

"Show me," she urged, slipping her arms around his neck and smiling when his mouth lowered to cover hers and he lifted her in his arms to carry her to the bed.